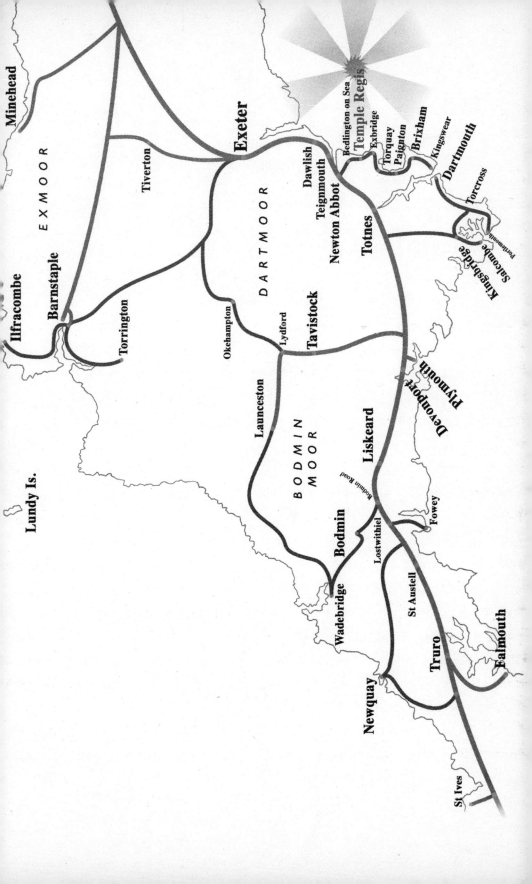

TP Fielden is a biographer, broadcaster and journalist. *The Riviera Express* is the first in the Miss Dimont Mystery series.

THE RIVIERA EXPRESS

TP FIELDEN

ONE PLACE. MANY STORIES

This novel is entirely a work of fiction. The names, characters and incidents portrayed in it are the work of the author's imagination. Any resemblance to actual persons, living or dead, events or localities is entirely coincidental.

HQ
An imprint of HarperCollins*Publishers* Ltd
1 London Bridge Street
London SE1 9GF

This edition 2017

1

First published in Great Britain by
HQ, an imprint of HarperCollins*Publishers* Ltd 2017

TP Fielden asserts the moral right to be
identified as the author of this work.
A catalogue record for this book is
available from the British Library.

ISBN: HB: 978-0-00-819368-3
C: 978-0-00-819371-3

Printed and bound in Great Britain by
CPI Group (UK) Ltd, Croydon, CR0 4YY

Our policy is to use papers that are natural, renewable and recyclable products and made from wood grown in sustainable forests. The logging and manufacturing processes conform to the legal environmental regulations of the country of origin.

For CRCW
Dei due, la migliore

ONE

When Miss Dimont smiled, which she did a lot, she was beautiful. There was something mystical about the arrangement of her face-furniture – the grey eyes, the broad forehead, the thin lips wide spread, her dainty perfect teeth. In that smile was a *joie de vivre* which encouraged people to believe that good must be just around the corner.

But there were two faces to Miss Dimont. When hunched over her typewriter, rattling out the latest episode of life in Temple Regis, she seemed not so sunny. Her corkscrew hair fell out of its makeshift pinnings, her glasses slipped down the convex nose, those self-same lips pinched themselves into a tight little knot and a general air of mild chaos and discontent emanated like puffs of smoke from her desk.

Life on the *Riviera Express* was no party. The newspaper's offices, situated at the bottom of the hill next door to the brewery, maintained their dreary pre-war combination of uprightness and formality. The front hall, the only area of access permitted to townsfolk, spoke with its oak panelling and heavy desks of decorum, gentility, continuity.

But the most momentous events in Temple Regis in 1958

– its births, marriages and deaths, its council ordinances, its police court and its occasional encounters with celebrity – were channelled through a less august set of rooms, inadequately lit and peopled by journalism's flotsam and jetsam, up a back corridor and far from the public gaze.

Lately there'd been a number of black-and-white 'B' features at the Picturedrome, but these always portrayed the heady excitements of Fleet Street. Behind the green baize door, beyond the stout oak panelling, the making of this particular local journal was decidedly less ritzy.

Far from Miss Dimont lifting an ivory telephone to her ear while partaking of a genteel breakfast in her silk-sheeted bed, the real-life reporter started her day with an apple and 'The Calls' – humdrum visits to Temple's police station, its council offices, fire station, and sundry other sources of bread-and-butter material whose everyday occurrences would, next Friday, fill the heart of the *Express*.

Like a laden beachcomber she would return mid-morning to her desk to write up her gleanings before leaving for the Magistrates' Court where the bulk of her work, from that bottomless well of human misdeeds and misfortunes, daily bubbled up.

After luncheon, usually taken alone with her crossword in the Signal Box Café, she would return briefly to court before preparing for an evening meeting of the Town Council, the Townswomen's Guild, or – light relief – a performance by the Temple Regis Amateur Operatic Society.

Then it would be home on her moped, corkscrew hair

blowing in the wind, to Mulligatawny, whose sleek head would be staring out of the mullioned window awaiting his supper and her pithy account of the day's events.

Miss Dimont, now unaccountably beyond the age of forty, had the fastest shorthand note in the West Country. In addition, she could charm the birds out of the trees when she chose – her capacity to get people to talk about themselves, it was said, could make even the dead speak. She was shy but she was shrewd; and if perhaps she was comfortably proportioned she was, everyone agreed, quite lovely.

Why Betty Featherstone, her so-called friend, got the front-page stories and Miss Dimont did not was lost in the mists of time. Suffice to say that on press day, when everyone's temper shortened, it was Judy who got it in the neck from her editor. Betty wrote what he wanted, while Judy wrote the truth – and it did not always make comfortable reading. She didn't mind the fusillades aimed in her direction for having overturned a civic reputation or two, for ever since she had known him, and it had been a long time, Rudyard Rhys had lacked consistency. Furthermore, his ancient socks smelt. Miss Dimont rose above.

Unquestionably Devon's prettiest town, Temple Regis took itself very seriously. Its beaches, giving out on to the turquoise and indigo waters which inspired some wily publicist to coin the phrase 'England's Riviera', were white and pristine. Broad lawns encircling the bandstand and flowing down towards the pier were scrupulously shaved, immaculately edged. Out in the estuary, the water was an impossible shade of aquamarine, its colour a magical invention of the gods – and since everyone in Temple agreed their little town was the sunniest spot in England, it really was very beautiful.

It was far too nice a place to be murdered.

*

Confusingly, the *Riviera Express* was both newspaper and railway train. Which came first was occasionally the cause for heated debate down in the snug of the Cap'n Fortescue, but the laws of copyright had not yet been invented when the two rivals were born; and an ambitious rail company serving the dreams of holidaymakers heading for the South West was certainly not giving way to a tinpot local rag when it came to claiming the title. Similarly, with a rock-solid local readership and a justifiable claim to both 'Riviera' and 'Express' – a popular newspaper title – the weekly journal snootily tolerated its more famous namesake. If neither would admit it, each benefited from the other's existence.

Before the war successive editors lived in constant turmoil, sometimes printing glowing lists of the visitors from another world who spilled from the brown and cream liveried railway carriages ('The Hon. Mrs Gerald Legge and her mother, the novelist Barbara Cartland, are here for the week'). At other times, Princess Margaret Rose herself could have puffed into town and the old codgers would have ignored it. Rudyard Rhys saw both points of view so there was no telling what he would think one week to the next – to greet the afternoon arrival? Or not to bother?

'Mr Rhys, we could go to meet the 4.30,' warned his chief reporter on this particular Tuesday. 'But – also – there's a cycling-without-lights case in court which could turn nasty. The curate from St Margaret's. He told me he's going to challenge his prosecution on the grounds that British Summer Time has no substantive legal basis. It could be very interesting.'

'Rrrr.'

'Don't you see? The Chairman of the Bench is one of his parishioners! Sure to be an almighty dust-up!'

'Rrrr . . . rrr.'

'A clash between the Church and the Law, Mr Rhys! We haven't had one of those for a while!'

Rudyard Rhys lit his pipe. An unpleasant smell filled the room. Miss Dimont stepped back but otherwise held her ground. She was all too familiar with this fence-sitting by her editor.

'Bit of a waste going to meet the 4.30,' she persisted. 'There's only Gerald Hennessy on board . . .' (and an encounter with a garrulous, prosy, self-obsessed matinée idol might make me late for my choir practice, she might have added).

'Hennessy?' The editor put down his pipe with a clunk. 'Now *that's* news!'

'Oh?' snipped Miss Dimont. 'You said you hated *The Conqueror and the Conquered*. "Not very manly for a VC", I think were your words. You objected to the length of his hair.'

'Rrrr.'

'Even though he had been lost in the Burmese jungle for three years.'

Mr Rhys performed his usual backflip. 'Hennessy,' he ordered.

It was enough. Miss Dimont noted that, once again, the editor had deserted his journalistic principles in favour of celebrity worship. Rhys enjoyed the perquisite accorded him by the Picturedrome of two back stalls seats each week. He had actually enjoyed *The Conqueror and the Conquered* so much he sat through it twice.

Miss Dimont did not know this; but anyone who had played as many square-jawed warriors as Gerald Hennessy was always likely to find space in the pages of the *Riviera Express*. Something about heroism by association, she had noted in the past, was at the root of her editor's lofty decisions. That all went back to the War, of course.

'Four-thirty it is then,' she said a trifle bitterly. 'But *Church* v. *Law* – now there's a story that might have been followed up by the nationals,' and with that she swept out, notebook flapping from her raffia bag.

This parting shot was a reference to the long-standing feud between the editor and his senior reporter. After all, Rudyard Rhys had made the wrong call on not only the Hamilton Biscuit Case, but the Vicar's Longboat Party, the Temple Regis Tennis Scandal and the Football Pools Farrago. Each of these exclusives from the pen of Judy Dimont had been picked up by the repulsive Arthur Shrimsley, an out-to-grass former Fleet Street type who made a killing by selling them on to the national papers, at the same time showing up the *Riviera Express* for the newspaper it was – hesitant, and slow to spot its own scoops when it had them.

On each occasion the editor's decision had been final – and wrong. But Judy was no saint either, and the cat's cradle of complaint triggered by her coverage of the Regis Conservative Ball last winter still made for a chuckle or two in the sub-editors' room on wet Thursday afternoons.

With her raffia bag swinging furiously, she stalked out to the car park, for Judy Dimont was resolute in almost everything she did, and her walk was merely the outer manifestation of that doughty inner being – a purposeful march which sent out radar-like warnings to flag-day sellers, tin-can rattlers, and other such supplicants and cleared her path as if by miracle. It was not manly, for Miss Dimont was nothing if not feminine, but it was no-nonsense.

She took no nonsense either from Herbert, her trusty moped, who sat expectantly, awaiting her arrival. With one cough, Herbert was kicked into life and the magnificent Miss Dimont flew away towards Temple Regis railway station, corkscrew hair flapping in the wind, a happy smile upon her lips. For there was nothing she liked more than to go in search of new adventures – whether they were to be found in the Magistrates' Court, the Horticultural Society, or the railway station.

Her favourite route took in Tuppenny Row, the elegant terrace of Regency cottages whose brickwork had turned a pale pink with the passage of time, bleached by Temple

Regis sun and washed by its soft rains. She turned into Cable Street, then came down the long run to the station, whose yellow-and-chocolate bargeboard frontage you could glimpse from the top of the hill, and Miss Dimont, with practice born of long experience, started her descent just as the sooty, steamy clouds of vapour from the Riviera Express slowed in preparation for its arrival at Regis Junction.

She had done her homework on Gerald Hennessy and, despite her misgivings about missing the choir practice, she was looking forward to their encounter, for Miss Dimont was far from immune to the charms of the opposite sex. Since the War, Hennessy had become the perfect English hero in the nation's collective imagination – square-jawed, crinkle-eyed, wavy-haired and fair. He spoke so nicely when asked to deliver his lines, and there was always about him an air of amused self-deprecation which made the nation's mothers wish him for their daughters, if not secretly for themselves.

Miss Dimont brought Herbert to a halt, his final splutter of complaint lost in the clanking, wheezing riot of sooty chaos which signals the arrival of every self-regarding Pullman Express. Across the station courtyard she spotted Terry Eagleton, the *Express*'s photographer, and made towards him as she pulled the purple gloves from her hands.

'Anyone apart from Hennessy?'

'Just 'im, Miss Dim.'

'I've told you before, call me Judy,' she said stuffily. The dreaded nickname had been born out of an angry tussle with Rudyard Rhys, long ago, over a front page story which had gone wrong. Somehow it stuck, and the editor took a fiend-ish delight in roaring it out in times of stress. Bad enough having to put up with it from him – though invariably she rose above – but no need to be cheeked by this impertinent snapper. She had mixed feelings about Terry Eagleton.

'Call me Judy,' she repeated sternly, and got out her note-book.

'Ain't your handle anyways,' parried Terry swiftly, and he was right – for Miss Dimont had a far more euphonious name, one she kept very quiet and for a number of good reasons.

Terry busily shifted his camera bag from one shoulder to the other. Employed by his newspaper as a trained observer, he could see before him a bespectacled woman of a certain age – heading towards fifty, surely – raffia bag slung over one shoulder, notebook flapping out of its top, with a distinctly harassed air and a permanently peppery riposte. Though she was much loved by all who knew her, Terry sometimes found it difficult to see why. It made him sigh for Doreen, the sweet young blonde newly employed on the front desk, who had difficulty remembering people's names but was indeed an adornment to life.

Miss Dimont led the way on to Platform 1.

'Pics first,' said Terry.

'No, Terry,' countered Miss Dim. 'You take so long there's never time left for the interview.'

'Picture's worth a thousand words, they always say. How many words are you goin' to write – *two hundred*?'

The same old story. In Fleet Street, always the old battle between monkeys and blunts, and even here in sweetest Devon the same old manoeuvring based on jealousy, rivalry and the belief that pictures counted more than words or, conversely, words enhanced pictures and gave them the meaning and substance they otherwise lacked.

And so this warring pair went to work, arriving on the platform just as the doors started to swing open and the holidaymakers alight. It was always a joyous moment, thought Miss Dimont, this happy release from confinement into sunshine, the promise of uncountable pleasures ahead. A small girl raced past, her face a picture of joy, pigtails given an extra bounce by the skip in her step.

The routine on these occasions was always the same – if a single celebrity was to be interviewed, he or she would be ushered into the first-class waiting room in order to be relieved of their innermost secrets. If more than one, the likeliest candidate would be pushed in by Terry, while Judy quickly handed the others her card, enquiring discreetly where they were staying and arranging a suitable time for their interrogation.

This manoeuvring took some skill and required a deftness of touch in which Miss Dimont excelled. On a day like today, no such juggling was required – just an invitation to old Gerald to step inside for a moment and explain away his presence in Devon's prettiest town.

The late holiday crowds swiftly dispersed, the guard completed the task of unloading from his van the precious goods entrusted to his care – a basket of somnolent homing pigeons, another of chicks tweeting furiously, the usual assortment of brown paper parcels. Then the engine driver climbed aboard to prepare for his next destination, Exbridge.

A moment of stillness descended. A blackbird sang. Dust settled in gentle folds and the reporter and photographer looked at each other.

'No ruddy Hennessy,' said Terry Eagleton.

Miss Dimont screwed up her pretty features into a scowl. In her mind was the lost scoop of *Church* v. *Law*, the clerical challenge to the authority of the redoubtable Mrs March-bank. The uncomfortable explanation to Rudyard Rhys of how she had missed not one, but two stories in an afternoon – and with press day only two days away.

Mr Rhys was unforgiving about such things.

Just then, a shout was heard from the other end of Plat-form 1 up by the first-class carriages. A porter was waving his hands. Inarticulate shouts spewed forth from his shaking face. He appeared, for a moment, to be running on the spot. It was as if a small tornado had descended and hit the platform where he stood.

Terry had it in an instant. Without a word he launched himself down the platform, past the bewildered guard, racing towards the porter. The urgency with which he took off sprang in Miss Dimont an inner terror and the certain knowl-edge that she must run too – run like the wind . . .

By the time she reached the other end of the platform Terry was already on board. She could see him racing through the first-class corridor, checking each compartment, moving swiftly on. As fast as she could, she followed alongside him on the platform.

They reached the last compartment almost simultaneously, but Terry was a pace or two ahead of Judy. There, perfectly composed, immaculately clad in country tweeds, his oxblood brogues twinkling in the sunlight, sat their interviewee Gerald Hennessy.

You did not have to be an expert to know he was dead.

TWO

You had to hand it to Terry – no Einstein he, but in an emergency as cool as ice. He was photographing the lifeless form of a famous man barely before the reality of the situation hit home. Miss Dimont watched through the carriage window, momentarily rooted to the spot, as he went about his work efficiently, quickly, dextrously. But then as Terry switched positions to get another angle, his eye caught her immobile form.

'Call the office,' he snapped through the window. 'Call the police. In that order.'

But Judy could not take her eyes off the man who so recently had graced the Picturedrome's silver screen. His hair, now restored to a more conventional length, flopped forward across his brow. The tweed suit was immaculate. The foulard tie lay gently across what looked like a cream silk shirt, pink socks disappeared into those twinkling brogues. She had to admit that in death Gerald Hennessy, when viewed this close, looked almost more gorgeous than in life . . .

'The phone!' barked Terry.

Miss Dimont started, then, recovering herself, raced to the

nearby telephone box, pushed four pennies urgently into the slot and dialled the news desk. To her surprise she was met with the grim tones of Rudyard Rhys himself. It was rare for the editor to answer a phone – or do anything else useful around the office, thought Miss Dimont in a fleeting aperçu.

'Mr Rhys,' she hicupped, 'Mr Rhys! Gerald Hennessy . . . the . . . dead . . .' Then she realised she had forgotten to press Button A to connect the call. That technicality righted, she repeated her message with rather more coherence, only to be greeted by a lion-like roar from her editor.

'Rrr-rrr-rrrr . . .'

'What's that, Mr Rhys?'

'Damn fellow! Damn him, damn the man. Damn damn damn!'

'Well, Mr Rhys, I don't really think you can speak like that. He's . . . dead . . . Gerald Hennessy – the actor, you know – he is dead.'

'He's not the only one,' bellowed Rudyard. 'You'll have to come away. Something more important.'

Just for the moment Miss Dim lived up to her soubriquet, her brilliant brain grinding to a halt. What did he mean? Was she missing something? What could be more important than the country's number one matinée idol sitting dead in a railway carriage, here in Temple Regis?

Had Rudyard Rhys done it again? The old Vicar's Longboat Party tale all over again? Walking away from the biggest story to come the *Express*'s way in a decade? How typical of the man!

She glanced over her shoulder to see Terry, now out of the compartment of death and standing on the platform, talking to the porter. That's *my* job, she thought, hotly. In a second she had dropped the phone and raced to Terry's side, her flapping notebook ready to soak up every detail of the poor man's testimony.

The extraordinary thing about death is it makes you repeat things, thought Miss Dimont calmly. You say it once, then you say it again – you go on saying it until you have run out of people to say it to. So though technically Terry had the scoop (a) he wasn't taking notes and (b) he wasn't going to be writing the tale so (c) the story would still be hers. In the sharply competitive world of Devon journalism, ownership of a scoop was all and everything.

'There 'e was,' said the porter, whose name was Mudge. 'There 'e was.'

So far so good, thought Miss Dimont. This one's a talker. 'So then you . . .?'

'I told 'im,' said Mudge, pointing at Terry. 'I already told 'im.' And with that he clamped his uneven jaws together.

Oh Lord, thought Miss Dimont, this one's *not* a talker.

But not for nothing was the *Express*'s corkscrew-haired reporter renowned for charming the birds out of the trees. 'He doesn't listen,' she said, nodding towards the photographer. 'Deaf to anything but praise. You'll need to tell me. The train came in and . . .'

'I told 'im.'

There was a pause.

'Mr Mudge,' responded Miss Dimont slowly and perfectly reasonably, 'if you're unable to assist me, I shall have to ask Mrs Mudge when I see her at choir practice this evening.'

This surprisingly bland statement came down on the ancient porter as if a Damoclean sword had slipped its fastenings and pierced his bald head.

'You'm no need botherin' her,' he said fiercely, but you could see he was on the turn. Mrs Mudge's soprano, an eldritch screech whether in the church hall or at home, had weakened the poor man's resolve over half a century. All he asked now was a quiet life.

'The 4.30 come in,' he conceded swiftly.

'Always full,' said Miss Dimont, jollying the old bore along. 'Keeping you busy.'

'People got out.'

Oh, come ON, Mudge!

'Missus Charteris arsk me to take 'er bags to the car. Gave me thruppence.'

'That chauffeur of hers is so idle,' observed Miss Dimont serenely. Things were moving along. 'So then . . .?'

'I come back to furs clars see if anyone else wanted porterin'. That's when I saw 'im. Just like lookin' at a photograph of 'im in the paper.' Mr Mudge was warming to his theme. ''E wasn't movin'.'

Suddenly the truth had dawned – first, who the well-dressed figure was; second, that he was very dead. The shocking combination had caused him to dance his tarantella on the platform edge.

The rest of the story was down to Terry Eagleton. 'Yep, looks like a heart attack. What was he – forty-five? Bit young for that sort of thing.'

As Judy turned this over in her mind Terry started quizzing Mudge again – they seemed to share an arcane lingo which mistrusted verbs, adjectives, and many of the finer adornments which make the English language the envy of the civilised world. It was a wonder to listen to.

'Werm coddit?'

'Ur, nemmer be.'

'C'rubble.'

Miss Dimont was too absorbed by the drama to pay much attention to these linguistic dinosaurs and their game of semantic shove-ha'penny; she sidled back to the railway carriage and then, pausing for a moment, heart in mouth, stepped aboard.

The silent Pullman coach was the *dernier cri* in luxury, a handsome relic of pre-war days and a reassuring memory of antebellum prosperity. Heavily carpeted and lined with exotic African woods, it smelt of leather and beeswax and smoke, its surfaces uniformly coated in a layer of dust so fine it was impossible to see: only by rubbing her sleeve on the corridor's handrail did the house-proud reporter discover what all seasoned railway passengers know – that travelling by steam locomotive is a dirty business.

She cautiously advanced from the far end of the carriage towards the dead man's compartment, her journalist's eye taking in the debris common to the end of all long-distance journeys – discarded newspapers, old wrappers, a teacup or two, an abandoned novel. On she stepped, her eyes a camera, recording each detail; her heart may be pounding but her head was clear.

Gerald Hennessy sat in the corner seat with his back to the engine. He looked pretty relaxed for a dead man – she wondered briefly if, called on to play a corpse by his director, Gerald would have done such a convincing job in life. One arm was extended, a finger pointing towards who knows what, as if the star was himself directing a scene. He looked rather heroic.

Above him in the luggage rack sat an important-looking suitcase, by his side a copy of *The Times*. The compartment smelt of . . . limes? Lemons? Something both sweet and sharp – presumably the actor's eau de cologne. But unlike Terry Eagleton Miss Dimont did not cross the threshold, for this was not the first death scene she had encountered in her lengthy and unusual career, and from long experience she knew better than to interfere.

She looked around, she didn't know why, for signs of violence – ridiculous really, given Terry's confident reading of the cause of death, but Gerald's untroubled features offered nothing by way of fear or hurt.

And yet something was not quite right.

As her eyes took in the finer detail of the compartment, she spotted something near the doorway beneath another seat – it looked like a sandwich wrapper or a piece of litter of some kind. Just then Terry's angry face appeared at the compartment window and his fist knocked hard on the pane. She could hear him through the thick glass ordering her out on to the platform and she guessed that the police were about to arrive.

Without pausing to think why, she whisked up the litter from the floor – somehow it made the place look tidier, more dignified. It was how she would recall seeing the last of Gerald Hennessy, and how she would describe to her readers his final scene – the matinée idol as elegant in death as in life. Her introductory paragraph was already forming itself in her mind.

Terry stood on the platform, red-faced and hopping from foot to foot. 'Thought I told you to call the police.'

'Oh,' said Miss Dimont, downcast, 'I . . . oh . . . I'll go and do it now but then we've got another—'

'Done it,' he snapped back. 'And, yes we've got another fatality. I've talked to the desk. Come on.'

That was what was so irritating about Terry. You wanted to call him a know-it-all, but know-it-alls, by virtue of their irritating natures, do *not* know it all and frequently get things wrong. But Terry rarely did – it was what made him so infuriating.

'You know,' he said, as he slung his heavy camera bag over his shoulder and headed towards his car, 'sometimes you really *can* be quite dim.'

*

Bedlington-on-Sea was the exclusive end of Temple Regis,

more formal and less engagingly pretty than its big sister. Here houses of substance stood on improbably small plots, with large Edwardian rooms giving on to pocket-handkerchief gardens and huge windows looking out over a small bay.

Holidaymakers might occasionally spill into Bedlington but despite its apparent charm, they did not stay long. There was no pub and no beach, no ice-cream vendors, no pier, and a general frowning upon people who looked like they might want to have fun. It would be wrong to say that Bedlingtonians were stuffy and self-regarding, but people said it all the same.

The journey from the railway station took no more than six or seven minutes but it was like entering another world, thought Miss Dimont, as she and Herbert puttered behind the *Riviera Express*'s smart new Morris Minor. There was never any news in Bedlington – the townsfolk kept whatever they knew to themselves, and did not like publicity of any sort. If indeed there was a dead body on its streets this afternoon, you could put money on its not lying there for more than a few minutes before some civic-minded resident had it swept away. That's the way Bedlingtonians were.

And so Miss Dimont rather dreaded the inevitable 'knocks' she would have to undertake once the body was located. Usually this was a task at which she excelled – a tap on the door, regrets issued, brief words exchanged, the odd intimacy unveiled, the gradual jigsaw of half-information built up over maybe a dozen or so doorsteps – but in Bedlington she knew the chances of learning anything of use were remote. Snooty wasn't in it.

They had been in such a rush she hadn't been able to get out of Terry where exactly the body was to be found, but as they rounded the bend of Clarenceux Avenue there was no need for further questions. Ahead was the trusty black Wolseley of the Temple Regis police force, a horseshoe of spectators and an atmosphere electric with curiosity.

At the end of the avenue there rose a cliff of Himalayan proportions, a tower of deep red Devonian soil and rock, at the top of which one could just glimpse the evidence of a recent cliff fall. As one's eye moved down the sharp slope it was possible to pinpoint the trajectory of the deceased's involuntary descent; and in an instant it was clear to even the most casual observer that this was a tragic accident, a case of Man Overboard, where rocks and earth had given way under his feet.

Terry and Miss Dimont parked and made their way through to where Sergeant Hernaford was standing, facing the crowd, urging them hopelessly, pointlessly, that there was nothing to see and that they should move on.

The sergeant spoke with forked tongue, for there *was* something to see before they went home to tea – there, under a police blanket, lay a body a-sprawl, as if still in the act of trying to save itself. But it was chillingly still.

'Oh dear,' said Miss Dimont, conversationally, to Sergeant Hernaford, 'how tragic.'

''Oo was it?' said Terry, a bit more to the point.

Hernaford slowly turned his gaze towards the official representatives of the fourth estate. He had seen them many times before in many different circumstances, and here they were again – these purveyors of truth and of history, these curators of local legend, these *nosy parkers*.

'Back be'ind the line,' rasped Hernaford in a most unfriendly manner, for just like the haughty Bedlingtonians he did not like journalists. 'Get BACK!'

'Now Sergeant Hernaford,' said Miss Dimont, stiffening, for she did not like his tone. 'Here we have a man of late middle age – I can see his shoes, he's a man of late middle age – who has walked too close to the cliff edge. When I was up there at the top last week there were signs explicitly warning that there had been a rockfall and that people should keep away. So, man of late middle age, tragic accident. Coroner will say he was a B.F. for ignoring the warnings, the *Riviera Express* will say what a loss to the community. An extra paragraph listing his bereaved relations, there's the story.

'All that's missing,' she added, magnificently, edging closer to the sergeant, 'is his name. I expect you know it. I expect he had a wallet or something. Or maybe one of these good people—' she looked round, smiling at the horseshoe but her words taking on a steely edge '—has assisted you in your identification. He has clearly been here for a while – your blanket is damp and it stopped raining an hour ago – so in that time you must have had a chance to find out who he is.'

She smiled tightly and her voice became quite stern.

'I expect you have already informed your inspector and,

rather than drive all the way over to Temple Regis police station and take up his *very precious time* getting two words out of him – a Christian name and a surname, after all that is all I am asking – I imagine you would rather he did not complain to you about my wasting his *very precious time*.

'So, Sergeant,' she said, 'please spare us all that further pain.'

It was at times like this that Terry had to confess she may be a bit scatty but Miss Dimont could be, well, remarkable. He watched Sergeant Hernaford, a barnacle of the old school, crumble before his very eyes.

'Name, Arthur Shrimsley. Address, Tide Cottage, Exbridge. Now move on. Move ON!'

Judy Dimont gazed owlishly, her spectacles sliding down her convex nose and resting precariously at its tip. 'Not *the* Arthur . . .?' she enquired, but before she could finish, Terry had whisked her away, for Hernaford was not a man to exchange pleasantries with – that was as much as they were going to get. As they retreated, he pushed Miss Dimont aside with his elbow while turning to take snaps of the corpse and its abrasive custodian before pulling open the car door.

'Let's go,' he urged. 'Lots to do.'

Miss Dimont obliged. Dear Herbert would have to wait. She pulled out her notebook and started to scribble as Terry noisily let in the clutch and they headed for the office.

Already the complexity of the situation was becoming clear; and no matter what happened next, disaster was about to befall her. Two deaths, two very different sets of journalistic values. And only Judy Dimont to adjudicate between the rival tales as to which served her readers best.

If she favoured the death of Gerald Hennessy over the sad loss of Arthur Shrimsley, local readers would never forgive her, for Arthur Shrimsley had made a big name for himself in the local community. The *Express* printed his letters most weeks, even at the moment when he was stealing their stories and selling them to Fleet Street. Rudyard Rhys, in thrall to Shrimsley's superior journalistic skills, had even allowed him to write a column for a time. But narcissistic and self-regarding it turned out to be, and of late he was permitted merely to see his name in print at the foot of a letter which would excoriate the local council, or the town brass band, or the ladies at the WI for failing to keep his cup full at the local flower show.

There was nothing nice about Arthur Shrimsley, yet he had invented a persona which his readers were all too ready to believe in and even love. His loss would be a genuine one to the community.

On the other hand, thought Miss Dimont feverishly, as Terry manoeuvred expertly round the tight corner of Tuppenny Row, we have a story of national importance here. Gerald Hennessy, star of *Heroes at Dawn* and *The First of the Few*, husband of the equally famous Prudence Aubrey, has died on our patch. Gerald HENNESSY!

The question was, which sad passing should lead the *Express*'s front page? And who would take the blame when, as was inevitable, the wrong choice was made?

THREE

It is remarkable, thought Miss Dimont, as her Remington Quiet-Riter rattled, banged, tinged and spat out page after page of immaculately typed copy addressing the recent rise in the death rate of Temple Regis. It really is remarkable . . .

Her typing came to a halt while she completed the thought. *It's remarkable how when there's an emergency everybody just melts away. Here I am, writing one of the greatest scoops this newspaper has ever been lucky enough to have, and with press day looming, and everyone's gone home.*

She was right to feel nettled. The newsroom resembled the foredeck of the *Mary Celeste*, with all the evidence of apparent occupancy but none of the personnel. It was barely six o'clock but the crew of this ghost ship had jumped over the side, leaving Miss Dimont and Terry Eagleton alone to steer it to safety. Call it cowardice in the face of a major story, call it what you like, they'd all hopped it.

Around her, tin ashtrays still gave off the malodorous evidence that people once worked here. Teacups were barely cold. Someone had forgotten to put away the milk. Someone else had forgotten to shut the windows – strictly against company regulations – and the soft late summer breeze caused the large sign over the editorial desks to gently undulate, as if a *punkah wallah* had been employed especially to fan Miss Dimont's fevered brow.

This sign was Rudyard Rhys' urgent imprecation to staff to do their duty. 'Make It Fast,' he had written, 'Make It Accurate.' To which some wag had added in crayon, 'Make It Up.'

There were wags aplenty at the *Express*. In the corner by Miss Dimont's desk was a gallery of hand-picked photographs, rich harvest of the paper's weekly editorial content, which showed off the town's newly-weds. For some reason the office jokers had chosen to pick the ugliest and most ill suited of couples – brides with snaggly teeth, grinning grooms recently released from the asylum. It was called the 'Thank Heavens!' board – thank heavens they found each other!

This joke had been running for a good few years and it was remarkable that on this evidence, in beauteous Temple Regis, there could be quite so many people – parents now, grandparents even – making such a lacklustre contribution to the municipality's gene pool. It was rather a cruel joke of which Miss Dimont did not approve.

Turning away, she ladled in some extra paragraphs of glowing praise to the life and achievements of Arthur Shrimsley, adding a few of her own jokes – 'His life was enriched by the sight of a good story' (he stole enough of them from the *Express* and peddled them to Fleet Street). 'He enjoyed the very sight of a typeface' (if it showed his name in big enough print). 'He was fearless' (rude), 'adept' (as thieves so often are), 'a consummate diplomat' (liar) . . . 'wise'(bore).

Gerald Hennessy she had already dispatched to the printer – a full page, motivated in part by his fame and the shock of the death of one so esteemed in humble Temple Regis, but also from a sense of personal loss: Miss Dimont had of course never met the actor before their recent silent encounter, but like all his fans, she felt she knew him intimately. There was something in his character as a human being which informed the heroic parts he played, her Remington had tapped out – instinctively his many admirers knew him to be the right choice to represent the dead and the dying of the recent war, as well as the nimble, the bold and the picaresque. It truly was a great loss to the nation and Miss Dimont, in writing this first of many epitaphs, captured the spirit of the man *con brio*.

The tumult from her typewriter finally ceased and, after a reflective pause, Miss Dimont fetched out the oilskin cover to put it to bed for the night. She had missed her choir practice, but then she already knew by heart the more easily accomplished sections of the Fauré Requiem with which the Townswomen's Guild Chorus would be serenading Temple townsfolk in a fortnight's time. She went along as much for the company as anything else, for Miss Dimont was a most able sight-reader with a melodious contralto that any choirmaster would give his eye teeth for. She did not need to practise.

She heaved a sigh of relief that it was over. How she would have hated to work on a daily newspaper, where deadlines assail one every twenty-four hours and there is no time to breathe! As she gathered up her things, her eyes travelled round the abandoned newsroom, about the most dreary working environment one could possibly imagine, and yet the very place where history was made. Or if not made, then recorded – for just as there is no point in climbing Mount Everest if there is no one there to chronicle it, so too what pleasure can there be in winning Class 1 Chrysanthemums (incurved) if not to rub their competitors' nose in it? All human life was here, recorded in detail by the diligent *Express*.

The room was dusty, untidy, littered, and from the files of back copies lying under the window there rose the sour odour of drying newsprint. Desks were jammed together and covered in all the debris which goes with making a newspaper – rulers, pencils, litter galore, old bits of hot metal used as paperweights. Coats were slung over chairbacks as if their owners might shortly return.

Being a reporter had not been what Miss Dimont was put on this earth for – there had been another career, most distinguished, which preceded her present occupation – but she was a very good one. Except, of course, on occasions like the Regis Conservative Ball last winter, but if ever anyone had the temerity to bring *that* up, she rose above.

Now she must find Terry, beavering away in the darkroom, and get him to take her back to Bedlington where, in their rush to get back to the office, her trusty Herbert had been abandoned.

As she made towards the photographic department, she heard the sound of a door opening, followed by a muffled squeak. Miss Dimont stopped dead in her tracks. There was nobody else in the building except her and Terry – what was that rustling sound, that parrot-like noise?

She swung round to be faced by a ghostly apparition – white-faced, grey-haired, long claw-like fingers, a rictus of a smile upon its features.

'Purple,' it whispered.

'Oh hello, Athene,' started Miss Dimont, 'you gave me such a fright.'

Then, like the Queen of Sheba, Athene Madrigale sailed into the room, her aura wafting before her in the most entrancing way. She was rarely seen in daylight – indeed she was rarely seen at all – but despite her advanced age she remained one of the pillars upon which the *Riviera Express* had built its reputation. For Athene wrote the astrology column.

What most *Express* readers turned to each Friday morning, immediately after looking to see who'd died or been had up in court, were Athene's stars. In Temple Regis, you never had a bad day with Athene.

'Sagittarius: Oh! How lucky you are to be born under this sign,' she would trill. 'Nothing but sunshine for you all week!

'Capricorn: All your troubles are behind you now. Start thinking about your holidays!

'Cancer: Someone has prepared a big surprise for you. Be

patient, it may take a while to appear, but what pleasure it will bring!'

These were not the scribblings of a simpleton but rare emanations from under the deeply spiritual cloak which adorned Athene Madrigale's person. Though not quite as others – her rainbow-hued costumes set her apart from the average Temple Regent, not to mention the turquoise finger-nails and violet smile – she exuded nothing but beauty and calm. It is quite likely her name was not Athene, but nobody felt the need to question it while she predicted such wonderful things for the human race.

Equally, nobody was quite sure where Athene lived – some said in a mystical bubble on the roof of the *Riviera Express* – but what is certain is that she needed the protection of night to save her from being swamped by an adoring public, her aura too precious to be jostled. It is true Miss Dimont encountered her from time to time, but only because she would return late from council meetings to diligently write into the night until her work was done. Most reporters on late jobs kept it in their notebook and typed it up next day.

'Purple,' whispered Athene again.

'But going green?' replied Miss Dimont.

'Mercifully for you, dear.'

'It's been a something of a day, Athene.'

'I can tell, my dear, do you want to sit down and talk about it?'

This was a rare invitation and one not to be denied. The strain of the day's activities had taken its toll on the reporter and she was grateful for a sympathetic ear. Almost as if by magic a cup of hot, sweet tea appeared in front of her and Athene arranged her rainbow clothes in a most attractive way on the seat opposite, the manner in which she did it suggesting she had all the time in the world. Even though she had yet to write the astrology page!

'It's not the first time I've seen dead bodies,' started Miss Dimont.

'No dear. That chemist with the pill-making machine.'

'Yes.'

'Lady Hellebore and the gardener.'

'I'd almost forgotten that.'

'The Temple twins.'

'So many, oh dear . . .'

Athene knew when to move on. 'What is it then, Judy? What's wrong?'

'I don't know,' came the reply. 'Maybe it's seeing two fatalities in one day. Two such different people – one so loved, the other so hated. But both lives at an end, equally, as if God cannot differentiate between good and evil.'

'That's not really what's upsetting you, though,' said Athene gently, for she was gifted with a greater understanding of people's travails. 'It's something else.'

Miss Dimont stirred her tea. 'Yes,' she said finally. 'I just feel something's wrong.'

'Like you did with the twins?'

'Oh . . . oh yes, something *is* wrong. I've been over it while I was writing my copy but I can't see what it is. There was something about Gerald Hennessy, he sat there so calmly, but he was pointing – pointing!'

'At what, dear?'

'Well, nothing. I thought when I looked at him that he was accusing someone. There was just that look on his face. Somehow trying to say something, but not quite managing it.'

'Go on.'

'And then, when we went to Bedlington, the way he – oh, did you know Arthur Shrimsley was dead?'

'Couldn't happen to a nicer chap,' said Athene crisply, her perpetual sun slipping over the horizon for a brief second.

'Mm?' said Miss Dimont, not quite believing such harsh words could steal from the benign countenance. 'Well, anyway, there was just something about it all. It wasn't just Sergeant Hernaford, though he was obnoxious, it wasn't even the way the body was lying. Just something about the way Mr Shrimsley had managed to get through that barrier right out on to the cliff edge. It didn't seem . . . logical. It didn't add up.'

Athene did not know what Judy was talking about, but she did know how to refresh a teacup. Once done, she sat there expectantly, waiting for the next aperçu.

'And, er, that's it really' said Miss D, disappointingly.

Miss Madrigale was far too conversant in the ways of the parallel universe to see a complete lack of evidence in what she had just heard. There was something here, most certainly. She was glad to see that she had eradicated the purple from Miss Dimont's aura and that it was almost completely restored to a healthy green.

'You've been such a help, Athene,' said Judy gratefully, but as the words formed in her mouth, she awoke to the fact that Athene had completely disappeared.

'Still 'ere?' barked Terry Eagleton, who had blustered into the room with a time-for-a-pint look on his face, startling Athene away.

'Yes. And you've got to take me back to Bedlington to pick up Herb— the moped.'

'Want to see what we've got?' asked Terry, eager as ever to show off the fruits of his day's labours. 'Some great shots!'

'Pictures of dead bodies? Printed in the *Express*?' marvelled Miss Dimont. 'Never in a month of Sundays, Terry, not while King Rudyard sits upon his throne!'

'Yers, well. ' Terry sniffed. 'I'll keep them back for the nationals. Take a look.'

And since Judy Dimont relied on Terry for her lift back to Bedlington, she obliged. The pair walked through into the darkroom where, hanging from little washing lines and attached by clothes pegs, hung the 10 x 8 black-and-white prints which summed up the day's events. They were not a pretty sight.

On the other hand, they were: an eery light percolated the first-class carriage containing the body of Gerald Hennessy ('f5.6 at 1/60th,' chirped Terry proudly). The image was so dramatic that, honestly, it could have been a publicity still from one of his forthcoming films. Terry had caught the actor in profile, his jaw as rugged as ever, the mop of crinkly hair just slightly ruffled, the tweed suit immaculate.

The hand was raised, index finger extended in imperious fashion. Gerald's lips appeared to be pronouncing something. It was indeed a hero's end – until Miss Dimont noticed the litter on the carriage floor. 'Thank heavens I got rid of that!' she told herself.

Her eyes switched to the pictures of Arthur Shrimsley, or at least the police blanket which covered Shrimsley – very little to boast about here in pictorial terms, she thought. A blanket – that's not going to earn Terry a bonus. But, as she moved along the washing line examining the various angles he'd taken the reality of what she'd seen, with her own eyes, supplanted the prints hanging before her. She recalled the odd feeling she'd had when craning around the obstructive body of Sergeant Hernaford and, as her eyes slid back to Terry's prints, she realised why. In one shot – and one shot only – Terry had captured a different angle, which showed a hand, as well as the middle-aged man's shoes, protruding from the blanket.

The hand was clutching a note.

Miss Dimont stepped back. 'Surely not,' she said to herself. 'Surely not!'

'Surely what?' said Terry, busy admiring his f5.6 at 1/60th. The light playing over Gerald Hennessy's rigid form, the etching of the profile, the shaft of light on the extended forefinger . . . surely, a contender for Photographer of the Year?

'He can't have committed suicide. Not Arthur Shrimsley. Why, he was the most self-regarding person I ever met!'

'Speaking ill of the dead, Miss Dim.'

'That's as maybe, Terry,' she snipped, 'but I don't remember you ever saying anything nice about him.'

'Man was a chump,' but Terry looked again at the picture in question. 'You're right,' he said. 'Looks like a note in his hand. Has to be a suicide. Unless it was a love letter to himself, of course.'

'Terry!'

The pair emerged from the darkroom, each wreathed in their separate thoughts. That last portrait of Gerald Hennessy is indeed a work of art, marvelled Terry, which might spring me from a lifetime's wageslavery at the *Express*.

Miss Dimont meanwhile was struggling to arrive at a logic which would allow the awful but never less than self-satisfied Arthur Shrimsley to do away with himself.

Then came the moment.

Miss Dim had had them before – for example when she discovered Mrs Sharpham's long-lost cat safe and well in the airing cupboard, when she suddenly knew why Alderman Jones had really bought that farm.

'Just a moment, Terry!'

She was back in the darkroom, staring hard at Terry's masterpiece. Part of her had admired, the other part recoiled from, this undeniable award-winner. When she'd looked before she had concentrated on Hennessy's face, the pointing finger, the irritating litter which nearly spoilt the picture. Now she concentrated on the light beams filtered by Terry's use of lens – light beams flooding from outside, throwing shadows on the thick carpet beneath the actor's feet.

'Come back here, Terry,' said Miss Dimont, very slowly. There was something in her tone of voice which made the photographer obey.

'Do you have a magnifying glass?' she asked.

'Got one somewhere. But you don't need—'

'Magnifying glass, Terry,' said Miss Dimont crisply. 'And another for yourself if you have one.'

He obliged. Both moved forward towards the print.

'Do you notice Gerald Hennessy's hand – his index finger?' she asked.

'Yes, the way I shot it, the light does a nice job of—'

'The finger, the finger!' interrupted Miss Dimont urgently.

'Yes,' said Terry, not seeing anything at all.

'The tip of it is dirty,' she said slowly. 'The rest of his hand appears clean.'

'Ur. Ah.'

'Now look at the window by his side. D'you see?'

'What am I looking for?'

'Where you have been so clever with the light. The light streaming through the window,' said Miss Dimont. 'The window is covered in a thin layer of dust. Your f8 at 1/30th has caught something on the window which you couldn't see – and neither could I – when we were in the carriage. Do you see what it is?'

Terry moved closer to the print, his eyes readjusting to

the moving magnifying glass. 'Ah,' he said. 'Yes. Looks like he was writing something on the window.'

'What does it say?'

'Not much . . . just three letters as I can make out . . .'

'And they are?' asked Miss Dimont, as soft as silk.

'M . . . U . . . R . . .'

FOUR

It was the fashion to mock the overblown grandeur of
Temple Regis Magistrates' Court, though it was actually
rather pretty – redbrick, Edwardian, nicely stained glass and
masses of oak panelling. Its solidity added weight to the
sentences handed down by the Bench.

Miss Dimont, who had spent more Tuesdays and Thurs-
days on the well-worn press bench than she cared to recall,
approached Mr Thurlestone, the magistrates' clerk, for a
copy of the day's charge sheet. The bewigged figure turned
away his head as she neared his desk and held up the requisite
document as if it had recently been recovered from a puddle.
He did not acknowledge her.

Curious, because it was hard to ignore such an amiable
person as Miss Dimont.

After all, Mr Thurlestone had never been the object of
the angry huffing and puffing, and the hefty biffing, from
which Miss Dimont's Remington Quiet-Riter weekly delivered its judgements. He'd never had to submit to a sharp
dressing-down in print like the disobliging council officials
she sometimes excoriated, nor had he ever been on the receiv-

ing end of the occasional furies directed at the judges at the Horticultural Society for the self-serving way they arrived at their deliberations.

In fact, Miss Dimont had always been perfectly sweet to Mr Thurlestone, but still he snubbed her.

Perhaps it was because, though this was his court and he virtually told the magistrates what to think, no mention of his life's work was ever made in the *Express*. The daily doings he oversaw in this room, with its heavy gavel and magnificent royal coat of arms, filled many pages of the newspaper, and quite often the stern words of one or other of the justices sitting on the bench behind him made headlines:

'JP ORDERS MISSIONARY "GO BACK TO AFRICA"' (at the conclusion of a lengthy case concerning an unfortunate mix-up in the public lavatories behind the Market Square).

'MOTHER OF SIX TOLD "ONE'S ENOUGH" BY THE BENCH' (the joys of bigamy).

'"YOU BRING SHAME TO TEMPLE REGIS," RULES JP' (something about Boy Scouts; Miss Dimont rose above).

Mr Thurlestone, for all his legal training, his starched wing collar and tabs, and his ancient and rather disreputable wig, yearned for recognition. But he would wait in vain, for he was no match for the vaulted egos, the would-be hangmen and the retired businessmen who made up his cadre of Justices of the Peace – for they it was who made the headlines.

Chief among their Worships, though not cast in quite the same mould, was Mrs Marchbank, the chairman of the

Bench, or, to give her the full roll-call, The Hon. Mrs Adelaide Marchbank, MBE, JP.

In many ways Mrs March, as she was generally known, summed up the aspirations of the town – hard-working, exquisitely turned out, ready always with a smile and an encouraging word. Fortunate enough to be married to the brother of Lord Mount Regis, she gave back to life far more than she ever took. Her tall, grey-haired good looks were tempered by a sharply regal streak, the combination of which went down well in a part of the country largely deprived of real Society. Everyone agreed she wore a hat exquisitely.

Her serene countenance often graced the pages of the *Riviera Express*, whether as chairman of this, a subscriber to that, or simply for being an Honourable. A lacklustre fashion show, staged by the Women's Institute in a determined bid to hold down the town's hemlines, would be sure of coverage if the smiling Mrs March were to grace the front row (though – poor models! – the photograph which accompanied the article would invariably feature the magistrate, not the matrons).

But Miss Dimont found it hard to like her.

And Mrs March did not much like Miss Dimont.

There was something scholarly about the corkscrew-haired reporter, something passionate, something humane – qualities Mrs March, as she peered down into the court, recognised that she herself did not possess. Apogee of correctness and charm though she was, the steely inner core which made her a most excellent magistrate (if too firm on occasion) disallowed her the luxury of these finer attributes.

For her part Miss Dimont hardly helped matters; she did not care for the unquestioning submission to privilege. On a number of occasions, she had pointed out in print where the Bench, under the leadership of Mrs March, had forgotten that old Gilbertian thing of letting the punishment fit the crime. Handing down a week's custodial sentence simply for having supped too deep in the Cap'n Fortescue did not find favour with this fair-minded reporter, and she did not mind saying so on the Opinion page.

For some reason Mrs March took these lightly worded criticisms badly. Were she less the Queen of Temple Regis, one might almost suppose that she felt threatened, but that could not be – her position in the town outranked the mayor, the rector, the chairman of Rotary, even the chief constable. A lowly reporter on the local rag presented no threat to her standing, no matter what appeared in print, and yet the unfinished business between the pair often had the power to lower the temperature in court by a good few degrees.

'All rise,' barked Mr Thurlestone. 'The court is in session.'

This morning there were usual crop of licensee applications – a form of morning prayers during which one could allow one's mind to wander – before the main business of the day began. Miss Dimont's eyes ran down the charge sheet automatically registering the petty thefts, drunken misdemeanours, traffic infringements and insults to civic pride which did nothing to diminish Temple Regis in the eyes of the world, but did not exactly shore up her faith in man's capacity to find that higher path.

'Call Albert Lamb!'

A furtive-looking fellow stepped forward, eyeing the court suspiciously as if one of them had stolen his bicycle clips.

'Are you Albert John Walker Lamb?'

'Yus.'

'Albert Lamb, you are charged with drunkenness in a public place. How do you plead?'

'Just a shmall one, shank you.'

Miss Dimont found, with her combination of immaculate shorthand and a sense of when to rest her pencil, that court reporting was a bit like lying on a lumpy sofa with a box of chocolates – the seating was uncomfortable but the work largely enjoyable. Gradually, as one traffic accident after another resolved itself, she allowed her mind to wander back to the events of the previous day.

All in all, it had been rather wonderful, snatching success as she had from the jaws of defeat – one moment no stories, the next, two – on Page One!

'Call Ezra Poundale.'

'Call Gloria Monday.'

'Call . . .'

What kept coming back to her, however, was the startling discovery she had made with Terry's magnifying glass. The pointed finger blackened by dust, the secret message left by the dying actor! The thrill of an even better story!! But what seemed certain at first examination seemed less so at second glance, and despite Terry obligingly putting another print through the bath to see if it came up more clearly, it was impossible to say that what was scrawled in the window-dust really was M . . . U . . . R . . .

She had ridden the trusty Herbert back to the railway station this morning in the hope of examining the carriage more closely, but the Pullman coach had been detached from the rest of the train and shunted into a siding where the Temple Regis police had thrown a barrier around it. She was forcefully reminded she was not allowed anywhere near – Hernaford's revenge for yesterday's small triumph in Bedlington.

There was no sense, she felt, that the police were treating this as anything other than a routine inquiry. She wondered, not for the first time in her eventful life, whether she wasn't reading too much into it all, jumping at shadows.

This morning the cases seemed to drag on, and the luncheon recess came as a merciful release. Normally, Miss Dimont joined like-minded members of the court proceedings for lunch in their unofficial canteen, the Signal Box Café, but she needed time to think. She boarded one of Temple's green and cream tourist buses and took a threepenny ride down to the promenade.

She alighted at her favourite spot by the bandstand and walked towards the shore. Bathed now in late summer sunlight, the turquoise sea stretched out to infinity, its wave-tops like glass beads glittering and cascading over the horizon. The sky was cloudless and a shade of innocent blue. Through the haze she could see fishing boats sliding out to meet the incoming tide while wise old seagulls circled in the heat, lazily awaiting their opportunity.

'This is why I am here,' said Miss Dimont, only half to herself. 'This is paradise.'

When compared to the fusty atmosphere of the Magistrates' Court, she was right. The irritants which go with any seaside town – late holidaymakers fussing over the price of an ice cream, Teddy boys with nothing better to do than comb their greasy hair and hang about with intent, or the eternal scourge of bottles abandoned on the beach – these things Miss Dimont did not see. The air was still, the only sound that eternal two-part harmony of surf and gulls.

She sat quite still on a bench and dragooned the various components of her considerable intellect into focusing on the events of the past twenty-four hours.

Last night there had been the shock, still with her, of confronting one of the most famous faces in the land so close upon the moment of his death. What she saw, what she had not seen . . . what did it amount to? In the bright hot sun it was hard to believe that in the darkroom with Terry by her side, both with magnifying glasses to their noses, she could smell murder. Apart from anything else there were no signs of violence, nothing to disturb the pristine tranquillity of that Pullman coach compartment – nothing sinister in the atmosphere, nothing disturbed.

But she had seen bodies like that before, and they hadn't died from a heart attack.

And yet her suspicions no longer seemed quite real, and so she turned instead to the question of Arthur Shrimsley. The fleeting glimpse of the note in his hand gave more than a hint that something was amiss. Miss Dimont had second sight about such things, as in when she found old Mrs Bradley's lost diamond ring in the clothes-peg basket. It had been a magpie, she deduced. Missing for a fortnight, but Miss Dimont intuited.

She had the same feeling now.

If there *was* a note, it meant something – the difficulty being, what? Mr Shrimsley, as Terry crisply summarised, loved himself far too much to contemplate self-destruction. What did strike as odd was that Sergeant Hernaford appeared to have done nothing about it. Shrimsley must have fallen down the cliff a good ninety minutes before she and Terry arrived on the scene – wouldn't he, while searching the man's wallet to establish his identity, have plucked the note from the man's lifeless fingers? Was police procedure so strict these days he would leave it to the detectives to pick up the paper and digest its contents? She didn't think so, in fact if anything the opposite.

Miss Dimont closed her eyes and let the sun do its work.

'Judy, *there* you are!'

Miss Dimont struggled for a moment and blinked. She had fallen asleep. There before her was Betty Featherstone, her friend and enemy – the one who was given the best stories, the one whose byline generally graced the front page of the *Express*. There was little animosity between the two over this – both knew that when it came to ferreting out stories, getting interviewees to confess, or even just how fast one could type or take shorthand, there was no competition. Yet Betty retained her competitive edge by doing no wrong in the eyes of Rudyard Rhys, whereas Miss Dim . . .

'Where *were* you last night?' quizzed the excitable Betty. 'We had the devil's own job with the Agnus Dei.'

Miss Dimont was shaken out of her somnolent meditation. 'Well,' she said slowly, 'I don't know if you heard, Betty, but we had two deaths yesterday. I was quite busy with the—'

'I know, I know,' trilled Betty, her blonde bob dancing a tango on top of her head. 'What a day for all of us! That planning committee went on interminably, and I almost didn't make the—'

'Choir practice,' remembered Miss Dimont. 'Lord, I forgot all about it! You see, we were late in the office and—'

'Yes, Rudyard *said* you left the window open,' said Betty accusingly. She liked to be in the right, or was it she liked Judy to be in the wrong? 'You know it's against regulations. He went on for quite some time about it. I *told* him it wasn't my fault when he complained to me, and then Terry said—'

'Terry could have shut it just as easily as me,' said Miss Dimont, now thoroughly awake and feeling peppery.

'Anyway,' said Betty, smoothing her pink sundress, 'I've been looking everywhere for you. The court, the Signal Box, everywhere . . . you have to come back to the office.'

'I've half-a-dozen cases to cover this afternoon.'

'Mr Rhys wants you back in the office,' said Betty smugly. 'Something about those dead bodies.'

The way she said 'dead bodies', you knew Betty had never seen one. Betty didn't care to think about death.

'Come on then,' she said. And the two set off companionably enough – for in Temple Regis it was not easy to find a friend in their line of work.

Everywhere there were still signs of the conflict whose name populated every other sentence uttered in Temple Regis. Though 'the War' had largely passed the town by, its effects had not. Bereaved families were still accorded a special respect, the services held around the War Memorial were well attended, the town's British Legion club was a thriving concern – and though its brightly lit bar turned out its fair share of over-lubricated fellows on a Friday and Saturday night, they were by common consent not to be subject to the attentions of the police or the Bench.

On the beach, at the far end of the promenade, rolls of rusty barbed wire bore witness to the town's long-ago preparations for invasion. Since the declaration of peace the gorgeous white sands had been swept again and again in case a defensive mine still lurked below the surface. Fire hydrants, their red paint peeling, dotted the pavements here and there. And military pillboxes, overgrown with buddleia and cracking at the corners, still stood on forlorn sentry duty – tired, overlooked, perceived now as an eyesore where once they had been the very bastions of liberty.

The walk back to the office took in all this, but Judy

and Betty were deep into the politics of their choir – Jane Overbeck's too-strident soprano, how Mabel Attwater came in late at the beginning of every line ('well, dear, she is eighty-three'), why the tea was always cold when they stopped for a break. Their conductor Geraldine Brent was a short, energetic woman with eyes that burnt like blazing coals – she instilled in her flock such a sense of urgency and importance in their delivery of Gabriel Fauré's sublime work that the composer himself would have left off his rehearsals with the cherubim and seraphim to smile down, especially upon their forthcoming performance at St Margaret's Church.

No summons from Rudyard Rhys was so urgent that it could not wait until Judy and Betty had bought their ice-cream from John, the one-armed 'Stop Me and Buy One' vendor who strategically placed his tricycle-tub on the corner where the promenade ended and the town proper started – only fourpence-ha'penny a brick. Then a quick dash into the Home and Colonial Stores.

'Three slices of ham, please.'

'One and six, madam.'

'Pound of sugar – can you pour it specially? You never know how long those bags have been sitting there.'

'Got a new bag of broken biscuits. Fresh in, thruppence to you.'

And then the air filled with the sound and smell of that most glorious luxury – coffee beans being ground – a recent innovation now that rationing was over. Both women sighed

over their rough blue-paper prizes with their precious contents.

Fortified by these invigorating delays they arrived at the
Riviera Express in excellent spirits, but one sight of Rudyard
Rhys striding down the newsroom towards them sent Betty
scuttling away.

'About time,' rasped Rudyard. 'I won't ask *where you've
been,*' he added, eyeing the Home and Colonial bag.

Miss Dimont was unbowed by the glowering presence –
she'd seen it too often before.

'Yes, Mr Rhys? You know there are six cases in court this
afternoon? 'Three traffic, but then there's—'

'Inquests!' snapped Rudyard. 'Inquests!'

'Yes, Mr Rhys?'

'You forgot, *Miss Dim*—' he dwelt heavily upon these
words '—to mention anything in your reports about the
inquests on Hennessy and Shrimsley.'

'Oh!' said Miss Dimont, colouring visibly.

'There are inquests to be held, *Miss Dim,*' snarled Rhys.
'Were you thinking these two gentlemen were happy now
they were reunited with their Maker? That that was the end
of the story?'

'Well . . .'

'Because I have heard from the coroner's clerk, via *Miss
Featherstone,*' growled Rhys, 'that there may be evidence of
foul play.'

Now why didn't she tell me THAT? fumed Miss Dimont.

FIVE

The weekend was not your own when you worked for the *Riviera Express*. Saturday mornings were devoted to writing up next week's wedding reports (and deciding who'd feature in the 'Thank Heavens!' board), and turning out the more run-of-the-mill obituaries of the town's great and good.

Quite often these careless and unthinking citizens would shuffle off the mortal coil without bothering to warn the *Express* beforehand, which could be irksome when it came to press day. Each new edition of the paper brought with it complaints from readers that their beloved one's journey to the Other Side had gone unmarked.

Rudyard Rhys did not like complaints. He drummed into Judy and Betty and the other members of staff – Terry, even – how they must keep eyes open and ears firmly to the ground on this fundamental point. Miss Dimont had once asked him, mid-tirade, if her job now was to walk about the town centre stopping people and asking, 'Know anyone about to die round your way?' But though this raised a snort of laughter in morning conference, Rudyard simply ordered her to add the town's undertakers to her lengthy list of morning calls.

Truth to tell, Miss Dimont was rather good at obituaries. Why, only the other month she had written a corker about William Pithers, one of the town's roughest diamonds who'd risen from obscurity during the War to become one of its most prominent citizens. His cerise Rolls-Royce, yellow tweed suits and the fat Havana sticking out of his breast pocket did not denote a man of breeding, perhaps, nor yet of great intellect, but Bill Pithers had made his mark all right. His fat-rendering business, though noisy, smelly, and hardly the town's greatest visual attraction, had made him richer than most. Money allowed him a voice in the community far louder than if he'd been elected to the Town Council or the Bench.

Pithers threw his money around ('noted for his extraordinary generosity', typed Miss Dimont pertly) and lorded it down at the golf club ('a sporting enthusiast'). After a lucrative week's work rendering fat, he would sit in the bar dishing out drink and opinion in equal measure to a befoozled audience made up of the thirsty, the hard-up, the deaf and the occasional owner of a rhinoceros skin.

'An enthusiastic conversationalist,' tapped Miss Dimont, who had bumped into the ancient Pithers when the Ladies' Inner Wheel invited her to their annual nine-hole tournament dinner, 'he often encouraged others into lively debate.' Indeed so; that night the lard-like entrepreneur had treated his audience to a twenty-minute peroration on how Herr Hitler was a much misunderstood man; it led, regrettably, to fisticuffs.

'Indeed his love of life (barmaids) and the Turf (he rarely paid his bookies) set him aside in the community (he had no friends) and will make him a much-missed figure' (three people went to his funeral, all of them to make sure he was dead).

Weaving such barbed encomiums was Miss Dimont's consolation, for through the office window she could see across the red rooftops to the promenade, the beach and the glorious turquoise sea which this morning was like glass. Young lovers strolled hand-in-hand, children built their dreams in the sand, the Temple Silver Band parped joyfully in the Victorian bandstand.

Miss Dimont sighed and picked up another green wedding form.

'It was love at first sight in the Palm Court of the Grand,' she rattled. 'Waiter Peter Potts and cleaner Avril Smedley met under a glittering chandelier and . . .'

This was an inspired introduction to the lives of two very nice but humdrum Temple Regents employed by the town's grandest hotel. The rest of her report – the guipure lace, the bouquet of white roses, stephanotis and lily of the valley, the honeymoon spent at a secret location – was standard pie-filling, but Miss Dimont adorned the crust with a little more care because she happened to know Peter. She was often in the Grand on business, and he was always most attentive. She was happy that he had found love with Avril for he was rather a sad boy. She would insist that their picture was not added to the Thank Heavens! board, but in truth it was a prime contender.

Her reports had only to be one hundred and fifty words long – on an average Saturday morning she would get through three or four – but she found it difficult to concentrate. Part of her longed to be set free from her desk so she could enjoy the glorious weather this lazy Indian summer was so generously providing, but another part kept returning to the deaths of Gerald Hennessy and Arthur Shrimsley.

The coroner's clerk had confirmed to Betty that one of the inquests might be troublesome because of certain suspicious circumstances, but refused to add a name or further clues. She would have to wait till Monday afternoon at 2 p.m., when proceedings would be opened and adjourned.

If it was suspicious it had to be Shrimsley, Miss Dimont decided, because of the note in his hand. But then again, as she thought about it, that of itself wouldn't be suspicious if indeed he'd gone against character and done away with himself – a suicide is a suicide. Where was the 'foul play' which Rudyard Rhys had hissed at her last night?

It must therefore be Hennessy. She had definitely felt a frisson of fear when she saw that 'M . . . U . . . R . . .' traced in the carriage dust, but distance lends clarity and it was quite clear that with no sign of violence or personal distress Hennessy could have suffered no foul play – and though she was no expert, it did indeed look like a heart attack.

It left her nowhere.

Her morning's work done, she covered up the Quiet-Riter

and gathered up the delectable bunch of asters Mrs Reedy had left at the front desk as a thank you for her glowing report on the Mothers' Union all-female production of *Julius Caesar*. It had taken a quite extraordinary suspension of disbelief to see this crinkle-permed bunch of ancients, clad in togas and brandishing knives, posing a serious threat to ancient Rome's democracy, but Miss Dimont had pulled it off magnificently, and here was her reward.

Such was the exchange of kindnesses in Temple Regis. It made it such a wonderful place to live.

Her ride home on the redoubtable Herbert took her along the kind of route that film directors dream about and scour the world trying to locate. But here it was, the coast road out of Temple Regis back to her cottage three miles distant, where the road gently rose to where you could see right across Nelson's Bay out into the English Channel. Out there, the faded blue of the sea met the white-blue of the sky at some point of infinity which, no matter how hard you tried, you could not pinpoint. The seascape was massive, blinding in its brilliance, making you feel that no other place on earth could touch it. Below, the ribbon of white beach skirted the waves modestly before turning into a sandbar dividing the sea from a freshwater lake which was home to a thousand contented species, winter and summer.

This was England's Riviera in its simple, unadulterated glory. Miss Dimont had been to Nice and to Cannes, but the Grande Corniche, which hemmed that southernmost part of France, was not a patch on the Temple Road – for here were no unsightly developments of blocks of flats and concrete villas vying with each other for a sight of the sea; instead just an open road with the occasional house on the headland to remind the traveller he was not quite in Paradise.

The thin ribbon of tarmac rounded a bend and made a steep descent to sea level, and as she urged Herbert ever onwards, the spume which rose from the rocks cooled her brow and moistened her lips with its salty zest. Her corkscrew hair bobbed in the wind and Miss Dimont was in seventh heaven.

These moments, of course, are fleeting, evanescent. Life's realities return all too soon and on arriving home she discovered a note from her neighbour Mrs Alcock complaining about Mulligatawny leaving his collection of mouse entrails on her doorstep. Again!

She unlocked her door, gazed fleetingly at the handsome face staring back at her from the silver frame on the mantelpiece, and made herself a cup of tea.

*

A weekend is what you make it, thought Miss Dimont, as she let herself into the *Express* offices on Monday morning. Domestic chores need not rule the roost – let there be music!

And so there was – the long-awaited visit from the Trebyddch Male Voice Choir to the village hall on Saturday night was a triumph, with their exquisite harmonies in 'All in the April Evening' bringing her to the verge of tears. Then the men pulled off their ties, brought out some guitars and a washboard, and sang some noisy skiffle songs to which she danced giddily.

At the reception afterwards – beer for the men, ginger beer for Miss D – she found that miners from the Valleys could be wonderfully charming. Muscular, handsome, incredibly dark, there was one who . . . but no! She moved her thoughts swiftly on to Sunday matins at St Margaret's – 003 in *Hymns Ancient & Modern*, 'Awake My Soul and With the Sun'.

But now back in the office, the sour smell from the back copies of the newspaper piled on the windowsill behind assailed her nostrils and reminded her that the weekend was over. It was time to go out and make The Calls.

Which was good, for Miss Dimont had been doing some thinking.

What, she asked herself, had happened to Gerald Hennessy's wife, the glorious Prudence Aubrey? Almost as famous as Gerald, she had starred in a string of black-and-white classics opposite her husband in the early fifties. Her style was about as sophisticated as it comes – sharply pulled-back hair, Norman Hartnell dresses, muted but expensive jewellery, perfect maquillage – and with that slightly sharp delivery which told you this was not a woman to stand any nonsense.

Less had been seen of Prudence on the silver screen of late, but that was probably because she was at home keeping Gerald's slippers warm, or translating Russian verse into French (her hobby, if you believed the publicity handouts).

Miss Dimont entered the battered portals of Temple Regis police station, a rugged edifice in local red stone as stout and dependable as the town's constabulary itself. Its interior, however, was another matter – dull paintwork, no carpets, dust and carbolic, and an air of barely controlled confusion. Her regular Monday morning colloquy with Sergeant Gull was now in session.

'The inquests, Sergeant.'

'Yes, Miss Dimont?' The sergeant took out his tobacco-pouch and stared at it doubtfully.

'Which is the suspicious one?'

'Couldn't say, nobody tells me nothing.'

It was always like this. It took ten very irritating minutes to warm the sergeant up before you could get anything out of him, even a cup of tea.

Miss Dimont changed tack.

'Strange, isn't it, that Mrs Hennessy hasn't come down?'

A rapt smile swept slowly over the sergeant's face. Here, clearly, was a fan of Prudence Aubrey. Was it *Shadows of the Night* which had enslaved him, or *No, Darling, No!*, possibly even her *Emmelina Pankhurst*?

'She be down this morning,' he said dreamily, as though already employed by her team of press spokesmen. 'Riviera Express. The 11.30.'

That would do – she and Terry would be there! The arrival of a film star on the Riviera Express was news, whether they were dead or alive, and this would be a useful follow-up story.

'Now, Sergeant, on to Mr Shrimsley. Was there a Mrs Shrimsley?'

A wintry smile. 'That's a joke, miss, iznit?'

'Come along, Sergeant, I'm late as it is.'

The sergeant clammed up – cither he didn't know, or wasn't saying. Always the same with the self-important Gull, and on such a small point too. His answer meant more time having to be spent tracking down relatives.

There seemed no more to be said. The reporter took herself off to the council offices to see what crumbs of information might be gleaned from the forthcoming week's proceedings, en route taking in the large public notice-board outside the Corn Exchange. This unassuming block of wood had proved a goldmine of stories over the years, a virtual town crier of tales in fact – from lost cats to appeals for assistance; from the emergence of new religious gatherings (they never lasted long) to announcements of the arrival of the latest phenomenon, beat groups. The town prided itself on staying *au courant*.

Miss Dim herself was much taken by beat groups. Temple Regis had already been visited by Max Bygraves and Pearl Carr and Teddy Johnson, but though there were whispers that Tommy Steele might make a surprise visit, the best they had had of this new music was Yankee Fonzie, just back from a barnstorming tour of France where there had been riots – though having watched his act at the Corn Exchange, Miss Dimont could not be sure quite why the French had gone so mad. Maybe it was his bubble-car; it certainly wasn't his hairdo.

*

The Calls completed, she retraced her steps to the office but as she approached the police station out popped Sergeant Gull.

'There you are,' he said. 'Got news fer you.'

'Oh?' said Miss Dimont. This was unprecedented.

'Hennessy.'

'Yes?'

''E were going to do a summer season. 'Ere, Temple Regis. Think of that!'

Miss Dimont asked Gull to repeat himself.

'Oh yers,' said Gull, as if he had discovered a nugget of gold.

'At the Pavilion?'

'Where else,' said the Sergeant smugly.

Miss Dimont adjusted her spectacles and stared Gull in the eye. 'How do you know?' she grilled. 'How could you possibly know that?'

She turned up the heat because it was the only way with Gull. On the rare occasions he had something worth telling, the policeman invariably prevaricated, wandered round the houses, kept the best wine till last. She hadn't got time this morning.

'Come on, Sergeant!'

Gull enjoyed this game of cat-and-mouse but was eager to demonstrate his superior knowledge. 'Card in Hennessy's pocket,' he declared proudly. 'From Mr Cattermole.'

Raymond Cattermole ran the Pavilion Theatre, an old actor-manager out to grass but clinging to past glories.

'Most unlikely,' said Miss Dimont firmly and stepped off towards her office.

'Card in his pocket,' called Gull as she rounded the corner.

Miss D swung round. 'What did it say?' she demanded crisply.

'Not much. Something about "looking forward to seeing you then",' said Gull.

'Doesn't prove a thing,' snapped the reporter, setting off again for the office. But, as she walked, she chewed over the possibility.

Or impossibility – for Gull's assertion made no sense. Gerald Hennessy was at the height of his fame as a screen actor – successful, admired, his career as a nation's favourite well established. Why would he want to spend six weeks in Temple Regis at the Pavilion, where turgid production after turgid production made successive generations of holiday-maker swear they'd never set foot in the place again?

Indeed the perpetrator of these epic failures, Ray Catter-mole himself, loved starring in them – so what place would there have been for Gerald Hennessy? Was Cattermole think-ing of retiring? Maybe planning a sabbatical next year? (*Oh, please*, thought Miss Dimont, whose duty it was each summer to review Ray's dreary fare.)

But no – he'd already informed her in lordly tones of next year's offerings: Bernard Shaw's *Saint Joan*, and a stage show starring Alma Cogan. There would be no male lead next year for Gerald Hennessy to play.

Unless, of course, Cattermole had been lying – as he often

did. Miss Dimont had doubted from the outset whether Temple Regents, while undeniably welcoming, could secure a star of Alma's lustre to spend six weeks among them any more than they could expect Gerald Hennessy ever to give them his King Lear.

No, there was something odd about the whole thing – what with no leading part for Cattermole, a too ambitious playbill, and the very idea Gerald Hennessy would think of treading the Pavilion's creaky boards. It must be something else.

But what? Without realising it, Miss Dimont was rapidly coming to the conclusion that if there had been foul play in Temple Regis' two celebrated deaths it must be to do with the actor, not the detestable Shrimsley.

Back in the office there was a rare daytime sighting of Athene Madrigale. 'Busy, dear?' she asked Miss Dimont indulgently.

'Well yes,' came the reply. 'What are you doing here, though? This isn't your time of day, Athene. It's Monday morning – you're a creature of the night!'

'I felt moved, dear. The spirit awakened within, and I knew I had to give my all to the stars this morning.

'Also,' she added, as if imparting a great secret, 'I needed to do some shopping.'

Athene made the tea while Miss Dimont found Terry to tell him about the impending arrival of Prudence Aubrey. As her cup cooled, reporter consulted astrologer.

'So you see, Gerald Hennessy – Raymond Cattermole – Alma Cogan,' she summed up neatly.

'Yes, I do see,' said Athene. She paused. 'Did you know that Gerald and Mr Cattermole were both in a West End play together? Before the War?'

'How interesting.' It wasn't particularly, actors being actors, but the tea wasn't cool enough to drink yet.

'Yes, *The Importance of Being Earnest*. I saw it myself, at the Globe Theatre – Edith Evans, oh! And Margaret Rutherford too!

'What was interesting is that Raymond was playing Jack, and Gerald, Algernon, then after the first few performances they were switched round so Gerald took the lead part. And *wonderful* he was! I never cared for that Raymond Cattermole,' added Athene.

'So they both had to learn another part?'

'Yes, and I remember an interview Mr Cattermole gave which said some quite unkind things about Gerald. Quite unusual in those days – created something of a stir. I mean, people in the theatre just don't talk like that do they, saying nasty things?'

'So,' said Miss Dimont, sipping her tea slowly, 'you might say there was no love lost between them?'

'Well,' said Athene brightly, 'everyone forgives and forgets. Don't they!' And with that she picked up her shopping bag and faded gently, a riot of colours, out of sight.

At last Miss Dimont felt she was getting somewhere. Once upon a time Hennessy and Cattermole were on an equal footing, co-stars in a West End production. Nearly twenty years later Gerald was a star and Raymond was . . . well, it still was something to be an actor-manager of a theatre, and Temple Regis was indeed the prettiest town in Devon, so he was very fortunate. But . . .

But, thought Miss Dimont, beneath the artificial bonhomie she had long ago spied an unhappy and, one might almost say, a tortured soul.

Why on earth had Raymond Cattermole lured Gerald Hennessy down to Temple Regis?

What *did* he have in mind?

SIX

It had taken Prudence Aubrey more than three days to arrive in Temple Regis to claim the mortal remains of her husband, one of the most famous men in the land. Clearly this was an actress who needed time to prepare for her big entrance.

At 11.30 precisely the Riviera Express pulled in to Temple Regis station. As the flood of disembarking passengers ebbed away, Miss Aubrey, swathed dramatically in black, stepped elegantly from the Pullman carriage and paused on the step as if waiting for a barrage of flash guns to pop off.

There was only Terry.

It did not take much persuasion to halt her forward progress however. Miss Dimont had her notebook at the ready, Terry his camera; Miss Aubrey repaired to the first-class waiting room in a mute acceptance that this was her lot in life, to be harried by the press. The fact that Miss Dimont had done no more than raise her eyebrows, and Terry check his lens, would not in the normal scheme of things rate as press harassment, but you had to be a celebrity to understand just how cruel newspaper people could be.

Miss Aubrey gathered her widow's weeds around her

and sat delicately on a hard oak settle. In deference to her new-found and sadly tragic status, Miss Dimont and Terry remained standing.

'I'm so sorry,' began the reporter but got no further.

'It is a complete tragedy. An actor in his prime, one so adored by the nation,' rattled out Miss Aubrey, 'so much loved by his friends and . . .' dramatic pause '. . . family. It is a great loss to the profession and the country.'

She reached into her bag for a small perfumed handker-chief and dabbed her nose, though not so much as to dislodge its maquillage. Her photograph had not yet been taken.

'I wonder if I could just—'

'He was telling me only last week how he loved my *Emmelina Pankhurst*. He said it is the one film he would have paid a large sum to have a part in, just to play alongside me. But, of course,' she went on, 'there was no role for Gerald in a film like *that*.' Just a sprinkling of contempt garnished her voice now. 'He took the populist path. And. Who. Can. Blame. Him.'

What rot, thought Miss Dimont. Gerald Hennessy was one of those actors who could do comedy, adventure, war – he even played Shelley once – while Miss Aubrey's palette was scattered with fewer, paler colours, her most successful films the ones where she dressed magnificently and said little. It really was quite remarkable how universally adored she had become, given everything.

Perhaps Miss Dimont was a little jealous of Prudence Aubrey's happy marriage to Gerald, perhaps she just preferred not to interview actresses. Perhaps, being a woman of a certain background, it was both – for an actress's lines, when scribbled in a notebook, always seem so weighty and rich with promise, but when you come to transcribe them, they seem so remarkably devoid of interest.

So far the interview had been about Miss Aubrey.

'Perhaps then he—'

'We were to make another film together,' this elegant steamroller continued, her voice sliding down a semitone, 'our pet project. An English version of *The Magnificent Ambersons,* only set here, of course. In England.' Her eyes for the first time focused upon the vaguely dishevelled middle-aged woman before her, clad in a macintosh tied tightly at the waist, with sensible shoes and a silk scarf at her neck – a combination which, if Miss Aubrey had chosen it, would have been carried off with considerable élan. On Miss Dim it all looked a bit haphazard. Maybe Miss Aubrey took her for an idiot.

'That must have been a—'

'Of course, we hadn't signed the contract. I had been waiting for the right director. I was to be the Duchess of Tintagel, Gerald the Duke naturally. It was a broader part for me, requiring many changes of costumes and, of course, the locations . . . stunning houses. Beautiful. Despite the War . . .'

'May I ask when you last saw Mr Hennessy?'

'What?' snapped the actress. 'What do you mean?' Suddenly her face was transfigured by a range of emotions considerably more extensive than her fans were generally granted onscreen.

'I meant . . .' started Miss Dimont, but then faltered. Her question appeared to have vaulted the actress from a cool if stagey presence into something more closely resembling a cornered animal.

She tried again. 'I'm sorry if I—

'Don't. Just don't.'

Suddenly the conversation was dangerously electric, and Miss Dimont drew back. Self-obsessed Prudence Aubrey may be, but she was also newly bereaved – and the *Riviera Express* had its standards of conduct towards its interviewees.

The interview concluded quite rapidly thereafter and Miss Aubrey was wafted away to the Grand by a uniformed chauffeur who materialised out of nowhere – as they always do in Temple Regis when film stars sail over the horizon. It was not a town, after all, peopled entirely by hayseeds.

Terry got his photos. You had to give Miss Aubrey that, she knew how to pose even in a railway waiting room. Somehow widow's weeds had never seemed more Parisian, more desirable. Cecil Beaton was said to have fallen in love with her, which seemed remarkable to those who knew Cecil, and here she was – in Temple Regis! She was front-page material wherever she went – it was just that she now seemed to be famous for being famous, for alas her millions of fans had been waiting a long time for her next film.

Terry drove Miss Dimont back to the office in the Minor.

'Did you notice how she suddenly turned – just like that?' said an unsettled Miss Dimont to Terry.

'Fabulous coat she 'ad,' said Terry, ignoring the question as usual. 'Did you see that twirl I got her to do? Talk about New Look all over again! The way that fabric just floated in the air!'

'A disgrace,' snorted Miss Dim. 'Twirling? They haven't even had the post-mortem on her husband yet, let alone the inquest!'

'No disrespect,' said Terry, scratching his head. But the whole encounter – its timing, its focus, and the unexpected bolt of lightning which concluded it – troubled the reporter.

It was lunchtime. Peter Pomeroy, the chief sub-editor, was jerkily dipping his head towards his desk like a heron stabbing at a fish. Seen from a distance this behaviour might seem odd to the newcomer, alarming even, but it was Pomeroy's way and nobody said anything. After you'd worked at the *Riviera Express* for a few weeks you came to realise that everyone had their quirks – after all, Miss Dim and Herbert, just think of that! – and if he wanted to pretend he wasn't eating sandwiches concealed in his desk drawer then who was anyone to say otherwise?

Miss Dim took an apple from her raffia bag and placed it next to her Quiet-Riter. 'Exclusive,' she rattled. '*Riviera Express* talks to Gerald Hennessy's widow, Prudence Aubrey.' (Exclusive because no other paper thought to turn up, a cause of intense dissatisfaction to the nation's newest widow.)

She ratcheted down the page with two swift stabs of her

left hand. There was no time to spare – the printers were waiting for her copy.

'The tragic widow of Gerald Hennessy revealed to the *Express* that she had planned to make another film soon with her husband,' she rattled.

'Prior to her husband's inquest on Monday, Prudence Aubrey disclosed that her ambition to make a British version of *The Magnificent Ambersons* was well advanced but . . .' and so went the tale, innocuous, sympathetically worded and lacking any clue to avid readers that its tragic star was a nasty piece of work capable of sudden and vicious twists of temper.

When she had finished, Miss Dimont pulled the copy-paper – three sheets sandwiching two carbons – from her Quiet-Riter and separated the component parts. The bottom sheet was hooked on to the spike on her desk – a handy filing tool in the ordinary course of events and, unbent, an even more useful murder weapon – handed one to the sub-editors, and the top copy went into Mr Rhys' in-tray.

Grabbing her apple she stalked off to the coroner's court, munching furiously, thinking hard. Prudence Aubrey's unwarranted savagery had upset her – and after all the effort she and Terry had taken to treat her with kid gloves! Well, thought Miss Dimont, not next time – next time she would get the full Sergeant Hernaford treatment.

Her presence in court was about as vital to the proceedings as that of anyone else's – that is to say, not at all. Dr Rudkin paid lip service to the occasion by donning a black coat and pinstripe trousers with a nice stiff collar and a suitably drab tie, and in return was shown the deference that all coroners must be shown; for they, and only they, hold the key to a dead man's future reputation.

In ten minutes the whole thing was over. Dr Rudkin opened and adjourned the inquest into the death of Gerald Victor Midleton Hennessy pending a post-mortem report, then did the same in the case of Garrick Arthur Shrimsley. This was the way things were generally done to give the key players time to properly prepare themselves before the full inquest at a later date. Everybody rose, decorously awaited the doctor's exit, made a mental note to be here again on Friday, then swarmed out into the September sunshine.

As they all paused momentarily on the pavement, Prudence Aubrey glanced over at Miss Dim, blinked hard, then turned sharply away and headed for her car. In that instant the reporter realised that her question, as to when the actress last saw her husband, had hit the nail squarely on the head.

Only she had no idea why.

Was it that Prudence had been out with a man friend? There had been several sightings of her in the company of handsome young chaps, written up by the *Daily Mail*'s diarist, Paul Tanfield ('the column which brings champagne into the lives of caravan dwellers'). Was it simply that this supremely self-centred prima donna could not remember when she'd last seen her husband? That her well-polished script, delivered to Miss Dimont and Terry, an actress's soliloquy which brooked no interruption, had failed to incorporate this fundamental in its preparation?

Or was it just that the question was, when it came down to it, about her husband and not about her? Certainly the posing of it had exposed a chink in Miss Aubrey's haute-couture armour and had momentarily left her vulnerable and exposed.

But Miss Dimont – even clever, perceptive, worldly Miss Dimont – was unable to see past the film-star artifice. Thus protected, Prudence Aubrey retained her beautiful enigma, the single quality upon which she had built her reputation, and one which she was not about to relinquish to a corkscrew-haired provincial.

Outclassed and – perhaps – outwitted, the reporter beat a hasty retreat back to the office. Her account of the proceedings would make a small Page One paragraph, no more, and anyway she had to quickly scan the minutes of the Highways Committee before its meeting to consider the siting of a new public lavatory, a matter which was proving highly contentious to the good people of Temple Regis.

*

Life on the *Riviera Express* consisted of passages of frantic activity followed by equal periods of stasis. There was a chance to telephone friends, make shopping lists, dream about holidays, or write the occasional letter. Fridays were generally such a time for Miss Dimont and on this particular day she had completed all her work-displacement activities by the time the mid-morning coffee came around.

After chatting to Betty Featherstone about her latest boyfriend, some big wheel in Rotary, Miss Dimont decided on a whim to pay a visit to Raymond Cattermole at the Pavilion Theatre. There was always the panto to talk about – so far Miss Dimont had resisted thinking about Christmas but it was sure to come around sooner or later, so she had an excuse.

The Pavilion, Edwardian in construction, was living proof that there are jerry-builders in every age. Time and tide had taken their toll, and though the posters which adorned its frontage were bright and fresh, that was as much as you could say about it.

Including the manager, Mr Cattermole. There had been a time, when he first arrived after the War, when there was a spring in his step and an air of promise about the place. He had even managed to get some of his old West End chums to come down for a summer season, though it has to be said they only came once, and as these stars wafted back to their firmament so Raymond took on their mantle, increasingly starring in his own productions until he could only see virtue in saving money *and* taking the applause.

Needless to say this was not a recipe for success, and as time went by the Pavilion's productions became as creaky as the building itself. It therefore fascinated Miss Dimont that Gerald Hennessy – oh! she thought, what a loss to acting, what a loss to the nation! – might deign to do a summer season here. Was it a last-ditch attempt by Cattermole to revive the theatre's flagging fortunes? Indeed, a generous gesture by his old thespian colleague to help out?

Or perhaps a decision by the film star to award himself a sabbatical holiday, away from the arc-lights and the premieres and the press-men? She had managed to slide in a question to Prudence Aubrey about Gerald's plans in Temple Regis, but the actress was too busy with Terry arranging her twirl to answer.

Miss Dimont paused for a moment before entering the theatre and looked down the pier towards the great wide ocean beyond. Its waters had many characters, far more than were ever played on the boards of the Pavilion, and this morning they were strong and silent, great giants like Othello and Lear. Only bluer.

The Pavilion was situated at the landside end of the pier, something of a design compromise by the Edwardians but one which ensured its foundations would never fail, whatever the fate of its superstructure. Miss Dimont entered, as was her habit, by the stage door which was tucked next to a row of redundant penny-in-the-slot machines.

Inside, she could hear a curious noise, a scraping sound accompanied by a strangulated version of what she decided must be the overture to *William Tell.*

'*Minamin minamin minamin-min-min,*
Minamin minamin minamin-min-min –
Minamin minamin minamin-min-min,
Mina MIIIIIIIIIIIIIIN ma-mina min-min-min.'

She came upon Raymond Cattermole crouching on the floor with his back to the wall.

'Ah, Miss Dimont,' he said, unsurprised. 'Would you give

me a hand up? Just doing my daily exercises. Learned them off Larry, you know.'

Miss Dimont blinked.

'Sir Laurence Olivier,' said Cattermole as if taking a bow. 'We trod the boards together, you know.'

The actor-manager struggled up from the floor, explaining that 'William Tell' sung through gritted teeth while bending your knees and sliding up and down a wall was far better than Stanislavsky when it came to an actor preparing. He was unselfconscious in her presence and went over to a mirror to settle his toupee more precisely on his big fat head.

'*Henry V*,' said Miss Dimont. 'You were the spear-carrier.'

Cattermole had forgotten he had misled Miss Dimont once before on the nature of his theatrical partnership with the colossus of British theatre.

'He had his off nights, you know,' he said testily. A non sequitur, maybe, but it re-established the fact that he had known Larry while Miss Dim had not.

'I thought we could talk about the pantomime,' said the reporter. 'People will want to start booking soon.' (Just like childbirth, Temple Regents had that blithe capacity to forget the pain they had endured last time around.)

'But first,' she went on, 'I wanted to ask you about Gerald Hennessy.'

Cattermole looked startled.

'I understand he was in Temple Regis to meet you,' said Miss Dimont, 'and I just wondered . . .'

It was always better to leave a question open. People you

were interviewing didn't care what you wondered, they just wanted to get on and give you the benefit of their superior knowledge. Furthermore, if you wondered the wrong thing, they would be put off by your complete and utter incomprehension of the situation in hand. The reputation of journalism rested on *not* specifying what precisely it was that you wondered.

Cattermole said nothing.

'I wondered . . .' tried Miss Dimont again.

'Drink?' said Cattermole. It was not quite midday.

'No thank you,' said Miss Dimont sternly. 'But don't let me stop you.'

Those were the words which sprang forth but they were not what she meant. What she meant was, if it helps you to talk, then drink the whole bottle. But you are the custodian of our theatre and you churn out rotten performances which help you maintain that old Bentley and keep that mistress of yours, but if you sobered up a bit and put your back into it the Pavilion could be saved and we would love you again as we once did.

But Miss Dimont, being the non-judgemental sort, said nothing of the kind. Cattermole got down the Scotch and sloshed a little into the glass on his desk. He looked warily at the water jug next to it but decided against.

'Ah, yes, Gerald,' he said in drawling tones. 'Dear Gerald. We trod the boards together, you know.'

'*The Importance of Being Earnest*,' said Miss Dimont, swiftly. 'With Edith Evans. The Globe Theatre, wasn't it?'

Raymond Cattermole did a wonderfully lugubrious double-take, his trademark *moue* that could still raise a laugh, even after all these years. 'Well you *do* do your homework, don't you?' He was now in character. Possibly Professor Henry Higgins, she couldn't be sure just yet.

'He played Algernon, you played Raymond.'

The Professor looked over his spectacles at the reporter. 'He broke my arm, you know,' he said rather wistfully. 'And then stole my part.

'We had an understudy, can't remember the name, and he took over while I was in hospital. There was a bit of Bunbury business onstage, bit of a rough-house, and he broke my arm.'

Cattermole drained his glass and looked forlorn. 'Never been the same since. I was so keen to get back onstage the doctor didn't set it properly. The director refused to drop the Bunbury rough-house and I had to carry on with it even though I'd only just broken the old arm. I was right-handed, but I had to learn to use my left to raise a sword, point a pistol, all that stuff. Really, it was the beginning . . .'

Miss Dimont saw it all in an instant. The Wilde was the last time Cattermole had set foot on the London stage. Maybe it was the arm, maybe his already-waning fortunes as a slightly too-old young lead, maybe his self-pity (ever-present in an actor, never to be displayed) – but to save his reputation and his self-esteem, Cattermole had nimbly effected a career-change which ended with his arrival down here in Devon. For every step Gerald Hennessy took up, it would seem, Raymond Cattermole took a corresponding one down.

'So why was he coming to see you?'

'I didn't say he was, did I?'

'Mr Cattermole,' said Miss Dimont, 'I think he was.'

The Professor had disappeared and an ageing pink-cheeked thespian, unsettled and edgy, had taken his place. Cattermole uncorked the bottle and poured himself another one.

'Sure you won't?' he asked, but he didn't mean it. He had become distinctly cooler towards his interlocutor.

'Everybody seems to think Gerald Hennessy was coming down to do a summer season.' There, Miss Dimont had said it. There was no earthly reason to believe this baseless assertion, but baseless assertions were a time-honoured way of worming facts out of the reluctant and the downright unco-operative. Apart from Sergeant Gull nobody, apart from Cattermole, had a clue why Hennessy travelled down to Temple Regis.

Raymond Cattermole had not trodden the boards with Sir Laurence Olivier for nothing. He lifted his head, turned it, flicked his eyes at Miss Dimont and set his jaw. At the same time, he shot his cuffs and straightened the knot in his tie.

He did not say a word.

If Cattermole's purpose was to unnerve the reporter, he succeeded. Miss Dimont was not used to sitting in silence, staring eyeball to eyeball, with people. She did her best work by getting people to chat. The man opposite was just sitting and gazing at her. She was . . . unnerved.

'A summer season?' she prompted hesitantly.

Finally, he spoke, though his lips did not move very much as he did so.

'*Over . . . my . . . dead . . . body,*' said Raymond Cattermole.

SEVEN

Unlike Miss Dimont, Betty Featherstone played no part in the War and, actually, it would be hard to imagine what useful contribution she could possibly have made. Despite her breezy charm and outward competence there was something missing which, had she been put in charge of men's lives as Miss Dimont was, might have led to some tragic outcomes.

Not that you would get Rudyard Rhys to agree with that, for the editor was a man of very firm opinions and his opinion of Betty was that she was the right sort for the *Riviera Express*. How Miss Dim had got herself a position on his staff – well, that was another story.

It was not that Mr Rhys was soft on Betty, but it would be fair to say she knew how to twist him round her little finger. When he marked up the diary – that is to say, allotted the known stories for the week ahead – Betty always ended up with the best. Miss Dimont might have asked herself whether this was because the editor knew the plum jobs were usually the easiest – in Betty he had a useful but totally uninspired reporter – and it was better to leave the more difficult work to be handled by her. Wisely, she did not waste time thinking up the answer to that.

Betty had arrived only recently, the veteran of one or two failed engagements (there may have been more), but she looked optimistically on the world of love and her continuing part therein. Her regular features, permed blonde hair, undulating figure and conservative choice of clothes somehow marked her out for what she was – competent, unexciting, and by now in her thirties, a stranger to life's more exacting challenges. But there was more to her than that.

That business of not telling Miss Dimont about the foul play was typical.

'Oh dear, Judy!' she wailed when tackled. 'I just – you know Derek and I had been having a tiff – I just forgot!' And you didn't know whether that was the truth or not. What can be said for certain is that she rarely did anything for Miss Dimont which took her out of her way.

The double-death sensation at Temple Regis had been handled extremely competently by his chief reporter but Rudyard Rhys, a belt-and-braces man if ever there was, could not leave well alone. He was nervous of his chairman and he was nervous of public opinion. The bonus of having a celebrity scoop in Temple Regis could easily be outweighed by any further developments uncovered by Miss Dimont which might tarnish Temple Regis' golden reputation. You could never tell with stories like this – they were, to some extent, an unexploded bomb and he didn't like it.

He ordered Betty to keep an eye on her colleague and

let him know if she felt things could be done better. Betty blushed and smiled – was she pleased to be put in a position of supervision over her older colleague? Glad her superior journalistic talents were recognised by old Rudyard? Or was it jealousy, pure and simple? For Betty could never quite get the measure of the woman who sat across the desk from her. Miss Dimont seemed to live a unique life, at once both deeply involved in the community and at the same time set apart from it. Betty needed constant reassurance about her looks and femininity; Miss Dimont did not. Betty could not exist without a boyfriend knocking about; Miss Dimont lived alone. Betty talked a lot about men; but though Miss Dimont was far from immune to their charms, she chose not to share her innermost thoughts.

And then there was the War. Nobody knew quite what Judy Dimont had done, but whatever it was you knew instinctively she would have executed her duties as she did on the *Riviera Express* – diligently, accurately, speedily, and in a wholly exemplary manner.

There were many in Temple Regis who talked about the conflict and their part in it; but then again, there were others who did not – not through shame or embarrassment but because they preferred it that way. They knew who they were, it did not take a regimental blazer badge or a jewelled lapel brooch for them to identify each other. You saw them in St Margaret's Church on Remembrance Sunday, usually sitting towards the back, united in their reluctance to display the shining emblems a grateful nation had planted on their chests.

Miss Dimont was one of these lone wolves, quiet people who shared memories only with themselves.

Any friend of Judy, therefore, alerted to Betty snooping on her colleague's professional activities might have raged against the iniquity of it. But were she to be made aware of Betty's peephole activities – and maybe she instinctively knew anyway – it would make no difference for, as always, Miss Dimont rose above. In any event she was the first to admit her occasional journalistic lapses left her wide open to criticism – and usually just at the point where she had scored some remarkable triumph.

Life, she often reflected calmly, is like that.

Betty took advantage of her colleague's absence to saunter round to the other side of the desk. There, an open notebook, festooned with the weird and inexplicable hieroglyphics invented by Mr Pitman to torment successive generations of secretaries and reporters, offered its secrets up for the taking. But Miss Featherstone's own shorthand accomplishments were courtesy of Pitman's rival, Mr Gregg, and so she could neither make head nor tail of the scribbles.

However, there was a handwritten note-to-self from Miss Dim which made interesting reading.

PA – didn't know where G was. That <u>horrible</u> reaction!
RC – something to hide – hated G I am sure.
Did R&P know each other?
Don't forget Shrimsley!

It didn't make sense but Betty made a mental note. It was obvious Miss Dimont had something up her sleeve and she did *not* want to see her rival occupying the whole of the front page again on Friday as she'd done last week – why, that was Betty's domain!

She went back to her desk and noted with distaste the most recent edition of the *Riviera Express*, lying on the subs' table nearby. And then she did a double-take – Shrimsley in Judy's note was obviously the late Arthur of that name whose death was recorded so graphically.

And so . . . G must be Gerald Hennessy! And . . . PA must be Prudence Aubrey!

This excessive use of grey matter rather exhausted Betty but she struggled on. Who was RC? And why did he hate Gerald? Why was Prudence horrible? And DID R and P know each other?

It was all rather exciting, just like a detective novel. She couldn't wait to tell Mr Rhys.

*

The Palm Court of the Grand Hotel, Temple Regis, was a home-from-home for anyone with upstart aspirations. Here, heavy doors swung open and the world swept through into its colonnaded rooms. Waiters bowed and smiled, ladies rustled their dresses, gentlemen adjusted their cuffs. The air was one of decorum; hotter passions inflamed by early evening cocktails were quickly doused by the trio of ancients who scraped and plinked their way through a menu of dusty Viennese composers. The mercy was that, acoustically, the Palm Court had always been something of a nightmare, and the clinking of glasses and cups and the raised voices of those on their second Sidecar drowned out the dismal musical offering which added tone but no bite to the evening's proceedings.

But pretentious it most certainly was not. The Grand had long lived up to its name, attracting an exceptional array of the rich and famous – writers, politicians, film stars – by virtue of its high standards, comfortable beds and Nelsonian eye to indiscretion. Nowadays, its swagger had evaporated a little, what with threadbare carpets and manservants to match, but it had lost none of its gravitas or charm. And in one way, the Grand was what kept the town's head above water – for all the time the well-known and the celebrated continued to check in, those who looked up to them would flock to Temple Regis just to rub shoulders with them.

It was tragic indeed that Prudence Aubrey now occupied the hotel suite intended for her dead husband – a sumptuous collection of long-windowed, pastel-shaded rooms overlooking a beach which even the merest splash of sunshine rendered idyllic. Gerald's agent, Radford, had paid for it all; and now Prudence had only to ring, and a boy would come running to open the champagne or race to find a swizzle-stick.

That invisible chain of porters which stretches from railway station to hotel room in any town worth its salt had delivered the bags; the temporary maid assigned to her had neatly filled the closets and drawers with her possessions.

There was nothing for Prudence to do except sit out the week until the inquest proper into Gerald's death.

She had brought newspapers and magazines, dark glasses, and a number of current novels. Once upon a time there would have been film scripts, too, but of late there had been fewer of these. On a low table by the window the maid had artlessly left a copy of last week's *Riviera Express*, and it came as quite a shock to see on its front page a face she had known so well and for so long staring out, unseeing, at her.

She looked at the *Express*'s headline and took in the details of Gerald's death, almost as if for the first time. Her beautifully painted face gave nothing away as she read Miss Dimont's account of her husband's final moments, but a twitch of disapproval corrugated her brow as she discovered that Gerald's demise had not been the only noteworthy departure in Temple Regis that week. She rather resented the fact that the local rag bracketed his tragic loss with that of another, a man whose name may have seemed vaguely familiar, but who was not one of her circle.

It must be said that Prudence Aubrey was quickly bored. A half-empty champagne glass signified this fact – normally by 6.45 she would be on a second or third, but this was still the first. She paced the room and wrestled with what to do, for at this hour in London she would be surrounded by friends, *good* friends, planning an evening at the Café de Paris or the Trocadero. Here, there was no one. Radford would arrive eventually, but for now he was busy sorting out Gerald's affairs.

To go down? Or to have supper on a tray?

She turned on the radio. Dance music murmured gently forth from the BBC's Light Programme, but it failed to catch her mood. She switched the apparatus off and, with a lingering glance in the mirror, picked up her evening bag and prepared to face her public. Anything was better than being cooped up in this dreary old room all night.

Miss Aubrey was quite surprised by the scene which presented itself on her arrival in the front hall. Women in floral dresses and jewels, men in sober suits or dinner jacket. Waiters weaving through the throng, drinks trays at shoulder level, waitresses skipping after them carrying linen napkins. Though the nation may have lost one of its leading actors and the hotel now sheltered his grieving widow, the party went on.

Prudence decided to join in. 'Martini, dry, straight up, olive,' she drawled to a passing young man in her best Bacall imitation. She had to repeat the instruction once or twice for though the ever-obliging Peter Potts knew his way around martinis he was unfamiliar with the 'straight up' business. Finally, the cocktail arrived and she took it on to the terrace.

The late summer sun lingered lazily, but people were already moving in to dinner and there was plenty of choice when it came to chairs and tables. She selected one which had a particularly beguiling view down to the hazy sea and was sitting down when a voice said, quite gently, 'Miss Aubrey.'

The actress looked up to see an elegant figure clad in an emerald silk dress with a nice-looking diamond brooch at its shoulder. The sloping nose carried upon it a pair of spectacles, the hair which might otherwise prove problematic held back by a toque, one hand conveying a cigarette holder, the other a glass containing a liquid not unlike her own.

'Er, have we . . .?' said Prudence, since from the tone of the other woman's voice, they had.

'Judy Dimont,' came the reply. 'We met this afternoon. At the station.'

'Ah, yes, the—

'Reporter,' finished Miss Dimont. 'I'm sorry, I feel I owe you an apology.'

Prudence was not sure what this meant. The woman had asked awkward questions. Was she about to launch into more? And anyway, was this even the same woman? Could it be some imposter? She looked so very different from the dumpy thing in that dreary old macintosh.

'I really don't want to talk to the press,' said Prudence snappily, though this was a lie. She loved talking to the press.

'May I join you?' asked Miss Dimont gently, bringing up a chair.

'No, I really don't think . . .' said Prudence, in a way which did not discourage Miss Dimont from quickly sitting down opposite her. *The way the press has of inviting itself into people's lives – quite outrageous!*

The reporter made hasty amends for their earlier clash and, as she did so, the film star cast a professional eye over this transformed character, puzzling – how could she look so down-to-earth one minute, and really quite regal the next? But then, despite a professional life of being exposed to flashbulbs and notebooks, Miss Aubrey had never really bothered to think about the life of those who put her name in the headlines; that perhaps they, too, were actors; the best of whom adopted chameleon-like qualities to suit the circumstances in which they found themselves.

At the railway station Miss Dimont looked like a nobody dressed for second-class rail travel. Here in the Grand Hotel she looked like a prized guest, with a gleam in her eye and a straight-backed deportment which might go unrecognised in the dusty offices of the *Riviera Express*.

'. . . and so kind of the Townswomen's Guild to invite me to their dinner,' she was saying softly.

Miss Aubrey rallied. 'Another.' She smiled as Peter Potts slid by. The waiter nodded his acknowledgement then flicked his eyebrows at Miss Dimont.

She flicked back. *Nice martini made out of water, thank you, Peter, don't forget the olive. The usual when I'm working.* He scurried away.

Miss Dimont was acting on a hunch. She had been shocked by that vitriolic response from the actress when asked a perfectly ordinary question – when had she last seen her husband? There was something wrong about Gerald Hennessy's death, and maybe here lay the answer – here, in front of her, in this famous actress with her haute couture smile and martini thirst, her layers of hostility and warmth, and her enviably crafted court shoes.

No doubt about it, Miss Aubrey was cautious and distant. A simple question had rattled her – though, thought Miss

Dimont, it may just have been the reaction of an actress interrupted in mid-soliloquy. That seemed a strong possibility now she had the measure of the woman. But beneath the cool exterior, that cut-glass accent and the beautiful clothes, lay very near the surface something else – another person altogether, a passionate woman never to be thwarted. She sensed before her a fighter and, yes, an animal.

Maybe all these qualities are needed to succeed in the acting profession, thought Miss Dimont as Prudence Aubrey launched once more into an account of the never-to-be film project with her late husband. Maybe to reach the very top, as she had done, took an almost manic determination.

'My favourite was *The Colour of Hope*,' Miss Dimont was saying admiringly. 'So much seemed to be expected of your character.'

The actress adopted a sardonic expression – oh, it was Hester Randall to a T! – and quoted, 'They'll never get me where *I'm* going . . .' while flicking up her eyelids and turning down the corners of her mouth, all at the same time.

The reporter professed astonishment that Prudence could quote so accurately a line she'd been paid a lot of money to remember, albeit a decade ago. When it came to interviewing film stars, the journalist who scored the greatest success was the one who laid it on thick.

'Wonderful! Magnificent! So I wonder . . . could you tell me . . .?'

She continued to toss Miss Aubrey questions designed to calm her fears, questions whose answers meant nothing but contributed to a growth in confidence between the two women, while she observed the actress's demeanour – was this a woman capable of murder? For, reading the runes, Gerald Hennessy's death could well be murder.

Or, was it Arthur Shrimsley who'd been murdered? Miss Dimont was glad her martini glass only contained water and an olive, for the answers infuriatingly continued to evade her.

Experienced – hardened, one might say – by years of interviewing, Miss Dimont realised she was getting nowhere with Prudence Aubrey. Maybe it was time to rejoin her hosts, the Townswomen's Guild, though the thought did not immediately overcome her with joy.

Just then a familiar figure wafted past in a cloud of Chanel or Dior or . . . Miss Dimont was not a great one for fragrances.

'Oh!' she cried. 'Isn't that Marion Lake?' Her question was aimed at her interviewee – for Miss Dimont assumed, as most people do, that all members of the acting profession know each other and, what's more, are friends. Marion Lake was this year's hot number, with *Charm School Graduate*, *Lady Godiva* and *The Chilly Wife* among the nation's favourite silver-screen offerings. She was tall, she was blonde, she was sinuous, and she was extremely shapely. And, really, still quite young.

Instead of the anticipated ready acknowledgement of her fellow-thespian, Prudence Aubrey stiffened in her chair, went white, and swallowed the remains of her martini at a gulp. 'I must go now,' she almost hissed. 'You know, you people in the press never know when to leave well alone. You really are the most awful shower.'

Miss Dimont blinked.

'Yes,' went on the actress, with just the mildest hint of two hefty martinis colouring her diction, 'you just have no idea, no idea at all!' Her voice rose further. 'You know, this is press harassment. There ought to be a law!

'Here I am, so very recently widowed, and there you are – drilling questions at me, upsetting me, making life awful when life already could hardly be worse. Have you no sense of compassion? No wonder the British press gets such a,' and here she ended lamely, 'bad press.'

With that, she snatched up her bag and stalked angrily off.

Murderer, thought Miss Dimont. *Quite possibly a murderer.*

EIGHT

It had taken Inspector Topham longer than most police officers to shed his uniform and adopt the cloak of detection.
Whether it was because he was not much good at exams,
or because there were no vacancies in Devon's CID for a
copper of his rank, was lost in the mists of time. Certainly
in the aftermath of war, when his soldierly figure first arrived
at Temple Regis, the crimes which occasionally occurred in
town hardly needed a detective to solve them.

If Cranch's sweet shop had been broken into, then it was
either the Luscombe brothers or that poor unfortunate Stanley Riddell ('Not *again*, Stanley!' was a catchphrase down
the station). White-collar crime of the sort you could get
arrested for was non-existent, though that did not mean it
didn't happen – when Alderman Jones, a man never known
to don gumboots, bought a farm just outside the town just
weeks before his planning committee allowed full consent
for Temple Regis' first housing estate, people merely shook
their heads. If the saintly Alderman had made a mint, well,
it must be above board, surely. Topham, if asked his opinion,

would have inspected his fingernails very closely and grunted non-committally.

It would be wrong to say there was nothing to do in the CID room at Temple Regis police station. After all, an inspector, a sergeant and two constables all dressed in mufti filed in in the morning and came out again in the evening. Something must have been going on in there, but nobody asked or was even interested.

However, correct form had to be followed on occasions such as the death of Messrs Hennessy and Shrimsley. Questions had to be asked, even if the coroner could get all the information he required to square away the nasty business of death in Temple Regis without any help from the CID.

But sturdy Inspector Topham was nothing if not diligent.

'I'm going over to the Grand,' he announced.

'Not *again*, Stanley!' came the ragged chorus from his underlings, a response which might be deemed humorous but only if you knew that Frank Topham took his beer of an evening in the private bar there.

'Very funny,' snapped Topham. 'Going to see Prudence Aubrey.'

And off he went, leaving behind a vacuum of envy and discontent among his officers, all of whom had, in their time, enjoyed private dreams about this most desirable of silver-screen stars.

Miss Aubrey had been looking forward to Topham's visit. A Londoner at heart, she was incredibly bored by Temple Regis, its Grand Hotel, the seaside and the messy business of her husband's death. Radford was making slow progress in unravelling Gerald's affairs and she wondered whether as he pursued unpaid residuals he was cutting himself too large a slice of the cake. But there was nothing she could do, because as a film star she knew how to write a cheque and that is where her comprehension of the laws of getting and spending stopped. Meanwhile, time stood still.

She answered his knock after a dramatic pause, so dramatic in fact that the inspector was about to turn on his heel and walk away. Her demeanour, heavily borrowed from her part in *The Chilly Wife*, was withdrawn, inaccessible. She wore cream, with a thin black chenille scarf thrown around her neck almost like a hangman's noose.

'Inspector.'

'Miss Aubrey.'

'I'm so glad you have come, Inspector, it's so reassuring to have the police on one's side at a time like this, a real comfort.'

'Thank you, Miss Aubrey. We do like to—

'It is *so* bothersome being hounded by the press.'

Topham looked startled. 'The press?' he said. 'Have they been giving you trouble?'

'There's a particularly obnoxious woman, Miss Dimmer or something, who won't leave me alone. She tackled me the moment I stepped off the train last afternoon, and then there she was again last night – bothering me. Here in the hotel!'

'Well, I expect she—' started Topham.

'Gutter press,' said Miss Aubrey, angrily. 'They ought to be locked up!'

'I'll see if I can have a word, madam,' said Topham, untrained in the protocols of combating undercover reportage.

'Would you?' said Prudence appealingly, smiling now. 'Do have a cup of coffee over here by the window. It's so delightful to be in your gorgeous town looking out over the . . .' She made a gracious gesture which somehow managed to embrace all of Temple Regis' finer points.

Topham settled in an armchair and allowed himself the tantalising luxury of being served coffee by one of the most famous women in the land. He caught a whiff of her perfume as she bent forward to place the cup in front of him and briefly wondered if he was in paradise.

'Now, madam,' he said, finally coming to, 'may I ask you a few questions? Just for form's sake?'

Miss Aubrey drew up her silk-clad legs under her on the sofa and eyed the detective over the rim of her cup. She was enjoying this already.

'Your full name and address, just for the record.'

'Janine Murgatroyd Hope-Simpson Hennessy,' purred Miss Prudence Aubrey conspiratorially, 'but do *not* tell another soul.'

Topham caught his breath. 'Prudence Aubrey' was an invention! To share such secrets of the rich and famous!

'Er, address, Mrs, er . . .'

'Call me Prudence,' said Prudence, sighing. 'I have learnt to live with the name over many years.' She frowned. 'And you have no idea what it was like being called Murgatroyd at school.'

'Address?'

'Regent's Lodge, Regent's Park, London. Such a divine little house. Do you know London, Inspector?'

'Very well, madam,' he replied stoutly. 'I was in the Grenadier Guards.'

Miss Aubrey glanced at Topham's heavy shoes – boots, really – and took in their mirror-like shine. 'You didn't know a Colonel ffrench-Blake, by any chance?'

'My commanding officer, madam,' said Topham happily. This was going terribly well.

The conversation swerved into personal reminiscence and the inspector laid down his notebook. He admired the flowers in the room, accepted another cup of coffee, and at the same time an invitation to drop in to the Lodge at any time he happened to be passing. Miss Aubrey was so wonderfully unaffected.

Half an hour passed, little of note was said and, despite a number of invitations, Miss Aubrey gracefully sidestepped the matter of when she had last seen Gerald. She rang the bell and soon this harmonious couple were sharing a thimbleful of dry sherry before Inspector Topham, with regret, picked up his hat and prepared to take his leave.

'One last thing,' he said genially, as he stuffed his notebook in his pocket.

'Yes?'

'When *did* you last see Mr Hennessy?'

The beautifully rouged lips froze together, and a wild look came into Miss Aubrey's eye. 'I thought you had finished,' she said, almost pleadingly.

'Just routine,' said Topham who, despite his teak-like exterior was no fool. 'You last saw him when?'

Were she a stage actress, the pause which followed before Miss Aubrey spoke again might be described by a critic as 'climactic'. Inspector Topham knew he'd got what he came for.

'I have something to tell you,' whispered Prudence. 'It must be in confidence. It will be in confidence, won't it?'

Not *again* Stanley, thought Topham. They all say that.

He pulled out his notebook again but Prudence Aubrey was having none of it. 'Really, Inspector!' she said. 'My husband dies of a heart attack on a train, and you are treating me as if I were a criminal!'

She has a point, thought Topham, and laid down the offending article. 'What, then, were you going to tell me in confidence, Miss Aubrey?'

'Marion Lake,' hissed Miss Aubrey. 'Marion . . . LAKE.'

'The actress, madam?'

'*You* might call her that, Inspector. I would not. I happen to know that she can take up to twenty attempts to deliver a single line – think of all that wasted studio time! All that film which has to be thrown away! The disastrous effect on the budget! All those poor fellow-actors dying to go home to their loved ones while she stumbles and bumbles and dumbles!

I deliver my lines word-perfect every time, and if there's a retake it's for technical reasons, and technical reasons alone.'

Topham was no cinema-goer but he read the newspapers. Once, Prudence Aubrey was front-page material, her glittering presence an essential adjunct to every film premiere, and her latest film always the subject of frenzied gossip. But that had been some years ago. Still she looked like a star, talked like a star, and acted as if she were a star; but by comparison with Marion Lake, well, her day had come and gone. Her contribution to cinema history was unassailable, but the wheel of fame turns inexorably, and now it was very much Miss Lake's time for the limelight.

These things Inspector Topham instinctively knew, indeed could intuit from Prudence Aubrey's rasping tone, and so he waited.

'What I'm concerned about,' went on the actress, smoothing her hair, 'is that there should be no scandal.'

'Well of course we'll do what we—'

'Scandal, Inspector, just at the moment when I have lost my husband.'

Topham nodded. No need for words, the floodgates were about to open.

'It is not easy living a legend,' said Prudence, eventually. 'There are . . . pressures.

'My husband and I were married for twenty-one years and as far as the world was concerned we were the golden couple. But—' she pulled in her skirt more tightly round her legs '—time moves on, things change.

'We had no children – he couldn't. And there comes a time in a man's life when . . . when he needs to feel young again. This film business – it's not what it seems. It tears the heart out of you, destroys your values, creates false priorities. Allows you to behave in a certain manner which is not the norm. And after a while you take it all for granted, and you become a different person.'

Inspector Topham nodded. At one level this was leading to an important revelation, he felt, with no need for any assistance from himself. At another, it was a gripping sidelight on the lives behind the cameras, in the dressing rooms, on the Côte d'Azur or wherever film stars played these days.

'Gerald had . . .' went on Miss Aubrey, her voice trailing, 'had the notion that he would stay younger in himself if he were around younger people. There are huge pressures on you when you're a star to remain as youthful as you were in your last picture, and the one before that. Age does not exempt us from its depredations just because we are famous. Gerald sought out the company of young people in an attempt to deny his years and to maintain his popularity with the . . . *fans*.' She spat out the last word with some vehemence. 'They can be so fickle!' Her voice was rising again. 'Do you know they have polls in the newspapers as to who's the most popular star? I'm certain it's all made up – just look at the state of the newspapers these days, it's all trash! – but these *inventions* carry weight with the producers.'

She was not talking about Gerald now.

'Because of these ridiculous articles your name can go up

and down the screen credits with no reference to the quality of your performance, or the loyal following you have built up over the years. That affects how much you earn. Ultimately, it affects what scripts you get offered – and one bad script can smash your reputation overnight.'

'So Mr Hennessy . . .' murmured Topham hoping for swift resumption of the main theme, away from this nonetheless fascinating glimpse into the slow descent of a star.

'Mr Hennessy,' said Prudence crisply, 'spent time away from home with his young friends. There were very many friends, and they were often very young.'

'Miss Lake?' prompted Topham.

'Well what do you THINK?' came the scalding response. 'They came down on the same train. They shared the same compartment. She was booked in at the Grand Hotel – here – *just across the corridor from this suite.*'

She looked the detective straight in the eye. 'I do not know where my husband was for the twenty-four hours before he boarded the Riviera Express. There – does that answer your question?'

Topham gently nodded his head in acknowledgement.

'We had a . . . we had an exchange of views about the way he was conducting himself. He left the house and did not return. He may have gone to his club or . . .'

Or spent the night with Marion Lake.

Whatever his limitations the inspector was a man of the world and it came as no surprise. He allowed himself the thought that of all the women in the country most men would like to dally with, Marion Lake had to top the list. It was all very absorbing but hardly altered anything. Topham had set himself the task of collating Gerald Hennessy's last movements in case there should be questions from the coroner on Friday. He would say that the actor had come down on unspecified business and that he had stayed the previous night at his club. That covered things nicely.

'One thing remains unexplained,' said Topham. 'Why did Mr Hennessy choose Temple Regis to bring Miss Lake? Do you have any idea?'

Prudence Aubrey's clear blue eyes turned to mud, and her gaze fell to the carpet.

'One of my sergeants understands he was considering doing a summer season at the Pavilion Theatre.'

'Are you mad?' shouted the actress, getting up from the sofa and leaning over him. 'Gerald? Here – *here*?' The gesture with which she had greeted the policeman was repeated but with quite another interpretation. Gone was the praiseful appreciation of Temple Regis' many charms and in its place a contemptuous dismissal of its funfair and toffee apples, its donkey rides and all the primary-coloured gewgaws splattered along the seafront. What looks magical one minute can look, well, tawdry the next.

'Whatever you may think of him as a person,' hissed the actress, 'he was at the top of the tree. Top of the tree! Why on earth would he want to come to . . . this . . .' The words failed her.

Topham looked at her. 'In his pocket,' he said in measured

tones, 'there was a card from Raymond Cattermole. Do you know Mr Cattermole, by any chance?'

'Of course,' said Prudence testily. 'A second-rater. Actor without a future even before he got started. Why they ever bother to enter the profession . . .'

'So they knew each other well?'

'I wouldn't say well. They were in the West End together before the War. Wilde. *The Importance of Being Earnest.* They swapped parts after Cattermole broke his arm. They didn't get on. Why would Gerald want to come here to see him?'

'Mr Cattermole manages the Pavilion Theatre. Puts on two alternating shows in the summer season.'

'Well, what does *he* say was the reason for Gerald coming down here?'

'We have not yet been able to ascertain that,' said Topham, an official tone creeping into his voice.

'He seems to have gone missing.'

NINE

Miss Dimont hummed and swung her raffia bag as she wandered back to the *Express* offices. Such a stimulating morning in the Magistrates' Court!

Once the bread-and-butter cases had been cleared away they came to the matter of Mrs Symington, a bleach-blonde of a certain age with a lumpy figure and a pugnacious expression. At a glance you could tell what a thoroughly dislikeable person she was, though evidently not Mr Symington, who sat next to the dock and whose adoring eyes never left his wife.

Mrs Symington was up before Mrs March for having lied, at her recent marriage, about her age. This deception may not have mattered to Mr Symington – one had only to look at the rapt expression on his foolish face – but it mattered very much to the registrar who had joined them in matrimony, and who had reported her transgression to the authorities.

'Eloise Mary Symington,' intoned Mr Thurlestone, adjusting his disreputable wig, 'you are charged that on the ninth of March of this year you entered into a marriage contract with

Herbert Trefusis Symington by making a false declaration, contrary to the Marriages Act 1949. How do you plead?'

'Ridiculous,' spat Mrs Symington.

'How do you plead?'

'Complete waste of time,' said Mrs Symington, and sat down abruptly.

This was an encouraging start for those who measured out their life in the cups of dreary coffee they swallowed in the Mag Ct canteen over the years. Everybody perked up.

'Stand up,' said the Hon. Mrs Marchbank, looking over her gilt pince-nez. Mrs Symington sulkily obliged.

'The magistrates' clerk has read out the charge to you. Do you understand this is a serious offence? You must enter a plea, or alternatively you can apply for an adjournment so you may be represented by a solicitor. How say you to the charge?'

'Don't know what all the fuss is about,' said Mrs Symington. You could see there was a strange gleam in her eye.

Mrs March looked at her clerk and they nodded to each other. 'We'll take that as a not guilty plea,' she announced. 'Sergeant Smith?'

The prosecuting officer rose to his feet. 'Your Worship, this is a simple case of a woman who persuaded a man to marry her by pretending to be ten years younger than she was. It was his first marriage and her second. She said she was fifty-three when in fact she is sixty-three.'

All eyes shot to the dock for a closer scrutiny of this

imposter. She certainly looked sixty-three, and then some. How could Mr Symington be so easily fooled?

'Her husband had been a lifelong bachelor. He lived alone at Enderby Manor. They were introduced and, Mr Symington has said in a statement, she entranced him. He was unfamiliar,' explained the sergeant, clearing his throat, 'er, unfamiliar with the opposite sex.'

Mrs Symington stuck out her bulky chest in what might be interpreted as an offensive manner. Her husband gazed up longingly.

'Mr Symington has further said that he took in Mrs Symington and her elderly mother after they were made to leave their previous home after an . . . incident. He felt sorry for both women.'

Mrs Marchbank did not like the sound of this. 'Are you saying the accused found refuge in this gentleman's home and then – er, sought out his affections?'

'He had never had his breakfast in bed before, Your Worship.'

The magistrate evidently felt a sense of disgust at such blatantly opportunistic behaviour. Old fool, large house, sitting target, she summarised to herself. 'Yes, Sergeant?'

'The offence was uncovered when the defendant applied for a new passport in her married name. The authorities alerted the registrar, who in turn informed the police. Mrs Symington was interviewed under caution but refused to acknowledge the offence. She maintains she is fifty-three, Your Worship. She will be sixty-four next week.' He sat down.

Mrs Marchbank looked towards the person in the dock. 'Stand up,' she said, those two words carrying the heavy weight of Temple Regis' moral outrage in them.

Mrs Symington ambled to her feet, stuck her nose in the air and looked unconcernedly around the court. To Miss Dimont, a veteran of many years on the press bench, this was a thrilling moment. If there was one thing Mrs March did not tolerate, it was a challenge to her authority.

'We have entered a plea of not guilty on your behalf since it would appear from the evidence that you do not accept the charge,' she said stonily. 'This is now your opportunity to tell the court why you made an unlawful statement with regard to your age. You are sixty-three, are you not?'

The accused stared back insolently. 'None of your business,' she said.

Mrs Marchbank had never been spoken to like this before. It took a moment for her to rally.

'A copy of your birth certificate shows you were born on the eighteenth of September 1895.'

The accused did not turn a hair. 'It's a woman's right to present herself as best she can,' she said. 'That's why we spend money on make-up, the hairdresser, the clothes we wear. That's what men want.'

Mrs March dismissed this evident truth with a sniff.

'HE—' she tossed her head in her husband's direction without actually bothering to look at him '—has a lot of love to give. He has been waiting all his life to give that love. He told me he wanted a son to pass on his estate to. Once we had become acquainted he thought that we could . . . you know . . .'

'But Mrs Symington, you are sixty-three!'

'You're as old as you feel,' snapped back the accused. This was something of a non sequitur, since in its lengthy and colourful history Temple Regis had not so far recorded a case of a woman achieving the miracle of childbirth after the official retirement age. But it did not diminish by one iota Mrs Symington's delusional self-belief.

Miss Dimont watched this fascinating verbal tennis match as if from the umpire's seat. Mrs March had the law on her side but Mrs Symington seemed to have the upper hand.

'So, if I have this correctly, Mrs Symington, you fooled Mr Symington into believing that you could bear him a son and heir.'

'I can and probably will.'

Mr Symington gave a chimpanzee's grin at the Bench.

'You broke the law and, if I may say so, you made a fool of a man who took pity on you and took you in,' said Mrs Marchbank, her own rigorous personal standards in danger of getting the better of her legal judgement. 'You applied womanly guile and, no doubt, have gained pecuniary advantage from the use of that guile. There is a word for that,' said Mrs Marchbank, simmering up to boiling point.

Mrs Symington smirked and patted her comfortable form.

'I therefore sentence you to six months. Take her down.'

And the Bench rattled as Mrs Marchbank brought down

her gavel with terrifying force to signify the end of the case and a suitable termination to Mrs Symington's liberty.

Mr Thurlestone jumped up, his dirty old wig bouncing on his head. He turned to face Mrs March and spoke urgently in an undertone. His head was so close to hers it was impossible to hear what he was saying, or her reaction, but after a minute or so he bobbed down again and Mrs Marchbank with a face like stone spoke once again to the accused.

'I am advised that in this case, a custodial sentence would be inappropriate,' she snarled. (Too right, thought Miss Dimont, three months maximum and as a first offender it would be probation – she knew her law.)

'Therefore on the charge before me I sentence you to one year's probation. I further sentence you to one year's probation for contempt of court.'

Mrs Symington, who had woken to the possibility she might be spared her nightly duties with old Mr Symington and get a good night's sleep for a few months, looked somewhat disappointed. But Mrs March had not finished.

'I have had the privilege to sit on this Bench for twenty-five years,' she said, her pince-nez wobbling on the end of her nose. 'In that time I do not think I have seen such a flagrant or depressing example of moral turpitude.

'You have lied,' she thundered. 'You have lied to your husband and you have lied to the court. You have deliberately sought to bury the truth. Your actions are morally indefensible and they bring shame and disgrace upon you and upon the good people of Temple Regis.'

This is going a bit far, thought Miss Dimont, her pencil scrubbing furiously at the page before her.

But the Honourable lady had not finished. 'It would be fair to say we have a duty, all we women, to set an example in our dealings with the opposite sex in order to maintain our right to the privileges we have earned in recent times.' (Does she mean the *vote*? thought Miss Dimont. That was years ago!)

The magistrate, robbed of her opportunity to jail Mrs Symington, was not going to let her go without a taste of fire and brimstone. But it was water off a duck's back, for the hotter the fusillade from the Bench, the cooler became the accused's demeanour.

Miss Dimont had seen nothing like this before. Mrs Marchbank was the town's idol – the very synthesis of aristocratic allure, modest elegance, moral compass and general good feeling that all towns with a modicum of pride wish for. It was extraordinary that such a trifling offence could bring out this torrent of anger and rectitude, and curiously it suddenly reminded Miss Dimont of Prudence Aubrey's outburst the previous day – outspoken, irrational. But just then Mr Thurlestone jumped up, adjourned the court, Mrs Symington strode out with her pathetic husband trailing behind, and everybody headed for lunch.

*

There was such pleasure, such freedom, in working on the *Riviera Express*, thought Miss Dimont as she made her way back to the office. Rudyard Rhys was a bit of a nightmare, but wasn't that true of all editors, everywhere? Didn't they always make jokes about 'the editor's indecision is final'? It was certainly true in old Rudyard's case.

Those years when they knew each other during the War – hadn't he always been like that? A good brain, but irresolute? She could never imagine that one day their roles would be reversed and she would be working for him. It had taken some getting used to.

But truth to tell, Mr Rhys gave Miss Dimont a free hand in the way she wrote up her stories, and though he liked to see the Betty Featherstone byline decorate his front page, the newspaper's reputation relied heavily upon the output and integrity its senior reporter brought to the job. And when it came to an account of this morning's standoff in the Magistrates' Court, the editor was in Miss Dimont's hands.

All too conscious of this, she mulled over the possibilities as she entered the *Express*'s front hall. She edged her way through the usual gaggle of complainants, advertisers, junior councillors hoping for a mention and future brides waving their green forms, and walked up the uncarpeted stairs to the office. It was lunchtime, and though she thought she caught a glimpse of Athene wisping out of the door she could not be sure and, in any event, though she would have enjoyed a cup of Athene's tea and some soothing words about her aura, she wanted to get the story written while it was fresh in her mind.

She plumped down her raffia bag, took out her notebook and an apple, pushed back the sea of paper around her, and

threaded the traditional sandwich of copy and carbon paper
into her Quiet-Riter. She flipped back through her notebook
without seeking to interpret the immaculate shorthand before
her, looking for the key for introducing her story to the readers.

The 'intro' was, after all, what drew them in. Should she
start by describing Mrs Marchbank's rant at the bovine Symington? Or entice them in by describing how a woman who
plainly looked sixty-three (Terry's accompanying photograph
was not kind) could have convinced her husband she was of
childbearing age?

Or lead off on the fact that a magistrate of twenty-five
years' standing – Chairman of the Bench, no less – had issued
a term of imprisonment she was not entitled to hand down?
That, yet again, she had overstepped the mark?

To Miss Dimont, who did not like Mrs Marchbank, this
would have been the favoured first paragraph. But she was
shrewd enough to realise that a tale of a lumpy sexagenarian
using her waning charms to bamboozle a sweet old boy into
believing he was about to procreate a longed-for son and heir
was what would capture popular attention best.

There was always the Comment page, where a few sharp
words rapping Mrs Marchbank's elegant knuckles for her
vindictive incompetence might do the deed. Sad to say, few
people actually read the Comment section because in Temple
Regis people were all too ready with a Comment of their
own – they needed nobody to tell them what to think. But
at least Miss Dimont's considered opinion would become a

matter of record – something, perhaps, for historians to linger over a century hence.

Miss Dimont had rattled off four hundred words of crisply paragraphed prose, thankful for the emptiness of the office, when Betty breezed in and plumped herself down noisily.

'How goes the Hennessy investigation?' she asked disingenuously, once the matter of who made the tea was tidied away.

'What investigation?' responded Miss Dimont, genuinely surprised. 'There's nothing more now till the inquest on Friday. I saw Mrs Hennessy last night and I might get a par out of it—' 'par' always being easier on the overworked tongue than the more sensible 'paragraph' '—but she's behaving oddly. For an actress, she doesn't seem to want to talk.'

'I wonder why,' said Betty, encouragingly.

Miss Dimont was not fooled. 'Been looking at my notes, Betty?' she asked sweetly.

The woman across the desk had the grace to blush. 'Reporter's nosiness,' she said lamely. Her attempt at spying on Judy was not going well but she pressed on: 'Looks like you've had some thoughts about this Hennessy business,' she said. 'I wonder what it's all about.'

Miss Dimont pushed her spectacles up her nose, finished her last par on the Symington case with a crash and turned her attention to Betty.

'Well, Betty,' she said. 'It does seem extraordinary that Miss Aubrey, the grieving widow, should take three days to arrive in Temple Regis. It does seem extraordinary that

when I asked her when she'd last seen her husband she flew
into a mad rage.

'It does seem extraordinary that Mr Cattermole had
arranged to meet Gerald Hennessy though he quite clearly
hates him. It seems inexplicable that, just in the run-up to
starting a new film such a prominent actor should travel all
the way down here to spend a couple of nights in the Grand
Hotel.'

'Girlfriend?' interjected Betty keenly, displaying all that
feminine intuition so beloved of the editor and so extraor-
dinarily absent in Miss Dim.

'Hadn't thought of that. But d'you know, then there's
the whole business about Shrimsley which we seem to have
forgotten about. Did he leave a suicide note?'

Betty's eyes, not her most attractive feature, popped wide
open. '*Suicide* note?' she parroted. Mr Rhys would surely
want to hear about this!

'There was something in his hand when he died. By the
time I saw the body it was covered up with a blanket but
Terry got a shot of it – but nobody seems to have said anything more about that. Mudford Cliffs was such a strange
place for him to be. What *was* he doing there?'

'It's odd, the whole thing is odd,' said Miss Dimont, and
disappeared into a brown study as she tried once again to
juggle the known facts on these two deaths and make sense
of them.

Betty got up, ostensibly to refill their teacups, but as she
glimpsed how deep Miss Dimont had plunged into her own

thoughts she slipped away down the corridor, past the subs' table where Peter Pomeroy was completing his heron-like stabs at his luncheon sandwich, and nipped into the editor's office.

Before she could vouchsafe her precious news – Prudence Aubrey, Ray Cattermole, Mr Shrimsley's *suicide* – Rudyard Rhys stopped her with a stare. 'You know Raymond Cattermole, don't you?'

Indeed she did. When first she arrived in Temple Regis the old ham had walked her out a few times, dazzled her with tales from the West End stage, and sat late with her in the Green Room drinking brandy and heavily embroidering his scant knowledge of some of the day's most famous stars. Whether it went any further nobody ever said, but it all came to an abrupt halt one day when Betty was asked to pop down to the Pavilion on some story or other and refused point-blank to go. 'Never! Never!' she said in a shocked voice, so shocked nobody pressed her. Cattermole was known to be a bit of an old goat.

Now the editor was bringing painful memories back. 'Cattermole?' said Betty. 'Barely at all. In fact I'd go so far as to say—'

'Terry tells me he's gone missing. I want you to go down to the theatre and see what you can find out.'

Betty looked dismayed. Asking people awkward questions wasn't her forte, and anyway she didn't want the theatre staff looking at her and giggling and recalling the day when Cattermole set up the spotlights, put her on a box in the centre of the stage and made her read from a script, telling her what a star she could be – with a little guidance, of course . . .

The reporter quickly reordered her thoughts. She could usually wriggle out of things with Rudyard when she wanted, and now she wanted it very much.

'Mr Cattermole,' she said slowly but with authority, 'hated Gerald Hennessy.'

'Yes?' said the editor, unmoved.

'Don't you see? Gerald Hennessy was going to meet him when he got here. There was a postcard in his pocket from Mr Cattermole confirming their meeting.'

'How d'you know that?' asked the editor, though he could not see where this was leading.

'Judy told me.'

'How does *she* know?'

'She didn't say. But she's got some theory about Mr Hennessy's death – and Mr Shrimsley's, too, come to that.'

Though the editor had asked Betty to spy on her co-worker, the intelligence she brought back was unwelcome. He was not such an incompetent journalist that he wanted to ignore news when it bubbled to the surface, but he preferred a quiet life. The *Riviera Express* was his ticket to retirement and he wanted the ride to be as comfortable and trouble-free as it could be. Why, oh why, was Miss Dim turning two perfectly explicable deaths into a riddle? And what would be the outcome of her unwelcome enquiries?

'Nothing we can do before the inquest,' he said with lordly

decision. 'We must not pre-empt the workings of the courts and their officers.'

Betty didn't mind either way.

'But,' he said, 'old Cattermole going missing – *that's* a story. Get along down to the Pavilion and see what you can rustle up.'

Betty did not like it. She crossed her legs and smiled winningly – that worked sometimes – then referred in some detail to a drive they had taken in Mr Rhys' car one day to no apparent purpose. That usually did the trick, especially if she suggested they go again to look at the Start Point lighthouse.

But the editor's decision was final. To the theatre Betty must go.

As she gathered up her handbag and notebook, Rhys brushed past her, stuck his head of his office door and bellowed, uncharitably,

'Miss DIM!'

TEN

Despite his undeniable charm Perce, the telegram boy, was an equivocal figure in the life of Temple Regis. When weddings and christenings were in the offing he was welcomed as if a family member, but at other times the scrape of his bicycle bell accompanied by a heavy knock could bring terror to townsfolk. The War was not so far distant that the sight of a small buff envelope could not still trigger feelings of horror, or sometimes the desire to rip the ominous article to shreds, sight unseen.

Like his fabled predecessor the benign god Hermes, Perce often knew what his messages contained though he always pretended not. Like Hermes he had curly hair, a noble profile and was clever; but unlike Hermes he could do nothing to change the fortunes of those whose doorsteps his duties attended.

He liked to hang around when he knew the recipient had won the football pools – there was always a drink or a tip in it – similarly a greetings telegram, sometimes lavishly wrapped up in a golden envelope, might be worth chancing a delayed exit while fiddling with his bicycle clips or his trusty steed's troublesome dynamo.

Other times, he skedaddled. Injury, death, divorce – you had to have a rhinoceros hide to withstand your customers' reaction if you hung around.

'One for you, Miss Featherstone,' Perce sang, as he way-laid his blonde-haired quarry departing the *Riviera Express* offices. He had delivered a number of billets-doux to Betty and had been rewarded, thanks to their content, with the occasional ecstatic kiss on the cheek. Not always, though.

This one was probably a skedaddler.

'Me?' said Betty, blushing. 'Oh, I . . .' and she turned as if to make off down the street. Perce politely stepped to one side, but thrust out his arm so she could not pass without appearing rude. Betty queasily took the telegram, dug in her pocket to give him a threepenny bit, then tore the flimsy envelope open.

Though still only nineteen, Perce was sufficient a student of human nature to have predicted it was curtains again for Betty. Last time it was Frank. This time, Derek. He wasn't quite sure whether to offer the threepence back again. His quarry went white and rushed back into the building from whence she had stepped so daintily just a moment ago.

Upstairs, Rudyard Rhys had just concluded his tête-à-tête with Miss Dimont and both were looking slightly flushed around the gills, but whatever had passed between them was finished by the time Betty flew back into the office.

She waved her telegram at Mr Rhys and, white-faced, told

a downright lie. 'D-death in the family,' she stuttered, and in that instant believed it. 'I have two days' overtime owing, Mr Rhys, and I will have to take them. Now.'

Despite his granite-like exterior, the editor caved in immediately. 'Off you go,' he said and turned to Miss Dim. 'Pavilion Theatre for you,' he ordered.

'Yes?' asked his chief reporter, who did not know of Cattermole's disappearance.

Soon however she did and, having overcome her disbelief, for it was only yesterday (or was it the day before?) she had been talking to the old poodlefaker, she strode off towards the pier.

It was perhaps an exaggeration to say Cattermole had disappeared. What was more strictly accurate was that he had not been seen since his uncomfortable encounter with Miss Dimont two days earlier. His lady friend Mrs Phipps, a Gaiety Girl type who these days expected little of her ageing Lochinvar, was nonetheless upset when he failed to show up for dinner that night and called the police.

This may have been from feelings of revenge rather than anxiety, for Mrs Phipps, who'd spent her career in the belief she would one day become a Lady Poulett, a Lady Drogheda, or a Lady Orkney, as Gaiety Girls were apt to do – but had instead ended up in mouldy old Temple Regis in a flat off the seafront where seagulls bred their young on the roof and her most frequent caller dyed his eyebrows and wore a tragic toupee.

Mrs Phipps did not like being abandoned.

'A worthless sort of fellow,' she spluttered between gasps of her Player's Navy Cut. 'Have a cup of tea, dear.'

Miss Dimont didn't mind if she did.

'He sometimes goes missing for the night but he's always at the theatre – that's one thing you can say about him, he loves that place almost as much as he loves himself.' Mrs Phipps gazed down with pride at a photograph of herself in her heyday, placed on a side table next to the ashtray. It may have been covered in dust but it showed what hot stuff she must once have been.

'Sugar, dear?'

'Mrs Phipps, there's something missing. I came to see Mr Cattermole the other day. He told me that when Gerald Hennessy came to Temple Regis, the two were due to meet.'

This was not strictly true – Cattermole had not confirmed the arrangement, but it is a reporter's trick to make a statement of fact in the expectation that the interviewee will assume its content is already general knowledge and, in answering, confirm what until then was mere hypothesis. Not strictly ethical, but it cut corners when a deadline was looming.

'Oh yes,' said Mrs Phipps, falling for it, 'Raymond and Gerry—' *Gerry?* thought Miss Dimont, how vulgarly theatrical . . . if ever there was a Gerald in this world, it was the dear departed '—Raymond and Gerry were to meet at the Pavilion to discuss a little business proposition.'

'What sort of . . .?' asked Miss Dimont, her spirits rising. The tea was filthy.

'I don't know, he always blethered on, I never knew any-body use the first person singular more than Ray. I this and I that – you tend to think of other things, nicer things, when he starts off like that. Did you ever see me on stage, dear?'

'Well, I . . .'

'Too young I suppose. I made my departure from the West End in 1936. A terrible show called *Transatlantic Rhythm*. My dear, the *unspeakable* things Lupe Vélez did on stage! The woman was just an animal, pools of water everywhere!'

'Is that where you met Ray – Mr Cattermole?' asked Miss Dimont, trying deftly to steer back the conversation.

'He was in a show next door, we were at the Adelphi. The orchestra walked out because they didn't get paid. Some frightful young whippersnapper of an American was the pro-ducer – Jimmy Donahue was his name, I think. Woolworth money, darling – we thought he had oodles. But it was all his mother's.'

'Ray, er, Raymond and Gerald would have been contem-poraries then?'

'Yes, I think Gerry was doing three short Coward plays at the Phoenix at the time. Brave soul – not that he *was* particularly brave.'

At last we are back on terra firma, thought Miss Dimont, with Gerald Hennessy. 'What do you mean, exactly?'

'Well, Ray used to say what a coward he was. All that business during the War.'

The reporter started to listen rather more intently. 'What business was that, exactly?'

'Oh, you know.'

'Well, no, I don't.'

'About how he avoided call-up and was generally lily-livered over the whole war business. I mean,' said Mrs Phipps, gasping as she lit her third Navy Cut, 'it's a jolly little joke, isn't it, that Gerry Hennessy – our so-called great hero actor – dodged the column?'

'I thought he was in ENSA.'

'That was later, dear. He was eligible for call-up at the outbreak, but he wriggled and he squiggled and somehow – I don't know how, but Ray does – managed to avoid going into uniform. I think he spent the first three years hobbling round Pitlochry on a stick pretending he'd been wounded. That was before the theatre opened up there, dear – they'd never seen an actor then, they were all taken in. I think he worked in the hotel.'

'But then he did ENSA?'

'They gave you a uniform to travel about in. Somehow Gerry's was more magnificent than a general's. It was ghastly behaviour. Really ghastly. I never really liked him after that, though he *was* gorgeous to look at, I will grant you that.'

This, if true, was shattering news to Miss Dimont, who'd sat through many a war epic starring the craggy-jawed Hennessy. She was far too clever to believe that the man had actually done the things he acted out on screen, but in the dark, with a nice ice cream, harbouring memories of her own part in the conflict, it was enjoyable to suspend one's disbelief.

'More tea, dear?' Miss Dimont blanched as Mrs Phipps dropped a cigarette end into her cup with a fizzle.

'No thank you, Mrs Phipps . . . but do tell me more about Raymond and, er, *Gerry*.'

'Not much to say, really. They appeared together in *The Importance of Being Earnest*. Edith Evans. Great success – eventually. In the dressing room one night, Ray made the mistake of ribbing Gerry about his part in the War and how ironic it was that he now was a greater hero than most of the people who'd taken part in the fighting.

'There was a fight and Gerry broke Ray's arm. It took him out of the show and gave Gerry the better part. A film director was in that night – and that's when Gerry's career took off.

'Meantime poor Ray found it difficult with a wonky arm to get the young-juve parts he'd specialised in and, really, that was the end of that. I will say this for him – instead of hanging around in the Stage Door Club getting drunk every lunchtime he hightailed it down here and *saved your theatre*.' These last words were delivered in quotation marks, a message from the great actor-manager himself, though not meant to be taken seriously between two grown women of the world.

Miss Dimont smiled. 'So, I don't really understand this,' she said, using her pencil to scratch her head. 'These two men disliked each other intensely and yet they were going to meet when Mr Hennessy came down to Temple Regis. In fact,' she added, 'it would appear to be the *only* reason why he came down here. Are you sure they hadn't patched things up and that Raymond was going to offer Gerald a summer season?'

Mrs Phipps' eyes popped open. 'You can't be serious!' she cackled. 'Ray despised Gerry – despised him! Don't forget, whatever you think of him, Ray did his bit during the War.'

'Army Pay Corps, wasn't it?'

'They also serve who stand and hand out the wages,' misquoted Mrs Phipps, not without irony. 'Ray is very proud of his General Service Medal.'

'So there was some business between them, then.'

'Yes, but I don't know what. It all blew up after he bumped into that wretched little man – colleague of yours, I think – nasty piece of work.'

Miss Dimont racked her brains. 'Mr Rhys?'

'No, nothing like that. Shrimp, or something like that.'

It took a moment for the penny to drop. 'Do you mean,' said Miss Dimont quite slowly, 'Arthur Shrimsley?'

'Could be,' said Mrs Phipps, who was bored now and thinking about a glass of gin. 'What I want to know is what are the police doing about finding Ray? I mean, if the theatre stays dark another night we'll all be in trouble. You don't know what a fuss there was last night at the box office when they had to turn everybody away.'

'He was doing *My West End Life*, wasn't he? His one-man show?'

'Yes, it fills the gap at the end of the season until we shut down for the winter.'

There'll hardly have been chaos at the box office, thought Miss Dimont. Word had got around the show was better than a cup of Horlicks for insomniacs. If more than a handful were in for the night, it would have been a miracle.

She walked back, slowly. The delicious smell of malting from Gardner's, the next-door brewery, wafted out to greet her and helped liven her steps back to the office, but as she walked, Miss Dimont pieced together the quite extraordinary scenario presented to her by Mrs Phipps.

Hennessy and Cattermole hated each other, yet they had planned to meet. Apparently the catalyst to this meeting – if Mrs Phipps' testimony was to be trusted – was a visit to Cattermole by Arthur Shrimsley.

Three men.

Two dead.

And one missing.

ELEVEN

Terry was such a mine of information, it was irritating. Miss Dimont could not tell one end of a camera from another and certainly the intricate settings, apertures and exposures Terry was apt to reel off in any conversation you had would blind you with science if you hadn't already died of boredom.

But though one might view Terry, in other circumstances, as something which had just jumped down from the trees – such was his rudimentary command of language, of domestic habit, and of knife and of fork – he really was very, very good at his job. Moreover, he was pretty good at Judy Dimont's job too.

'Shrimsley,' he said brightly by way of greeting, once the reporter had made her way along the corridor to the news-room.

'Yes?' came the snippy reply, for Miss Dimont was deep in her own thoughts. 'Inquest on Friday. Nothing more till then.'

Some might take this as a snub but to Terry it was water off the proverbial. 'Bit of a mystery,' he confided, forefinger touching nose. 'He wasn't where he should have been.'

Miss D blinked. 'What do you mean?'

'Shrimsley.'

'Yes, I *know* Shrimsley. What about him?'

'Apparently he took his dog for a walk up on Mudford Cliffs and for some reason walked out beyond the safety barrier.'

'Yes?'

'You remember we ran a story, two to three weeks ago, about that cliff fall. Barriers put up to stop the public snooping around and finding themselves on the rocks two hundred and fifty feet down. Plenty of warnings from the fire brigade to keep back because of an unstable cliff edge.'

'Yes.'

'Well, old Shrimsley somehow got beyond the barrier and – you know the rest.'

'Yes.' Miss Dimont really was finding it hard to concentrate. What Mrs Phipps had told her was weighing heavily on her mind.

'What I can't understand,' said Terry, waxing philosophical for a moment, 'was what he was doing there. Mudford Cliffs are a long way to take your dog for a walk from Exbridge. It's a fifteen-minute car ride or thirty minutes by bus. Did he come to follow up our front-page story about a cliff fall? Did he think he could sell it to Fleet Street? Nah,' said Terry. 'All a bit comical really.'

Miss Dimont usually thought Terry a bit comical too – heavens, he'd never even tried the *Daily Telegraph* crossword – but slowly, like a great Leviathan, she awoke to what he was telling her. No reason for Shrimsley to be on a cliff top so far from home. His death would remain, until the inquest, a mystery, but clearly the circumstances in which he fell suddenly seemed that much more mysterious.

Her senses sharpened. 'What happened to the dog?'

'What?'

'The dog, Terry. He was walking his dog. We saw him, you and I, where he ended up at the bottom of the cliff – there wasn't a dog. Where was the dog?'

'No dog that I saw,' said Terry, and in truth if there had been one, he'd not only have seen it but got a shot of it at f3.5.

'Police haven't said anything about a missing dog?'

'Not to me.'

'Not to me, either. Who saw him up there?'

'Mabel Attwell, you know, she works in the circulation department.'

Typical, thought Miss Dimont crossly. All those people who work in a newspaper office who have no idea they're sitting on a story. Just wander about keeping the news to themselves. Selfish. Short-sighted. They should be . . .

Aloud she said, 'Old Mrs Attwell? How would she recognise Arthur Shrimsley?'

'She lives in Exbridge too. Apparently he's a bit of a square peg in the village.'

And not only the village, muttered Miss Dimont, thinking ill of the dead.

There was nothing else for it. She checked the Diary and saw that nothing was expected of her until a meeting of the

Council of Social Service at 6.30. 'I'm going over to Exbridge,' she said. 'Want to come?'

Terry nodded without much enthusiasm. He picked up the keys to the Minor and they walked out of the office together.

The road to Exbridge skirted Dartmoor and plunged between hill and vale in a sinuous thin ribbon. On either side, behind massive Devon banks, rose huge fields whose green made you gasp, or whose red earth made you believe there must be some great god who once came to visit this corner of a wonderful land and spilled his blood in tribute to its beauty. White farmhouses stood importantly upon hilltops while scattered about were the reason they were there in the first place – herds of rust-coloured South Devon cattle, their coats catching the sunlight.

Terry drove efficiently but not fast. Once, Miss Dimont had made the mistake of thinking that, being a photographer, he had no soul, but in his own way Terry was enjoying the journey every bit as much as she; just in a different way.

'That ridge.'

Judy was looking at a new-born calf nuzzling its mother as they drove slowly by. 'Yes?'

'Hard edge of sunlight coming over the top. I'd need my Leica for that.'

His companion was not sure whether this was a camera or a cookbook. 'Mmm,' she said. 'It would be wonderful just to stop for a moment and drink all this in.'

'The technical challenges which you face when—'

'Oh, Terry, do shut up. Is this beautiful, or is it beautiful?'

Terry turned and smiled, very slowly, at her. 'It's beautiful,' he said.

Exbridge itself was little to write home about, or even to send a postcard from – a clutch of once-handsome dwellings which had weathered the worst of Devon winters over countless centuries and were now showing their age, not in a nice way. In summertime open-top tourist buses, en route to somewhere more attractive, jammed the streets and, when winter came, it would seem that every major haulier had instructed his drivers to take a short cut through the town.

The Minor found its way to the late Arthur Shrimsley's cottage without difficulty. Neither Miss Dimont nor Terry knew whether he had been married or what his domestic circumstances were. All that was known was that he once worked in some elevated capacity for *The Nation*, that cock-a-snook broadsheet paper beloved of chippy people who liked to look down on their betters.

At a stroke, Miss Dimont knew Shrimsley had lived alone – you only had to look at the state of the front-door mat! At a stroke, she intuited Shrimsley was not a dog owner – not because of physical evidence for or against the proposition, but just because of the feel of the place. It was what made Athene her friend – Judy had an uncanny feel for the unspoken, the unknown, when it came to certain things. After all, wasn't it she who had found Mrs Sharpham's cat in the back of the airing cupboard after it had been missing for a fortnight?

'No dog,' she said to Terry, who was casing the joint.

'Bet there's a window open round the back,' he said, as if relieved he wouldn't have to get the jemmy out of his camera bag.

'No, Terry!' said Miss Dimont. 'Certainly not! What *would* the neighbours think?'

'Flash 'em your press card,' said Terry, voice of experience. 'That should do it. You wait here, I'll let you in the front door.'

It was at times like this, thought Miss Dimont, that British journalism demonstrates what a broad church it is. Last night as she turned out the light she'd put down her volume of George Eliot, composing her thoughts around the moral dilemmas of Daniel Deronda and poor Gwendolen Harleth. Terry meanwhile had snuggled down dreaming of a chance to break and enter some poor innocent's property.

But in their different ways each now brought something to the moment. Terry hopped round the back while Miss Dimont engaged, as only she could, a nice-looking lady in a detailed discussion about the overgrown village green.

Two minutes later the door was open and Miss Dimont stepped in to the sound of a whistling kettle. 'They hated him,' she said to Terry, who was busy doing the honours with cups and saucers.

'Ur,' he said.

'Busybody. Made himself a nuisance. Couldn't adjust to country life. Made an ass of himself doing a book-signing in the town hall. Nobody turned up.'

'Books?' said Terry. 'You'll have to do without milk. It's off.'

'Really, we shouldn't!' squeaked Miss D, embarrassed at his sheer brass neck. But she seemed in no hurry to leave.

She told the photographer of her gleanings: that Shrimsley, who once nearly had an important biography published by the great Victor Gollancz himself, had by now sunk to ghosting memoirs of the not-particularly-rich and often not-very-famous. 'He called himself an author, but he was just a hack,' she said unkindly.

This was opinion, but she had hard fact as well. 'He was down in the saloon bar of the Silent Whistle every night, boring everybody to death. Said he was writing his memoirs, *Headlines All My Life*, or some such inflated nonsense. Meanwhile he paid his bills by filching stuff from the *Riviera Express* and selling it to Fleet Street.'

'Nasty piece of work,' said Terry.

'Well yes, but did you ever meet him?'

'Just look at that,' said Terry. It would appear that in the short time it had taken Judy to debrief the nice lady in the beige macintosh as to the nature and character of Arthur Shrimsley – no mean feat from a standing start – Terry had stormed the barricades, opened the front door, produced a cup of tea and no doubt laid a fire and was ready to light it. To that could be added the detection of a piece of paper he now handed his opposite number.

In Shrimsley's typewriter was an unfinished letter.

Dear Ray,

Good to see you today. I have to admit to being surprised by what you told me – not what I was expecting at all.

It's not something for the memoirs. There's nowhere where a story like that would fit in. On the other hand, what you have is priceless – or, put another way, has a price on it. And a pretty handsome one at that.

Blackmail is such an ugly word but it has its rewards. You really should . . .

And that's where the letter ended. Like Schubert's Unfinished Symphony, the beauty of it lay in what was yet unwritten, and now a theory was starting to form in her mind. She sipped her tea as Terry wandered from room to room, whistling in a decidedly unsympathetic way given the recent occupant's most unfortunate demise.

Miss Dimont squiggled absently on a piece of paper. Shrimsley had come to Cattermole for information to pad out his memoirs. Who knows what that information was, but given they had both been in London immediately after the War – Shrimsley in Fleet Street, Cattermole in the West End – it's likely they knew each other then, and something occurred which involved both men but which was too controversial even for the limelight-adoring Shrimsley to put in his book.

But like the amoral fellow that he was he saw no reason why he and Cattermole – a bear of little brain but one in need of cash (as, evidently, was Shrimsley) – why he and Cattermole should not extort money from some poor unsuspecting individual. That word, 'blackmail'.

But who?

The most likely candidate, of course, was Gerald Hennessy, since the two men – Cattermole and Hennessy – were due to meet on Gerald's arrival in Temple Regis. Indeed, there seemed no other purpose at all for the actor to come to Temple Regis. The postcard in Gerald's pocket confirmed their rendezvous.

Then again, Cattermole didn't strike Miss Dimont as the confrontational type. Cowardly might be a more appropriate word. If he was going to blackmail Hennessy, wouldn't he have done it by phone or letter?

No, it had to be someone else.

'Blackmail's nasty,' opined Terry, now standing behind Miss Dim and reading over her shoulder. 'Don't get much of that round here.'

'You probably do,' said Miss D, 'you just never get to hear about it. Surely you remember the FitzConachie case?'

'Ur,' said Terry, and wandered off again.

No, the blackmail victim had to be someone else. Could it, for example, be Prudence Aubrey? There had been rumours of an *affaire* between the two during the run of *Importance* – that was when Raymond Cattermole still had his hair and a promising career ahead of him.

These thoughts, she realised, were a side issue. Terry and she had come to Exbridge to discover whether Shrimsley had a wife or family to whom they could put questions about his puzzling death, and the answer was that he had not. They wanted to discover whether he had a dog – he did not.

So a man, thirty minutes from home with a dog that was not his, walked round the safety barrier on Mudford Cliffs and fell two hundred and fifty feet to his death.

He was involved in a blackmail plot, or was about to instigate one – victim unknown.

Looks like murder, thought Miss Dimont.

*

Inspector Topham swung through the revolving door of the Grand Hotel and made for the Palm Court.

Not *again*, Stanley! his subordinates would have cried had they known. But they did not know, for the inspector was here on a delicate mission, to ascertain whether Marion Lake and Gerald Hennessy had indeed travelled down in the same Pullman car from London's Paddington Station and whether they intended, well . . .

He pulled out his pipe and clamped it unlit between his lips. Domestic intrigue was not really his forte, but there was something disconcerting about this case which his generally unsuspicious mind ordered him to urgently pursue.

He knocked on Miss Lake's door – most conveniently placed opposite Gerald Hennessy's – and was let in by the maid.

'She'll be with you shortly,' came the pert reply even before he'd had a chance to say who he was or show his warrant card. The maid, evidently, already saw herself in a walk-on part in Miss Lake's next movie.

Inspector Topham had had a useful war in the Guards and had seen many places and many things. But to meet two of the most illustrious stars of the silver screen within the space of twenty-four hours was beyond any experience in that eventful life.

He heard her before he saw her. There was a gentle swishing noise which grew progressively louder as the shapely star made her entrance – caused, he soon was able to note, by the heavy hem of her evening gown trailing along the carpet. It was about as theatrical an entrance as you could imagine, with wafts of Chanel No 5 preceding her. All this, and she was just twenty-seven!

The slinky star poured two measures from a cocktail shaker without asking and handed the inspector a glass containing liquid of a rather bilious hue. It was only 5.30 p.m.

'Chin-chin,' Marion sighed, as if she was about to give her heart to the shiny-booted policeman.

'Er, well, good health,' said the inspector and took a sip of the poison. 'Inspector Topham.' This was superfluous since each knew who the other was, but he felt he had to start proceedings on an official footing.

'I can see you are preparing for an evening out so I will not delay,' he said. 'You were close to the late Gerald Hennessy?'

'You could say *very* close,' said Miss Lake, yet Topham could detect no emotion at her recent loss.

'You travelled down on the Riviera Express together?'

'Yes, we did.' Her answer was factual, clear, no-nonsense.

'And you came here to conduct an illicit liaison?'

'Really, I don't think that's got anything to do with Gerald, has it?'

Topham didn't understand. 'You, er, you came down here with the purpose of spending time with, er, a married man.'

'Yes, Inspector, I did. You know, in this business, these things happen.'

'So you and Mr Hennessy . . . you were . . .' There could be no doubting the meaning of his strangled words.

'Oh!' squealed the film star and jumped up in horror. 'Oh!'

'Oh! What *can* you be thinking of! Honestly, you police, what goes on in your minds?!' She threw down her glass – empty already – and her blonde hair threatened to become unpinned as she shook her pretty head from side to side.

'Inspector, I am appalled. How could you imagine I was sleeping with . . .?' She was unable to continue.

Topham was embarrassed. Clearly there was something wrong with this theory – and yet Prudence Aubrey had been so certain!

'Erm,' said the inspector hesitantly, 'the two of you travelled down together. In this hotel, Miss Lake, you had practically adjoining suites – I think some explanation really is required.'

The nation's number one film star stood up, drew herself up to her full height, and looked down witheringly upon the seated detective. 'You . . .' she hissed. 'You . . . *police*.' The word was full of poison. She paused dramatically.

'Gerald Hennessy, Inspector, was my father.'

TWELVE

Bedlington Harbour was, as ever, joyously busy. The harbour master's magnificent barge, all gold and black and white, surged powerfully from its pontoon on some important mission, its red ensign and personal pennant crackling in the breeze. Tanned fishermen puttered out to sea in small boats, faded brown sails catching the wind, while the Coatmouth Ferry – a riot of red, yellow and blue, dressed overall in bunting and lightly laden with late holidaymakers – made its way purposefully round the point and off to the next town along the coast.

Miss Dimont took off her headscarf, unhitched her raffia bag from Herbert's handlebars, and made for the Seagull Café where her dear friend Auriol Hedley made a point of making everyone feel especially welcome.

With a glass of Auriol's delicious home-made lemonade in front of her, she sat and thought.

Behind her the cliffs rose like skyscrapers, and further away from the harbour when she turned to look she could see the landslip which had taken off Arthur Shrimsley – a great red gash of earth and rock in an otherwise green landscape, like a giant finger pointing to the clue she could not decipher.

Auriol came to join her, and in return for the considerable pleasure of her company, Miss Dimont relayed the story of Gerald Hennessy and Arthur Shrimsley and Raymond Cattermole.

This was no idle chat, for Miss Dimont greatly respected Auriol, who had distinguished herself in her work for the Admiralty during the War. To her customers she was a sweet and plump lady of middle years, with a zest for life and a determination that you should have that second slice of cake. Seated next to Miss Dimont, however, she presented a rather different aspect.

'Well, Judy,' she said, seriously. 'There can be no question that something *irregular* has occurred.'

The word fell from her lips like a denunciation of all things bad. If irregular things had happened during her time at the Admiralty, it would not take Auriol long to regularise them again – and woe betide anyone who did not assist in that re-regularisation.

'Indeed,' sighed Miss D, helplessly, 'but something is missing.'

'Let's be clear,' said Auriol in her brisk, shipshape sort of a way, 'the clue lies in the blackmail, doesn't it? What Cattermole told Shrimsley, but Shrimsley said he couldn't write into his memoirs?'

'I'm certain of that,' said Judy, who was anything but certain.

'But it couldn't be that Shrimsley was encouraging Cattermole to blackmail Gerald Hennessy?'

'I don't think it can be that simple. I think the intended victim has to be Prudence Aubrey – or even Edith Evans.'

'I think more likely the former. I don't know much about Dame Edith's life but she seems too boring to me to have got up to much,' said Auriol, energetically stirring the coffee in front of her. 'On the other hand, you'd have to be a hermit not to see that Miss Aubrey was a woman who saw very little of her husband. They are a childless couple, are they not?'

Miss Dimont nodded assent.

'She is photographed here, there and everywhere,' said Auriol, waving her spoon, 'and never is she seen with her husband. This young man, that young man. Might one suppose she is vulnerable to the charms of the stronger sex?' Here the two friends exchanged smiles. Both might thus be described – vulnerable to male charm – but not at the cost of losing their heads to a gender which was not as strong as it liked to think it was.

'You may be right,' sighed Judy. 'But if Prudence Aubrey has been leading a secret life of that kind, it certainly didn't evince itself to me when we spoke. She strikes me as a woman who demands complete devotion but who gives very little back in return.'

'All the more reason for Gerald Hennessy to stray.'

'Well, there you are, then! It has to be Gerald who was the object of the blackmail plan!'

'You've already discounted him.'

'Ohhhhh!!!' expostulated the reporter, clanking her lemon-ade glass firmly down on the table. 'I wonder why I bother! Tomorrow is the inquest of the pair of them and there'll be no evidence of foul play – I know old Dr Rudkin. And as for Inspector Topham – he's a nice enough fellow but as a police-man he'd have difficulty detecting the first rays of dawn.'

'That seems a trifle unkind, Judy,' said Auriol, who knew of her friend's past run-ins with the detective. 'What about Cattermole?'

'Oh,' said Judy, 'I daresay Ray Cattermole will come home with the milk tomorrow morning.'

There seemed little more to say. Miss Dimont helped clear the table and the two women took a last look around the harbour before going inside. Waves chased in on the turn of the tide as if eager now for an early homecoming. The wind was getting up.

The Seagull Café was empty in the late afternoon, and the two women – as they had so often before – shared washing-up duties in companionable silence. On the wall in the little office was a photograph of Auriol in her WRNS uniform – slimmer in those days, perhaps, but no younger-looking than now. It was typical of Auriol's modesty that the number of stripes on her cuff, denoting her seniority in the Service, were deliberately obscured by a saucy postcard jammed into the corner of the frame.

Judy Dimont allowed her gaze to slip sideways for just one moment to the accompanying portrait, that of a young, handsome, devil-may-care face which could not quite dispose of the tendency to make a joke of everything, even for the photographer. It was the same face which stared out, kindly, tenderly, watchfully, at Miss Dimont when she reached home after her long and arduous day's work at the *Riviera Express*.

'His birthday next week,' said Auriol, almost to herself.

*

Herbert sturdily transported Miss Dimont up the hill back to Temple Regis. Bedlington was all very well but it was more than a trifle snooty, and anyway the reporter wanted to visit the cliff top from whence Arthur Shrimsley had tumbled to meet his maker. She'd seen where he'd ended up on that last journey, now she would inspect where he started out.

If you stood on the edge of Mudford Cliffs you could look down on to Bedlington Harbour – in fact if you screwed your eyes up you could even spot the Seagull Café – but as Mr Shrimsley must have discovered in his final moments, it did not do well to stray too close to the edge. When Miss Dimont parked Herbert and looked around the cliff top she saw nothing but order and regimentation – a precious greensward where dog-walkers met to chat (their dogs too) and to perambulate in leisurely fashion while gazing out to sea.

It was a heavenly place, perched somewhere between the earth and the sky, made all the more thrilling by the height of the cliffs and their vertiginous drop to the rocks beneath. Across the green, towards the edge, Miss Dimont could see the barriers hastily erected after the rockfall – sturdy wooden stakes holding up a lengthy picket fence you could neither vault nor breach. Despite the sternly worded warnings pinned to the fence, Shrimsley must have quite deliberately ignored their message and slipped around the end of the fencing in order to make his fall.

But why? asked Miss Dimont. As Terry had pointed out, this was a man too much in love with himself to want to end it all. And then again, what about the dog?

Did it escape before he fell? No canine corpse was found in the vicinity of his dead body. Nor, upstairs on the Mudford cliff top, was there any report of an abandoned or stray dog. How could it have just disappeared?

As she walked back and forth, Miss Dimont tried hard to ignore the celestial view spread before her, a vast panoply of sea and mist and azure horizon, instead fixing her gaze on the grass at the cliff edge as if it could offer up a clue. Disobligingly, it did not.

She looked to Herbert in the faint hope he might assist, but no. Just then, as she took out her headscarf and looped her raffia bag over the handlebars, an old gentleman walked by, gently led by his equally ancient dachshund.

'Excuse me,' said Miss Dimont. Not for nothing was she known as the best interviewer in the South West. 'That's an awfully sweet boy you have there. May I say hello to him?'

The gentleman smilingly assented.

'Bruce,' he said, after a moment. 'Called him Bruce because he ate a spider when he was a little puppy. Robert the Bruce, dontcha know.'

Miss Dimont did know, and thereby an introduction was made and a most pleasant conversation ensued, the upshot of which was that Captain Hulton had been widowed for seventeen, no, eighteen months and it was Bruce who kept him going.

There were some stern words for the late Mrs Hulton for having forced such a soppy dog on him, a man who should be seen with a retriever or nothing, but they did not fool Miss Dimont. His master a prisoner of loneliness, Bruce was Captain Hulton's saviour.

He loved Mudford Cliffs – the captain, not Bruce, though Bruce loved them too – because they offered him membership to an exclusive club. Since he first started coming here he had met virtually every dog-owner in the area, and it really was very pleasant to see how others' dogs were coming on – whether they'd learnt any new tricks, whether they were behaving themselves, whether there may be new puppies in the offing. It took quite a part of the day to dispatch all these most necessary conversations.

The captain, as Miss Dimont could quite easily see, was a shy man. The dog walk had given him a new purpose.

'Every morning. Rain or shine. People are so kind.'

Miss Dimont bit her lip at this solitude so bravely borne, but eventually could no longer resist. 'Last Thursday,' she said, her hopes rising giddily. 'Were you and Bruce up here last Thursday?'

'What time?' asked the captain.

'About midday,' said Miss Dimont, issuing a silent prayer to anyone who might be listening up there.

'Alas no. Bridge on Thursday afternoons. Don't like the people but it keeps the old grey matter going. We came earlier.'

Miss Dimont felt that sufficient information had now been exchanged between them that she could reveal her purpose.

'On the *Riviera Express*, you see.'

'Ah yes,' said the captain. 'Athene!'

Why do they always say *that*? she thought. A meteor could have landed on the town hall, the *Riviera Express* could have won an international press award for its coverage of the phenomenon, but all people ever wanted to talk about was Athene. Just as well she was her friend.

'So you see, I'm keen to find out about a man who walks his dog here – or at least was walking it that day.'

'What sort of dog?' asked the captain.

'Well,' said Miss Dimont, who up to this moment had not even considered the question, 'I have no idea. We have an eyewitness account of a man answering Shrimsley's description being up here with his dog at about midday. He was speaking to a lady, then he wandered off and, well, you know what happened.'

The captain nodded. He'd seen more than a few dead 'uns in his time. He knew when to offer a momentary pause out of respect.

'If he'd been here I would have noticed him,' he finally replied. 'That time of day there are very few men – in fact I might go so far as to say I am the only male member of this dog-walking club. We call it the She-Club, don't we, Bruce?'

Bruce sat down and scratched vigorously, his tiny leg going like the piston of a steam train.

'I wonder,' asked Miss Dimont thoughtfully, 'whether in your subsequent conversations you may have discussed Mr Shrimsley's unfortunate, ah, accident, with other members of the She-Club?'

'Mostly we talk about dogs.'

'Yes, but—

'Sometimes bridge.'

'There must have been a moment when—'

'We avoid the weather. It changes so much that the conversation is redundant before it's begun. Also, rather banal, dontcha think? Like those people who say "How are you?" – they aren't interested when they ask and I'm not interested in replying. No weather, no personal stuff. That way we all get on fine.'

These rules seemed rather hair-shirt to Miss Dimont, who could carry on a conversation about anything at the drop of a handkerchief. How would you ever know anything about anybody if you didn't ask?

But the honorary male member of the She-Club had taken on its rules as the price of his membership. People he had known for sixteen or seventeen months – he had no idea what their names were. Though cordial, everyone kept at arm's length from each other.

Miss Dimont realised what an utterly useless witness she had on her hands.

'Well, how lovely,' she said sweetly, and bent over Bruce to give his nose a quick fondle. 'I must be getting back now.'

The captain looked at her with gratitude, and suddenly she realised that possibly he had exaggerated his full membership of the She-Club. Maybe he spoke less often – maybe they spoke less often – than he had implied. He was old. He wore his regimental tie over a not altogether clean shirt. His shoes were well polished but the trousers had not seen a steam iron any time recently. Perhaps the smart ladies did not wish to dally too long with the owner of Bruce.

Miss Dimont wanted in that moment to hug him – this brave, this worn-out, old soldier.

'So lovely talking to you,' and she meant it. You are a human being first and a journalist second, she'd decided when she found herself quite by chance in this arcane profession. Never forget how important the person standing in front of you is.

'Just one thing,' said the captain, and Miss Dimont immediately wondered whether she hadn't been too kind. Was he now going to cling to her coat sleeve and not allow her to leave?

'Bruce and I were, as you know, detained at bridge when the unfortunate incident took place. But we did come up here after tea, didn't we, old chap?'

Bruce was equivocal. He wanted more walkies.

'Yes?' said Miss Dimont encouragingly.

'Went and had a look, of course. The police had come and gone by then – all the action was down the bottom of the cliff, dontcha see, they were down there then. Most people had done their dog-walking for the day but Bruce and I had a wander round. Blow me down if he didn't find a trophy.'

Miss D was not a member of the She-Club. She was only mildly interested in dogs. Really you were either a cat person or a dog person and frankly anybody who set eyes on her Mulligatawny would agree there could be no contest. So dogs digging up bones were not of compelling interest, especially as she was still officially on duty and her trip up to Mudford Cliffs had been a personal whim.

'Well I'll be getting—'

'I hung it on the picket fence and next day it had gone. Rather expensive, I'd say. Nice perfume.'

Something held Miss Dimont back from letting out Herbert's clutch.

'It was a . . .?'

'Ladies' scarf. White, silk. Torn. I found it beyond the barrier – I know we shouldn't, but Bruce and I wanted to see where the chap had gone down, didn't we, boy?'

'Er, anything else?' asked Miss Dimont, suddenly very interested.

'Not a thing. Don't know why it was there – probably blown over on the breeze. It gets windy up here, even in summer.'

'So you hung it on the fence and it had gone next day?'

'Yes. Expect the owner came along to collect it.'

'Well,' said Miss Dimont, 'that *is* interesting.'

Herbert took her, at no great speed, back to the *Riviera Express*. Part of the reason Miss Dimont so loved her old moped was because he allowed her time to think. And now she used the journey to reorder her thoughts once more.

Despite his apparent failure as a witness, the captain had said something quite important. It was almost unheard of for men to walk dogs up on Mudford Cliffs. The She-Club dominated the day – though doubtless husbands did their duty in the early morning or at night after work. So to find a man up on the greensward in the middle of the day would be remarkable.

And, again, why would Shrimsley be walking a dog half-an-hour's journey from his home when he didn't even possess one?

Answer, thought Miss Dimont, wobbling a bit as she came down the hill past Tuppenny Row. There can only be one answer.

It wasn't his dog.

It wasn't his dog and he had gone up to the cliffs to meet someone who *did* have a dog. Something had occurred between them. Arthur fell. The lady – it must have been a lady – took her dog and disappeared.

And . . . Could this be connected? A white scarf – a damaged white scarf – had been left behind at the scene of the crime – by now surely it *must* be a crime – though now it had disappeared.

Shrimsley was a hateful character. He had written of

blackmail. Was this the blackmail victim, who took the law into her own hands and saw him off?

Herbert arrived safe and sound in the *Express* car park and Miss Dimont alighted, happily patting her corkscrew hair back into some semblance of shape.

THIRTEEN

Rudyard Rhys was in typical mood – grumpy, indecisive, distracted. He struggled with his nasty briar pipe.

'What time do you call this?'

'Been out to Bedlington on the Hennessy story,' said his chief reporter happily.

'Please come into my office.'

This did not augur well. If Mr Rhys had something to say, he said it wherever he stood and didn't care who heard, and as he shut the door behind him Miss Dimont had a presentiment of ugly things to come.

'You appear to be playing detective,' he said, not kindly.

'Well in a manner of—'

'Again.'

'I don't go out of my way to discover dead bodies, Mr Rhys.'

'Betty tells me you have some theory about these deaths.'

'In a manner of speaking, yes.'

'Well, let me tell *you*, in a manner of speaking' rasped Rudyard Rhys, 'I've had a complaint.'

Miss Dimont's heart sank. No matter how hard you tried,

there was always someone. She hadn't meant to put the cat among the pigeons at the Regis Conservative Ball last winter – these things just happen. As for the mix-up over the winners of the Class Two Chrysanthemums (incurved) . . .

It always gave the Editor an unfair advantage. Implicit in his every instruction was the order to stick one's neck out, yet the moment someone complained the fault was yours, not his. He never took risks himself but wanted you to do it on his behalf.

'What is it this time,' asked Miss Dimont rhetorically, with a deflationary sigh. She had plenty of work to do and complaints took up precious time.

'Prudence Aubrey,' said the Editor.

Miss Dimont quailed inwardly. It was the inquest tomorrow.

'I saw Inspector Topham at the Club at lunchtime. He has been talking to Miss Aubrey. Miss Aubrey,' Rhys repeated the name with a degree of reverence before turning his fire on the reporter, 'is complaining of press harassment.'

'Well, those people from the *Western Daily Press* are nothing short of animals,' said Miss Dim. 'Jackals. The worst kind of—'

'Miss Aubrey,' snarled Rhys, 'was talking about *you*.'

Miss Dimont sat for five minutes while her editor relayed with some relish the actress's complaints as divulged to Topham. It may not have helped Miss Dimont's cause that in the past – especially in the Pillsbury case – she had called

into question the efficacy, even the existence, of Temple Regis'
CID department.

The head of that department clearly believed in the dish-
served-cold philosophy. The Pillsbury case, through which
he had marched painfully slowly, and to no great effect, had
been almost a year ago.

'I will say this, Mr Rhys. There's something odd about
Miss Aubrey. She's jumpy, angry, evasive and doesn't respond
in the way most actresses do to gentle questioning by the
press.'

'She's just lost her husband, what do you expect!'

'It's not that. There are things going on we don't know
about, Mr Rhys. I think you should trust me. There are things
going on.'

The editor looked at his chief reporter. The last time Miss
Dimont had used the 'trust me' line he had received a personal
letter of congratulation from the managing director of the
Riviera Express. He had taken it home and shown it to Mrs
Rhys. Miss Dimont's report had gathered widespread praise
and Mr Rhys had naturally taken his share, perhaps more,
of credit for having the courage to print it.

'Well,' he said, caught in a quandary, 'that's as may be. But
until you have anything more to write you must remember
that the *Express* represents the people of Temple Regis. It has
a responsibility to be above reproach. I don't want people
coming in from outside and criticising the way we do things.
You watch your step.'

Tight-lipped, for she had done no wrong – quite the opposite in fact – Miss Dimont rose to go.

'And, Miss Dim. I want you to go round and apologise to Miss Aubrey. Take some flowers for heaven's sake, put them on your expenses. It's the inquest tomorrow – I don't want her getting up in court and saying things about my newspaper.'

'I really don't think that's necessary, Mr Rhys.'

'Please, Miss Dimont, do as I say,' he replied testily. For once the editor's decision was final.

It was just as well Athene was in the office. One glance at Miss Dimont could tell her aura had turned to black.

'Cup of tea, dear?'

'Hemlock more like,' sniffed Miss Dimont, but ten minutes in Athene's glorious company put some semblance of sunshine back in her life. Between them they worked out which flowers Judy should take round to the Grand, and what words of contrition might be chosen which did not compromise her legitimate search after the truth.

The cups washed, Miss Dimont set off. In September, in Temple Regis, a suitable offering is those autumn chrysanthemums so beloved of harvest festivals and late Horticultural Society open days. Not perhaps the most celebrated in the floral pantheon, they nonetheless carry a very special message of hope and warmth. Miss Dimont had found just the right ones, in a delicious array of browns and golds.

Nonetheless her approach to Miss Aubrey's door on the Grand Hotel's second floor was not without its moments of doubt, regret and annoyance. She knocked, and waited.

No silk sheath for the film star this evening – evidently she was a planning a night alone with the wireless. A faded cashmere sweater, clearly comfort clothing, was wrapped around her spare frame and on her feet a pair of worn Turkish slippers. The hair was not quite so perfectly set, the make-up had rubbed thin.

'Come in, come in, don't stand on the doorstep.'

Miss Dimont couldn't get from her tone quite what mood she was in, but mood there was, aplenty.

Not for a humble reporter the glass charged with turbo-powered cocktails, as for Inspector Topham. Instead, without invitation, Miss Dimont was handed a hefty glass of sherry. It was just what she needed to get the ball rolling.

'Look, Miss Aubrey, I gather I have rather put my foot in it. I was a great admirer of your husband and I wanted to give him as comprehensive and as fitting a farewell as it is possible for a local newspaper to make. We do not, as a rule, see so many of his stature here in Temple Regis.'

'You did,' said Miss Aubrey, subsiding on a couch and tucking up her knees, 'a really wonderful job.'

Miss Dimont blinked. *What did she just say?*

'Vincent Mulchrone in the *Daily Mail*, Jack Higgins in the *Daily Herald* – they all tried to capture Gerry in their obituaries, but his was an elusive character. He had many flaws but he had a magical side to him as well. But I loved your phrase, "Angel with one foot in the . . ."'

'Gutter,' finished Miss D.

'That dreadful character Jack Spivimo he played in *The*

Devil's Quartet – he did that just as well as all those tiresome war heroes he played, didn't he?'

'I thought so,' said Miss Dimont.

'I'm sorry,' said Miss Aubrey, 'we got off on the wrong foot. The press have always been very kind to me. It was just – well, you know, the shock, the readjustment. I like to have a script and I like to stick to the script. Suddenly there was no script. I haven't been quite myself.'

And with that she got up and poured more sherry. The long windows giving out on to the balcony, with the sea beyond and the still effulgent clouds suspended above, allowed eventide to enter the room and bestow upon its furniture a special glow.

The sherry, the elegance of her surroundings, the extraordinary turnabout in Miss Aubrey's attitude, caught Miss Dimont off-balance. It was comforting, it was enjoyable, but wasn't it all just an act – and had she just suspended her disbelief in Miss Aubrey's innocence? Had she, unawares, been made to, by some unseen force?

After all, the woman before her was caught up in a blackmail plot. Her husband was dead, and his rival, the man with whom she had had a brief *affaire*, was missing.

Yet this evening Prudence Aubrey looked alone and slightly afraid. The hauteur, the grandiose gestures, were missing.

'I'm glad you've come,' she said. 'There are some things I want to say. I tried to tell the inspector but, fine fellow though he is – I knew his commanding officer – he's not what you might call *sympatico*. He doesn't understand family matters, and really this is at the heart of it all.'

Miss Dimont sipped her sherry and waited.

'It's all been a terrible mistake. Gerry came down on the *Express* with a woman – *that* woman, Marion Lake. It would not take an Einstein to work out what was going on. I just felt so terribly hurt, not only that he should do it – though Lord knows how many times there have been before – but that he should die so publicly and offer the public the opportunity to see that our marriage was not what we pretended it to be.

'He could always do that rueful smile, scratch his jaw, waggle an eyebrow and make you believe that that's what chaps do. But an actress . . . like me . . . at a certain time in her career . . . and him dead in the arms of the latest *sex siren*. I mean, there's been rather a long gap since my last film, which could only be made all the more prominent by the fact that Miss Lake is half my age and has made a handful of movies since I last stood in front of the camera.

'A word of that in the press and what little chance I have of getting a good part again would be dashed. So you will see why I was a little . . . er, cautious . . . in answering your questions.'

On the face of it all this seemed quite plausible, but Miss Dimont had a reporter's instinct that this was merely a version of the truth, not the full bag of tricks.

But her task here was not to enquire further, merely to smooth the ruffled feathers of this elegant swan seated before her. Two glasses of sherry and very little said by Miss Dimont seemed to have achieved that purpose and now, perhaps, the best course of action would be to retire. But Prudence Aubrey was in no mood to draw the interview, if that's what it was, to a close and they started to discuss the following day's inquest.

Here Miss Dimont was of some comfort and assistance, for she had attended many such occasions while Miss Aubrey had never set foot in a coroner's court. Naturally she was keen to learn how many press might attend, what might be her best outfit, where the best place would be to pose for the cameras – inside or outside the courtroom? Miss Dimont soon put her mind to rest on the latter point: 'The coroner will probably have you arrested for contempt if you encourage the photographers to snap you indoors.'

Little hints like this fostered a growing sense of trust in Prudence. She rang the bell and ordered sandwiches. It encouraged the irrepressible Miss Dimont forward, for here she was in the presence of the one person who might know the connection between her husband's death and that of Shrimsley, and possibly had some inkling as to why Cattermole had disappeared. It was not the moment to back off – a reporter has a duty to his story, after all.

'Tell me,' said Miss Dimont casually, 'do you know the name Arthur Shrimsley?'

Miss Aubrey's eyes narrowed. 'Shrimsley? Wasn't he the one who died soon after Gerry?'

And halved the front-page coverage of her husband's demise, thought Miss Dimont. In the acting profession it's all about how big the headline is – it would have been preferable if the wretched Shrimsley could have saved his cliff fall for another week.

'He was rather a disgusting figure. Drank too much and leeched off other people's lives,' said Miss Dimont in a rare bleak judgement, for generally she saw the best in people.

'The name seems familiar. Did he not work in Fleet Street after the War? He may have interviewed me. Or Gerry. Or both. Forgive me, Miss Dimont, but there have been *so* many interviews, one does not remember them all. And one most determinedly does not remember the ones which went wrong.'

Let's hope this one doesn't, then, thought Miss Dimont guiltily.

'I'm just wondering whether . . . he didn't get in touch with you recently, did he?'

'Why would he?'

'Didn't write to you?'

'No.'

'Raymond Cattermole,' said Miss Dimont. 'Did *he* write to you?'

'No. He did write to Gerry, though. I seem to remember Gerry and I at breakfast recalling what a terrible fraud Cattermole was when we were in the West End. You know I was playing Sybil in *Private Lives* at the Apollo while those two round the corner were doing *Earnest*?

'Gerry disliked him intensely. "Glad I broke his arm," he used to say. There was something between them, I'm not sure what.'

'Jealousy?' prompted Miss Dimont. 'Rivalry?'

'I see you are a clever woman,' said Miss Aubrey drily. 'You mean jealousy and rivalry over me. Well, yes, it could have been that. And since you are asking by the arch of your eyebrows was there an *affaire* between Raymond Cattermole and me, the answer I regret to say is yes.

'We all saw a lot of each other in those days. It was just after the War and there was a sense of, I don't know, liberation. That we had got through it all intact and now was the time to make hay. We were young – ish' she added after a brief pause, 'and we had the West End at our feet.

'Naturally, Gerry took the opportunity to run around with Gloria Westerby, who was playing opposite me in *Lives* – she was Amanda – it made me furious the way they would sit there at lunch saying "Sollocks" to each other all the time. Utterly infuriating! So I retaliated with Ray Cattermole.

'It was hideous, my dear – a torment I would not wish to put anyone through. As lovers go it would be hard to give him even a one-star rating – he was ugly, inconsiderate, and . . . a beast.' Her voice lowered dramatically and Miss Dimont could not even begin to imagine what indignities this beauteous flower of the silver screen had undergone at Cattermole's hands.

'It lasted a very short space of time and it was the last time I was unfaithful to Gerry. He carried on in his own sweet way, of course, but I really didn't have the heart for all the subterfuge and the lies. Frankly, my dear, I would rather press dried flowers.'

This took time to sink in. As with most fans, if Miss Dimont pictured him at all in her dreams it would be as the craggy-jawed soldier/sailor/airman who against all odds battled through and came home to his one true love. The notion that Gerald Hennessy could be a womaniser jarred, and jarred badly – though she was quite worldly enough to know that these things happen. Especially in the acting profession.

Miss Dimont gathered together the threads of the conversation and decided to plough on. Miss Aubrey did not seem to mind.

'So I take it that your husband and Mr Cattermole really thoroughly disliked each other?'

'My dear, the understatement of the year.'

'It's difficult, then, to understand why Mr Hennessy would want to meet Mr Cattermole, and vice versa. What was the purpose of their meeting?'

Miss Aubrey stood up. Her manner had changed abruptly.

'What's this all about?' she asked sharply. 'My husband is dead. It would appear he died of a heart attack. A very sad occurrence – and quite apart from that, I have to say with some regret that it comes at the wrong moment. We were going to do the *The Magnificent Ambersons* together, an opportunity to revive . . . my . . .'

She was close to tears. She would probably never make a film again. All that was left of her future now was wretched television.

'I'm sorry,' said Miss Dimont, 'you're quite right. Some-times one can read too much into things.'

'What was the purpose of your question?' The tears were drying and, Miss Dimont slowly realised, Miss Aubrey was rather enjoying the drama of it all.

'I'll be frank,' said Miss Dimont, taking a chance. 'I have been speaking to Geraldine Phipps, who—'

'Geraldine *Phipps*? I thought she died years ago!'

'No, she lives here in Temple Regis.'

'Good Lord! She must be ninety!'

'Well, not quite. She is actually the, ah, close friend of Mr Cattermole.'

'Ray . . . and Geraldine Phipps?' The thought appeared hilarious to Prudence. 'Old enough to be his mother! Ha! Ha!'

'Well,' said Miss Dimont rather primly, because despite the gin and the cigarette extinguished in the filthy tea, she had rather liked Mrs Phipps. 'She told me something interest-ing. But I wouldn't want to upset you over Gerald, er, Mr Hennessy.'

Miss Aubrey looked at her evenly. 'Nothing you could say about Gerald would upset me,' she said, and paused. 'Our marriage was over.'

It took a moment for this to register. It would explain the delayed arrival of the widow Hennessy in Temple Regis, and her slightly odd behaviour ever since. It also meant that some of the assumptions Miss Dimont had previously made were probably wide of the mark. Most importantly, though, it meant that she could plough on with the torrent of questions which kept rising to her lips without the fear of hurting her interviewee.

'Let me put it like this,' said Miss Dimont, still not quite sure whether she could trust Miss Aubrey, but taking a chance, 'I believe that the death of your husband and Arthur Shrimsley, and the disappearance of Raymond Cattermole, could all in some way be linked.

'And,' she added, 'if I am correct, your husband did not die of a heart attack. Mr Shrimsley did not fall by accident. And it may well be that Mr Cattermole is also dead.'

Miss Aubrey's face showed no sign of emotion. 'Go on,' she said, with just the shade of a tremor.

'Let's start with Mr Shrimsley. It would appear that he encouraged Cattermole in the idea that he could blackmail somebody – I thought it must be you.'

'Good Lord!' said Prudence. 'What on earth would he have to blackmail *me* about? I've certainly got a few things on him – I could earn a mint blackmailing Ray Cattermole! But not the other way round, I do assure you.'

'I wondered whether . . . maybe something to do with all those escorts you were seen in the papers with?'

Miss Aubrey erupted in laughter. 'More interested in each other!' she trilled, flouncing her hand. 'Safe in taxis! Safe as houses!'

'Oh,' said Miss Dimont, momentarily deflated.

Out beyond the balcony the sun sprinkled its last dazzling rays into the aquamarine blue. The songbirds, such as remained at this time of year, had exhausted their repertoire for the day. A chill wind ruffled the curtains of the long windows and Prudence Aubrey rose to shut them, draw the curtains, and turn on a succession of low lamps which cast a muted glow across the pastel-shaded boudoir.

This small domestic task she acquitted with grace and neatness, as if the actions were borrowed from some drawing-room drama she once starred in. It was clear she used the moment to collect her thoughts and consider what to say next.

Finally, she returned to the couch, tucked up her legs, sipped the last of her sherry and set her head at an angle.

'I am going to tell you some things which I do not want repeated in your newspaper. Do I have your agreement that you will keep this private?'

Miss Dimont groaned inwardly. It was not the first time someone had asked her that question. The dilemma which faces all reporters in a similar situation is whether to agree, and consign to history's dustbin the best story they would ever have; or agree, only to break that promise later. No self-respecting reporter would take the third option – to say 'either you tell this to me on the record or not at all' – for all reporters are nosy and cannot resist the sharing of a confidence. The more they are told a secret, the more they want to share that secret.

Miss Dimont paused before answering.

'Yee . . . ees,' she said. In the way her reply was intoned you did not know which of the options she had plumped for, but her nuanced response passed the film star by. As far as she was concerned they had an agreement.

'If there was any blackmailer, it was Gerald,' she began. 'At least, that's the way it felt to me.'

'What?'

'You know, Miss Dimont, times are changing. There is new drama in the air – all this kitchen-sink stuff. There's new music in the air. The world is changing fast. It would seem that for the first few years after the War all people wanted to do was look backwards to pre-war days – "pre-war" seemed to be the byword for all that was good and great. So it was a good time for actresses like me, playing for Noël Coward and Terry Rattigan.

'People didn't want change, they wanted to revisit the past and live there. But then, around the time of the Coronation, things started to shift – you got the beatniks and the Teddy boys, and jazz and poets and coffee bars. Things are moving on, Miss Dimont, and I don't mind telling you it's not something I like. My kind of acting is probably over – it's those dolls like Marion Lake who are leading the way now.'

She pointed to the sherry decanter and the reporter obliged.

'I can tell you were a fan of Gerry,' she said sympathetically. Miss Dimont nodded. 'Then you will have seen the metamorphosis he underwent in the past seven years. Once upon a time he was like all the others – Gielgud, Richardson, Olivier. He would give those enigmatic, clipped interviews which said very little and were designed to preserve what he thought was a god-like status.

'But then he sensed the change – he used to talk to me about it all the time. I find change frightening, but he seemed to thrive on it. Slowly he began to let his hair down – he would start out interviews by lying on the floor, repeating the reporter's questions, interviewing the reporter – any trick that would draw attention to the fact that he was part of the new wave. He would dress all in black or appear drunk – anything.'

Miss Dimont nodded. It was all part of Gerald's fascination for her – the fact that he continued to play stiff-upper-lip parts and yet appear to be so deliciously unconventional.

'It drew him a whole new raft of fans. He enjoyed the extra publicity it brought. And,' said Miss Aubrey in chilly tones, 'it *encouraged* him.'

The actress went on. 'He decided to do his memoirs. I think Radford, the agent, encouraged him. But unlike those actors who create their character in life and then live by it for the rest of their days, he decided he wanted to do a warts-and-all portrait, telling ghastly true stories that really should be consigned to the wastepaper basket.

'He wanted to talk about his failures as well as his successes. And,' added Miss Aubrey bitterly, 'he wanted to write about *me*.'

'Well,' said Miss Dimont, clearing her throat, 'I would think that must be—'

'Cheek!' snapped the actress. 'That's what it must be. He decided that since we were seen always as British cinema's happiest couple, it would be wrong to leave my story out of it. So he wanted to write up where I came from, how I struggled and . . .' here she paused and caught her breath '. . . and what I had to do to get parts. And all my successes and failures too. Especially, for some reason, the failures.

'I tell you, Miss Dimont, we had row after row about it. I told him my life was my own property, not his.' Miss Aubrey's voice was now rising to fever pitch and its timbre reminded Miss Dimont of her earlier, hysterical, outburst.

'It was NOT his story to tell!' she shouted, and swilled back her sherry. 'NOT his to tell!'

And with that she burst into tears. Miss Dimont recognised in that instant that *The Magnificent Ambersons* would never have been remade, that either Miss Aubrey would have won the day and Britain's most adored couple would part – or Gerald Hennessy would win, with the same result.

'He blackmailed me,' sobbed Prudence Aubrey. 'He said, let me write it my way. You can have the house. You can have the money. I'm off on a new adventure and you aren't part of it. Agree, and you can have the money. Disagree, and I'll make it worse for you.

'Oh yes,' sobbed Miss Aubrey. 'I was ready to kill him. I'd worked it all out.'

FOURTEEN

'Just in time, dear,' said Athene Madrigale as Miss Dimont, with one glass more of sherry on board than was strictly necessary, plumped her raffia bag down on the desk with a thud.

'It's late,' said the reporter absently.

'Just my time of day,' said Athene sweetly. 'You don't know how hard it is to connect with the spirit world when the office is full of . . .' she nodded vaguely towards the editor's office '. . . hooligans.'

It *was* late, and as Miss Dimont had tramped back from the Grand Hotel, her head buzzing with thoughts, the streets echoed to her footsteps. Out of season, Temple Regis put itself to bed early and with decorum: they may still be dancing and drinking in the Palm Court, but as the mist swept up slowly from the sea, the rest of the town was quiet as the grave.

The tea Athene made contained a magic ingredient. Drink it in her company, and you felt a different person. Maybe it was Athene's soothing clucks which went with the consumption of it, for after all what was it? Merely an infusion of dried leaves from some far-flung place, with a splash of Devon milk added. Yet it restored and invigorated in a way that no cup of tea which Miss Dimont made could ever do. That was the miracle of Athene.

The horoscope column was complete, so the two sat and chatted as the great newsroom clock clicked on towards midnight. There was something eerily dramatic about being alone in a newspaper office which had ceased its business for the day: in the mornings and afternoons there was a sense of perpetual motion, that this well-oiled piece of machinery was too restless, too energetic, ever to sleep. Copy-boys ran, sub-editors demanded, executives conferred, photographers splashed happily in their darkroom, and everywhere there was the tumultuous clatter of typewriters and the ringing of telephones.

At night, to sit in this abandoned room gave one the feeling of being in the eye of a storm. The tumult had passed, but it would come again. And meanwhile the electrical energy generated during the day still hung in the air, as if waiting to expend itself at any moment in a lightning flash.

Both women, as if aware of this, talked in lowered tones. Judy brought Athene up to date with the latest from the Grand, but curiously Prudence Aubrey's murderous words left the clairvoyant unmoved.

'It's not her, dear.'

'What?' said Miss Dimont. She needed more tea.

'Not Prudence Aubrey. I know, I can tell.'

'Well, I suppose it's unlikely. How could she have murdered

two men while she was apparently in London at the time? But how can you be so certain? You haven't even met her.'

'I have been casting about in my mind. I think you should be looking at this another way.'

This was the sort of advice Miss Dimont might welcome from Auriol Hedley who, after all, in another life had considerable experience in the dark arts, but Athene?

'I'm trying to do that,' said Miss D with some frustration. 'But I can't see anything.

'Cattermole,' said Athene with authority. 'Raymond Cattermole. All this time you have been assuming that Mr Cattermole is somehow the victim of the same horrific mind that has done away with Gerald Hennessy and Arthur Shrimsley. Did it never occur to you that, instead of being in league with them, Cattermole was in fact the architect of their joint ends? That it was he who caused their deaths?'

No, thought Miss Dimont, it had not occurred to me. All the evidence points to the three men involved in some distasteful action together – why would Cattermole kill? And frankly, when you looked at him with his wobbly toupee, who would think him possible of such a definite act?

And not once, but twice?

She cast her mind back to when she last saw the actor-manager. 'Over my dead body' is what he said, referring to the idea posited by her that Gerald Hennessy would take centre-stage on the Pavilion Theatre boards in the next summer season.

'Over my dead body' didn't sound like a murderer. Or did

it? Wasn't it just a line from one of the many melodramas he'd staged – actors always like to talk in quotes – or was it something more sinister? Had he, like Perce, skedaddled once his bloody work was done?

Or was it – was it? – that the story or stories which Shrimsley couldn't use in his memoirs had triggered some insane desire to see both men dead?

And, frankly, was he capable of it?

Miss Dimont didn't think so.

'Wasn't Cattermole,' she said to Athene, who was gazing into middle-distance.

'You're right, dear,' trilled the clairvoyant without a second's hesitation. 'Sometimes when I look into the ether I forget to put my specs on. I've just been talking to my spirit guide – it's all right, Judy, I don't expect you to believe – and he was shaking his head. Saying no, Athene, you've got it all wrong.'

These mixed-up thoughts remained with Miss Dimont on the journey home and even accompanied her to bed. Normally she had a good long chat with Mulligatawny and quite often some new thought came from it, but she was exhausted and could do no more than feed him, cuddle him, put him out and plump up the pillow in his basket.

She almost forgot – but no, she could never forget – to give her last gaze to the young man in his silver photograph frame, and utter some unspoken words to him before turning out the light.

*

Inspector Topham finished the last of his toast and marmalade and bade farewell to Mrs Topham. Theirs was a companionable but monosyllabic partnership as undemonstrative as his choice of necktie.

The coroner's court was a stiff ten-minute journey and as he walked with measured tread – a sergeant-major's pace-stick would approve his thirty-inch regulation step – Inspector Topham thought about what evidence he had gathered, and how much of it he would share with the coroner.

The inspector was not a secretive man, rather he was a pragmatist. Too much detail can swing an inquest jury around until it's pointing in the opposite direction. Anything salacious should be kept back because of the headlines – and the coroner, Dr Rudkin, did not like headlines in his court, any more than he would stand for film stars executing a twirl for the photographers.

The doctor was an old-school GP whose civic pride was barely camouflaged by his crusty exterior. His position allowed him, or so he felt, to exercise a preference for community good over the need to tell the whole truth. Fastidious to a fault, he guarded against the sort of lurid detail which will spawn in a more careless coroner's court when left to breed unchecked.

Topham had learnt over the years just how much to feed Dr Rudkin, and how much to leave out. The two men had never discussed it because they never met socially, but each understood the other's needs perfectly. The coroner would ask, the inspector would reply, but many, many facts would remain unspoken. Honesty, truth, transparency, clarity were less important than a respect for the dead – and, more importantly, for those the dead left behind, often in harrowing circumstances.

The inspector therefore discarded much of what he'd been told by Prudence Aubrey, as much for her benefit as for Hennessy's. The actor's womanising, Prudence's falling star, the card from Cattermole to Hennessy – the fact that Cattermole was missing – none of this mattered to the coroner. And as far as Inspector Topham was concerned, that meant it was nobody else's business either.

He had pondered the business of Marion Lake – the fact that she turned out to be the daughter of Gerald Hennessy, not his mistress. How did that affect the death of the actor or, come to that, the death of Mr Shrimsley? Not at all. So that could be struck from the record as well. *Honestly*, the inspector would say to his wife in a rare moment of confession, *I could write a book with all the stuff I hear but never repeat!*

The inspector's motives may be honourable, but they made for pallid copy when the likes of Miss Dimont and her colleagues on the press bench read back their notes. Where was the quotable quote, the juicy detail? Nowhere, if Frank Topham had anything to do with it!

But neither police nor press were prepared for the drama which was just about to unfold in this grey civic backwater. As the witnesses and observers filed into the dusty coroner's room, the inspector at their head, there was suddenly an almighty kerfuffle outside. Topham could hear women's voices raised to fever pitch and the unmistakable sound of a physical dust-up.

The inspector pushed back through a crowd which was only just waking up to the realisation that something was going on. He broke through the crush to discover the two famous women he had come to know in the past week standing, sobbing, dishevelled, angry and, in Prudence Aubrey's case, almost mad with rage.

If she had a knife she would use it, thought Topham, who'd had experience of such things in India. But in a second he had his hand on her shoulder and was issuing restraining words which, though gently spoken, were an order not to be disobeyed. Nor would Prudence do such a thing – for hadn't she known Colonel ffrench-Blake, Topham's commanding officer?

Further down the hall Marion Lake turned her face to the wall and wailed.

'Now what's this?' asked the inspector sharply, more perplexed than anything else. 'This is a coroner's court, madam, a place where you must show some respect. We are here to hear evidence of your late husband's death.'

A knot of spectators had gathered and it grew larger by the second – court officials, policemen, secretaries – because to witness a catfight between two of the most famous women in the land, for that is what it had been, was a remarkable spectacle.

Out across the parquet floor billowed the contents of Miss Aubrey's alligator-skin bag – make-up, handkerchiefs, banknotes, coins. The bag itself was some way down the hall and Topham's experienced eye could tell at a glance that the older woman had come off worst in the encounter.

'What's this all about?' he asked the actress, nodding to a uniform sergeant to take hold of Marion Lake.

'How could she,' sobbed Miss Aubrey. 'How *could* she? How could that piece of stuff have the temerity to come to this place when we are just about to hear about the last day of my late husband's life?'

'Well,' said Topham logically, 'she could be called as a witness. You see, she was on the train with—'

'I KNOW SHE WAS ON THE TRAIN WITH HIM!' shouted Miss Aubrey, all pretence of control now gone. 'She was coming down for a dirty weekend with him! How could she possibly show her face here, the brazen—' Suddenly she sat down, hard, on the floor. Her legs had given way beneath her.

Topham kindly leaned over Prudence Aubrey just as Miss Dimont hove into view. Between them, they lifted the distraught woman and helped her into a chair. Topham leaned forward and tried to whisper something in Prudence's ear. But such was her distress it was clear his message went unrecognised.

But Miss Dimont heard it all right. What the inspector had said explained everything.

Miss Dimont felt she needed a chair to sit down on too. Could it be true? Could Gerald Hennessy, that urbane and rakish charmer, have fathered Britain's number one sex siren without anybody knowing? And who was the mother? Clearly not Prudence Aubrey!

So far Miss D had this scoop to herself and, as she recovered her wits, she was keen to keep it that way. Mercifully, the other members of the press who were there were still in the courtroom, assuming that the business of the day must start any moment.

She whisked across to where Marion Lake was standing, now reapplying her make-up and showing a degree more composure than her assailant.

'Judy Dimont, *Riviera Express*,' she said briskly. 'Just one question: are you, were you, Gerald Hennessy's daughter?'

Miss Lake looked down her long nose with her lustrous big blue eyes. 'Ye-es,' she said slowly.

'Could you explain how . . .?'

Miss Lake had a reputation of never letting the press down, and now was not the time to quit.

'Twenty-five years ago, while he was engaged to Prudence Aubrey, he had an affair with my mother,' she said calmly. 'He did the decent thing – paid up and disappeared. My mother refused always to say who my real father was – they'd come to an arrangement – and in any case I didn't care because she married my adoptive father before I was born. It all happened very quickly.'

Miss Dimont trod very carefully. 'I interviewed Miss Aubrey very recently,' she said. 'She told me that she and Mr Hennessy had never had children because he was unable to.'

Marion Lake realised that this may be a lynchpin moment

in her career. She could already see the national newspaper headlines the next morning. She was only sorry there was just one reporter in front of her with whom to share the news.

'I finally found out who my father was only very recently,' she said, as if she had rehearsed the story in front of the mirror that morning before breakfast. 'I had employed a search agent. I was intrigued to know where all this acting – *talent*—' she dwelt on the word '—had come from.

'To be honest when they told me it was Gerald, I wasn't in the slightest surprised. I got in touch with him and we found we hit it off very well. But obviously it wasn't a secret he was going to share with his wife, given the circumstances.'

'But,' said Miss Dimont, never afraid to press the point, 'Gerald Hennessy was unable to have children. Miss Aubrey told me so.'

Marion Lake's smile was almost pitying. 'It was she who could not have children,' she said, with just the faintest hint of triumph in her voice. 'Once it emerged there were difficulties, Gerry went to the doctor and he discovered the truth. He told me all this at our first meeting. He loved her – then – and didn't want to upset her so he took the blame.'

It seemed plausible, but it left Miss Dimont on the horns of a dilemma – the story was not complete without Miss Aubrey's response to this quite extraordinary revelation. It meant the reporter would have to go back down the corridor and confront a woman who was facing the wretched ordeal of hearing her husband's last moments being lingered over in a public courtroom.

She could see Prudence Aubrey, still seated and in some distress, surrounded by a circle of admirers and that small knot of helpful souls who spring from nowhere in courtrooms to support and protect those bemused at finding themselves in such an alien environment.

This was not going to be pleasant. On the one hand, repeating what Marion Lake had just told her removed the sting of Hennessy's apparent adulterous intentions on the last day of his life. On the other, Miss Dimont was about to tell a woman of a certain age that the reason she had never had children with Gerald Hennessy lay with her, not her husband.

It is at moments like this that the average reporter shrugs their shoulders and blunders straight in, using the surprise element to extract the maximum amount of quotes before their victim rightly shuts up. Miss Dimont was not an average reporter.

She had little time to deliberate because the coroner's clerk was calling people back into the courtroom where proceedings were about to start.

Walking up to Miss Aubrey, she took the situation in hand. 'You are not ready to face the court,' she said. Miss Aubrey, through her tears, mumbled incoherently. 'I will explain to the clerk that proceedings cannot go ahead without you, but you need time to compose yourself.'

Miss Aubrey nodded dumbly.

'Let me take you to the waiting room once I've done that,' she said firmly but caringly. 'Sit here for the moment.'

The reporter caught the coroner's clerk at the door and

briefly explained the situation. After a hurried consultation he returned and nodded. 'Dr Rudkin will grant Mrs Hennessy a thirty-minute recess to allow her to regain her composure, but there are other witnesses here and he will have to go ahead without her if she is not ready by eleven o'clock.'

Miss Dimont nodded. What she was about to vouchsafe was not exactly guaranteed to put the actress in a more stable frame of mind, but with fortitude she returned to Prudence Aubrey's side and helped her into the waiting room. A kind helper suggested a cup of coffee and skipped away to fetch it.

'Now, Miss Aubrey,' said Miss Dimont, 'I am going to tell you something to ease your distress.' The actress looked her hopefully. 'Then I have something more uncomfortable to impart.'

The actress's gratitude was such that she appeared not to hear this second statement.

'Miss Lake was not Mr Hennessy's lover.'

Miss Aubrey looked disbelieving.

'She was his daughter. The inspector said so.'

A sudden movement, a hand clutching at a mouth, then a heart. A terrible, long silence. No words, just silence.

'I am telling you this,' said Miss Dimont, gently, as if speaking to a small child, 'because whether I write it or not, it will be in the national newspapers tomorrow. I know this will come as a terrible shock to you, but it would appear to be the truth.'

'Nnn . . . Not . . .' murmured Prudence Aubrey. 'Not . . . now . . .'

Miss Dimont did not quite understand this, but carried on. 'Miss Lake says that her mother and Mr Hennessy had a brief affair when you became engaged to him.'

'I was away a lot on tour,' said Prudence, as if through a mist.

Miss Dimont pressed on. 'She says that it was brief and her mother went on to marry the man she had intended to from the first. He still believes that Miss Lake is his daughter.

'Miss Lake says that despite what you told me the other night, Mr Hennessy was in fact capable of fathering children – as demonstrated by the fact that he paid for the child and her education.'

'I often wondered why we were so poor.'

'You don't seem surprised,' remarked Miss Dimont. 'I should have thought—'

'Well, I didn't know about the child,' said Prudence sharply. 'And of course it *would* have to turn out to be Marion Lake.' She hissed the name.

'But of course I knew it was me who wasn't capable of becoming pregnant. It has been a source of deep and bitter regret every day of my adult life.'

Curiously, uttering this statement helped clear away her tears, and emotion was replaced by the addressing of a lengthy personal history.

'So you . . .'

'Gerry was the one who made the decision to tell it that way. He reasoned that, as a female star, I should appear perfect in every way – unattainable, that sort of thing. That's really been my image, ever since he took control of my career. To women fans, therefore, there must always remain the possibility that I – like them – would one day have a child. It is in the nature of celebrity that people live their lives through yours.

'Take away that possibility and you become flawed, damaged goods. Or that was Gerald's thinking.

'On the other hand, he had this devil-may-care image which somehow it didn't matter that he couldn't father children. If anything it made him all the more exciting.'

Miss Dimont looked puzzled.

'Oh, you haven't seen the fan mail,' she said witheringly. 'The things they say! Gerry was very good at manipulating his image, and as soon as he realised that the fans who adored him loved him all the more – the fantasy, I think, was that they could bed him without their husbands knowing or there being any untoward consequences.'

'I have the feeling,' said Miss Dimont carefully, 'that now the cat is out of the bag, Miss Lake will be only too happy to add to her collection of front-page headlines. Are you going to mind that?'

Prudence looked at her as she dried her tears and took out her powder compact. 'I think that will put the final nail in the coffin of my career,' she said slowly. 'Don't you? My husband. This woman, his daughter. The humiliation . . .'

'I don't see why,' said Miss Dimont, though she did really.

The actress shook her head. 'In a sense I've known it was over for some time. Very few women reach my age in the film world and continue to work regularly. The ones who do character parts can go on indefinitely but actresses like me, with a special attraction I suppose you can call it, only go on as long as the crow's feet don't show.'

She sniffed. 'There's always television. I don't know much about it but I daresay some producer will pick me up when all this comes out. He'll get the headlines for casting me, I'll get the work. It could be worse.'

Miss Dimont marvelled at such a pragmatic approach, but acting is a cruel profession and you cannot continue in it for long if you do not confront its ugly realities. Miss Aubrey would survive, and maybe this untoward publicity (to which Miss Dimont now felt released to contribute) could bring a new lease of life to her career.

Miss Dimont rose and smiled down at the actress, now fully restored. 'Are you ready? Shall we go in?'

FIFTEEN

Coroner's courts are never very inspiring places, and Dr Rudkin diligently sought to make his as uninspired as possible. Whatever antics took place outside its doors, in here all was decorum; his was, after all, a branch of the undertaking trade and all the hallmarks of that business could be found in his grey-painted courtroom.

Having secured the presence of a refreshed-looking Prudence Aubrey (Marion Lake took care to sit at the back of the court), Dr Rudkin proceeded first to review the death of Gerald Victor Midleton Hennessy, of Regent's Lodge, Regent's Park, London.

'Inspector Topham.'

'Sir. The deceased was discovered in the penultimate first-class carriage of the Riviera Express when it arrived at the railway station last Tuesday afternoon. The 4.30. He had travelled from Paddington having stayed the previous night at his club, the . . . ah, Savile, sir.'

Dr Rudkin nodded approval. He knew people who were members there.

'The ambulance was called and a doctor attended the

scene. It would appear he had died of a heart attack some time after the train left Exeter. He had been dead approximately twenty minutes, as far as the doctor could judge.'

'No signs of disturbance in the carriage?'

'None, sir.'

'Was there anyone else in the compartment during his journey?'

Topham cleared his throat. 'Er, no. Sir.' Marion Lake studied her shoes intently.

'Evidence of identification?'

This rather threw the policeman. 'Well, sir, the deceased was a very well-known actor.' A chuckle from the packed courtroom.

'Yes, yes,' said Dr Rudkin testily, as if drawing attention to the fact might trigger a few more abominated headlines.

'Just about anybody in Temple Regis could have identified him, sir. He looked very much the way you see him on the cinema screen.'

This was not going well for Dr Rudkin – the policeman was now drawing attention to the fact the chap was a film star. It had to be stopped. 'Inspector,' he said tightly. 'You know very well we stick to correct procedure in this court. There will have been a formal identification. That was undertaken by . . .'

'Mrs Hennessy, sir. She is better known as Prudence Aubrey.'

Dr Rudkin was gnashing his teeth now and would have

eaten his moustache if he could. He'd had enough of Topham and his headline-making.

'Dr Protheroe.'

'The deceased was a man of forty-seven years of age, sir,' said the pathologist. 'It is my opinion he died of myocardial infarction. I took the trouble of consulting his London doctor, who told me that given Mr Hennessy's, ah, heavy work schedule – the stress in his profession is considerable – given his history, a heart attack was entirely possible. I believe they say, "he worked hard and he played hard".'

Dr Rudkin snarled. 'Please confine yourself to the facts, Dr Protheroe.'

'The body of a well-nourished male, reasonably physically fit. The post-mortem revealed some fatty degeneration around the heart, otherwise organs undamaged.'

'Any previous heart problems?'

'Not that I know of, sir.'

'Liver?'

'All in order,' said Dr Protheroe blithely while cursing under his breath. That last question of Rudkin's was a googly – he hadn't had the liver tested, and why would he? Chap died of a heart attack, for goodness' sake!

Dr Rudkin, who was never very keen on the testimony of others in his profession, had scored his point. He smiled in a sardonic way down at Protheroe, who looked away in disgust.

'Anything else?' The question was rhetorical.

'No, sir.'

'Mrs Hennessy.'

The packed courtroom sat upright, drew in its breath. So far nothing had been said that hadn't already appeared in last week's *Riviera Express*. Now, at last, they were going to get what they'd come for – Britain's newest and best-known widow. What's more they were not paying 1s 9d or 2s 6d for this performance – it was free!

'Your name, please, madam.'

'I am known professionally as Prudence Aubrey.'

Dr Rudkin did not like this. Another person using his court to try to milk some publicity for themselves!

'The name as stated on your passport, if you please.'

'Janine Murgatroyd Hope-Simpson Hennessy,' said Prudence. She'd hoped to avoid all that – and especially the thrill of wonderment which rippled round the courtroom. So depressing when people are reminded of your real name – in her mind she had jettisoned it years ago. The public were getting a feast of revelation, and the proceedings had only just begun.

'How long were you married to the deceased?'

'Twenty-five years. I—'

'Thank you,' the coroner jumped in. He did not like his witnesses offering random thoughts, especially ones which might lead to more headlines.

'You last saw your husband?'

'The night before his death.'

'Was he in good spirits?'

'Very much so,' lied Prudence. They'd had a blazing row before he stormed out.

'But he did not come down to Devon that night, I think?'

'No, he went to his club for a rubber of bridge. He stayed there the night because he was leaving first thing in the morning to catch the Temple Regis train.'

Dr Rudkin nodded. He did not ask why Gerald Hennessy chose to come to this golden town – because *anybody* in their right senses would want to be in Temple Regis if they thought about it for a second or two.

'Had he been unwell in recent times?'

'No. He exercised and watched his diet. I was shocked . . .' and here, suddenly, Melpomene clasped the proceedings in an awesome grip. Prudence Aubrey's eyes fell away, her hand went to her throat, and those who fondly remembered her peerless appearance in *The Beautiful and Damned* could be forgiven for almost thinking themselves back in that 1949 classic.

'Shocked,' said Prudence, slower this time. 'I . . .'

Dr Rudkin fidgeted in his seat. He did not like this at all. Normally his courtroom accommodated no more than a score of interested parties but this morning every seat was filled. It was a large room at the back of the Magistrates' Court building deemed too spacious for everyday crimes and licence applications, but today its copious seating was found wanting.

And every single pair of eyes was on Prudence Aubrey.

There was nothing Rudkin could do. He could bully his

police and his pathologists, but old-fashioned good manners would never allow him to interrupt a widow as she slowly broke down in the witness box. However infuriating, however self-indulgent those actions were, his hands were tied. He fidgeted again.

'Are you ready to go on, Mrs Hennessy?'

Prudence, a seasoned actress – even if not the most sought-after by casting directors this week – read the runes. She got to the end of her evidence in short order and resumed her seat in the well of the court. Nevertheless, her audience was on the verge of tears by the time she had done.

Some official business had to be run through – a couple more witnesses including the incomparable Mudge, station porter, who wore his Great War medals for the occasion – but quite soon the official inquiry had run its course.

'I find the deceased, Gerald Victor Midleton Hennessy, died of natural causes. The sympathy of the court is extended to his widow and family.'

And that was that.

Miss Dimont was floored. She sat in her customary seat on the press bench and scratched her corkscrew hair with her shorthand pencil. It didn't make sense.

It didn't make sense because Gerald Hennessy had been murdered.

Of that she was convinced, but there was nothing more she could do. She caught Prudence Aubrey making her way slowly out of court, signing autographs and posing for the cameras (nothing Dr Rudkin could do!) – and agreed they should meet at the Grand Hotel later in the day. That business with Marion Lake had made Prudence look more kindly on the person she had so recently accused of press harassment.

Meanwhile, after a short adjournment Dr Rudkin returned to finish his day's business.

'This is an inquest into the death of Garrick Arthur Shrimsley,' he said, obviously.

The usual forms of procedure were duly observed and soon it was Inspector Topham's turn again. They had heard the witness statement of Sergeant Hernaford – man at top of cliff, crumbling cliff top, man at bottom of cliff – and Dr Rudkin was, as usual, eager to discover what the shrewd questioning of the CID had uncovered.

'Man of sixty-seven,' said Topham. 'Widowed. A resident of Exbridge. Well known in Temple Regis for his letters to the local paper.'

Dr Rudkin shot him a warning glance.

'Walking his dog on Mudford Cliffs. Seen by an eyewitness at about 11.50 a.m. Shortly afterwards he went behind the protective barrier and fell to his death. He chose to ignore the large signs warning of the recent cliff fall. It would appear he had been drinking.'

'Dr Protheroe.'

'Body of a well-nourished man, sir. Cause of death multiple injuries consistent with a fall from a cliff top on to rocks two hundred and fifty feet below. He had ingested quite a large amount of whisky.'

'Anything more?'

'No.'

'I hereby record that the said Garrick Arthur Shrimsley died from multiple injuries sustained from a fall from the cliff top at Mudford Cliffs,' said Dr Rudkin briskly. 'Accidental death.'

'Court rise,' intoned the coroner's officer, and it was all over. Almost nobody had stayed behind once Gerald Hennessy's case had been dealt with, and the few people still remaining now dribbled out into the September sun.

Inspector Topham made his way past the press bench on his way to lunch.

'Just a moment, Inspector!' There was a chill in Miss Dimont's voice.

'Ah,' said the inspector, edging past.

'Man was out walking his dog. What happened to the dog?'

Topham eyed her warily.

'Man had a note in his hand. What happened to it?'

'You're wrong there,' said Topham loftily.

'Got the photograph,' said Miss Dimont, with an edge of triumph in her voice.

'I think not, Miss Dimont.'

The trouble with Miss Dimont was, she believed the police. She believed in their honesty and steadfastness. Many a constable's stuttering first appearances before Mrs Marchbank she had turned into moments of high drama via the court pages of the *Riviera Express*.

She wavered. If Inspector Topham said there was no letter,

perhaps there was no letter. That, coming after the apparently innocent death of Gerald Hennessy, had blown her murder theory wide apart. The blackmail conspiracy had disappeared in a puff of smoke as well. Any moment now Ray Cattermole would pop his head round the door, waggle his absurd eyebrows, and ask if she would join him in a chota peg.

Ridiculous, humphed Miss Dimont.

'I distinctly saw in a photograph of Terry Eagleton's a letter in Mr Shrimsley's hand.'

'You were there at the scene, I believe, according to Sergeant Hernaford.'

'Yes, I was.'

'Then you would have seen there was no letter.'

'The sergeant kept us away from the body. Terry took a photograph on his long lens.' (f8 at 1/125th, as a matter of fact.) 'And there it was, under his right hand. Was it a suicide note?'

Topham wanted his lunch. 'If you *must* know,' he said shirtily, 'there was a scrap of cloth in his hand, not a letter. Get your facts right!'

But then he relented, because Miss Dimont seemed so downcast. 'An awful lot of rubbish came down that cliff with him. Underneath his body there was a croquet mallet and a ball. Nearby there was a kid's tin bucket. There was debris all over the place, you must have seen it yourself. The place where he stood at the top of Mudford Cliffs was highly unstable and ready to go, after that earlier cliff fall. He did a stupid thing and ignored the warnings. He was drunk. And when he went over he took a lot more earth and rock – and whatever was resting on the earth and rock – down with him. He wasn't a pretty sight.'

Miss Dimont had been no fan of Arthur Shrimsley – who was? – but she felt sorry for him. The end must have been horrific.

'How did you know about Marion Lake being Gerald Hennessy's daughter?'

'She told me,' said Topham. 'The thought that she could be his mistress was hilarious to her. She'd brought someone else down on the train to share her pillow at the Grand.'

'Oh,' said Miss Dimont dully, who was as broad-minded as the rest. Most of the time.

'I really must get along,' said Topham. 'I can see you were hoping for more out of this morning's proceedings.'

'On the contrary,' said Miss Dimont, 'I have quite enough to keep me busy. It's not every day that the nation's number one matinée idol is exposed as having fathered a daughter who is now the nation's number one *sex siren*.' She uttered the words with mild distaste.

'Not quite as good as a double murder, though, eh?' winked Topham, for he was no fool.

He could tell what was on Judy Dimont's mind.

SIXTEEN

To suggest Betty Featherstone was desolated by Derek's telegram would be an overstatement. It was humiliating to be given the brush-off in quite such a public way – in the street, with Perce bearing that anxious look which meant he'd probably read the contents before sealing the envelope – and, anyway, if anyone was going to be doing the off-brushing it should be she.

After all, Derek was a big wheel in Rotary but pretty insignificant in Temple Regis – his small electrical shop in Lemon Street struggled to make its way – and the thing had run its course. True, two telegrams in a row for Betty smacked of carelessness in an Oscar Wilde sort of way, but in affairs of the heart she remained an optimist. She set her sights low and, as a result, was rarely without companionship and that was all she needed; for Betty was incapable of love.

Tonight found her simultaneously at work and play at the town's Coronation Ball. Held annually since the new Elizabethan era had been proclaimed six years earlier, it was a glamorous affair, though obviously pitched at a different level from what went on behind the doors of the Grand. Some of the old diehards wore tails, but the trend these days was more towards a dinner jacket with a white handkerchief in the breast pocket. Ladies wore court shoes and calf-length ball gowns, setting off their newly permed hair, and the music was jolly but retrospective – not a guitar in sight.

Betty was there on behalf of the *Riviera Express* and such was the status conferred by her employment that she was seated next to the mayor, Mr Brough. Across the circular table littered with red, white and blue ribbons sat the monolithic Mrs Brough, not demonstrably pleased to see her husband so concerned about the future of the town's ancient newspaper. And understandably so – Betty's hair was objectionably blonde tonight, her lipstick too glossy, even for a gala occasion such as this.

Out of the corner of her eye, Betty spotted Derek on the dance floor with Beryl Couzens, one of the town's few lady councillors, who from the soft expression on her face seemed not to have noticed the cut of his clothes, the shape of his head or the size of his feet. Could they all have been quite so ugly only as recently as last week, Betty asked herself. She had never noticed before quite what a leaden figure he cut.

Before she had time to answer that question, Mr Brough had breathtakingly swept her on to the dance floor to the strains of 'On a Little Street in Singapore'. His Worship might be a butcher, but he knew how to cut his way through the crowd and Betty went with him, swirling and turning and smiling – especially as they whizzed past Derek and Beryl – in wonderful gay abandon. This was where she felt most at home, caught in an in-between world filled with music and laughter and gracious manners, and the clanking of the heavy mayoral chain wedged between her and Mr Brough only offered the mildest dampener to proceedings.

Before long Betty and Mr Brough were the centre of attention – for she was as skilled as he on her feet and it turned out they were natural partners. Betty looked up at handsome Mr Brough and Mr Brough gazed down at melting Miss Betty as they completed a spectacular circuit of the floor and . . .

And . . .

But no, Betty had Certain Rules.

Drenched with applause, they returned to the table only to discover Mrs Brough, brief witness to this considerable social success for her husband in his mayoral year, had disappeared. His Worship knew what this meant and, after extending the courtesy of pulling back Betty's chair and quickly seeing her safely into it, beat a hasty retreat.

The evening was hotting up and most people were on the floor or at the bar – there must have been two hundred people there, what a triumph! Betty thought she should take the opportunity to make a few notes, for this sort of event not only reminded Temple Regis that it had an identity of its own when not submerged by happy holidaymakers, but it was a reaffirmation – less often mentioned, but very much in everyone's thoughts – that their great ship of state was now at peace, in calm waters and, after years of privation, had turned its prow towards prosperity and a golden future.

This was what Rudyard Rhys wanted for his newspaper,

not death! And Betty's reward for her coverage of the evening's events would be a big byline with a Page One turn (to
the uninitiated, her name in exaggeratedly large print and her
story spilling over from the front cover to page three – maybe
even four!).

It was exactly the sort of affair at which Miss Dimont
struggled professionally, for her ever-questing mind found it
difficult to construct a celebration out of an evening where
the town's bigwigs got together, drank copiously, and bragged
each other down while their wives sat marooned at their
tables, smiling vacantly across the void. But Betty had no
difficulty on such occasions, and with a few swift notes jotted
down, neatly put her purse away. She was looking radiant
this evening, though the combination of coral-pink lipstick
and lime-green ball dress indicated perhaps a lack of coherent
thought; no doubt Mrs Brough would be making the point
with His Worship later that night.

Betty took a sip of her Babycham and gazed out at the
exhilarated crowd. Her eye was attracted to the sight of Claud
Hannaford, the coal merchant, whose get-up would not have
disgraced one of Prudence Aubrey's costume dramas. Though
twice Derek's age, his tailcoat was a perfect fit, the white tie
and dimpled waistcoat dazzled in the revolving lights, his
dance pumps glittering in an old-fashioned but, to Betty,
very reassuring way.

Claud did not waste time by asking Betty for a spin.
Instead, he brought two glasses of something interesting-
looking and settled down beside her. He was old enough to

be Betty's father – older – but he didn't care. And, she found somewhat surprisingly, neither did she.

'*Express*, isn't it?'

'Yes.'

'Thanks heavens they didn't send that other one. Miss . . . er . . .'

'She's not very keen on this sort of thing,' said Betty, truthfully enough.

'So I've noticed,' laughed Claud, drawing out a cigar from his top pocket. 'We haven't forgotten the Conservative Ball last winter.'

'The *Express* printed an apology. But people do seem to go on about it still.'

'You should have been there!' laughed Claud, but his thoughts had evidently moved on. 'You're not married?'

'I have a number of engagements rings which I keep in my kitchen drawer,' sparkled Betty, her stock response to this oft-put question. 'Won't tell you how many!'

There was rather more talk along these lines but Betty soon settled to the realisation that this rich widower wanted nothing more than to spend time in the company of a younger woman. He charmed, he yarned, he brought more drinks, and at all times behaved impeccably. His was not an approach the worldly-wise Betty had encountered before – all he seemed to want to do was entertain her.

'And old Bill Pithers,' he was saying, 'you must remember him.'

'I don't think . . .'

'You know, the old fat renderer. Biggest crook in South Devon. You've seen him – pink Rolls-Royce, those appalling tweed suits. Died last year.'

'The Golf Club.'

'Always.'

'I tended to avoid him. He had . . . creeping hands.'

'That's old Bill,' roared Claud. 'I used to go racing with him at Exeter and Newton Abbot, and oh! the ladies! But he never paid his bookies, it was an embarrassment.'

'So what about him?' asked Betty, more for form's sake than anything else. She had detested the overblown caricature who could never leave a woman's skirt alone.

'He left me his Rolls, I've got it outside. Can't quite believe it, because he was mean as mouse-shit in life.' Claud smiled as he said this, hoping to bring a blush to Betty's cheeks. She'd heard worse.

The coal merchant was happy to muse on his good fortune, knowing that in Betty he had a captive audience. Hannaford knew about women and he could see she had no date that night; Betty was his for the next hour if he wanted.

'It's taken all this time for the probate to come through,' he said, drawing on his cigar. 'I'd love to know where all the money went.'

'Was he rich?' This interested Betty.

'Multimillionaire. Nobody wanted to do what he did for a business – not even me, and I'm a coal merchant! Filthy, dirty, smelly – horrible. But he made a packet.

'Then, of course, all the things you never heard about

– shipping Dartmoor ponies to Ireland to be used for dog food. The property swindles. Wasn't above threatening his way into a bargain. I liked him because he amused me, but I'm the only one who ever did.'

'Who got the money, then?' asked Betty, idly watching the back of Derek's square head.

'Well, it's interesting – there were two daughters but he last saw them when they were toddlers – his wife Honoria made a mistake. She thought she could polish up a rough diamond, turn him into a gentleman, then when she discovered she couldn't, she hightailed it.'

'I doubt it was the rough diamond business,' said Betty, not without experience when it came to matters of the human heart. 'More like all those other women.'

'That may have played a part,' acknowledged Claud. 'Anyway, according to the will there are two grandchildren who've copped the lot. I got my Rolls-Royce, but they are both very rich now.'

'I wonder who they are,' said Betty, though perhaps in retrospect she should have wondered a bit more.

The idle acquisition of money seemed to fascinate Claud, who'd had to earn every single penny of his not inconsiderable fortune. He no longer came home as black as a coalminer – others did that for him now – but he remained strong, fit and energetic. Compared to old Bill Pithers, who resembled a crushed sponge cake when last seen at the golf club, he looked like a teenager.

As is the way, the conversation turned to other rich people, to the newly launched Premium Bonds, which for a £1 outlay a delightful £1,000 might tipple into your lap, and to the football pools where, on a good Saturday, a fellow might find himself £75,000 better off.

By 10.30 p.m. the Coronation Ball had reached its zenith. Betty could see Terry on the other side of the dance-floor taking the pictures which brought extra revenue to the *Express* coffers, since for many Temple Regents this was their one night in finery, and they were more than happy to troop into the front hall over the next few days to order expensive copy prints to paste into their scrapbooks.

Betty had secured from the mayor's secretary a list of the most prominent guests, and her work was done.

'Want to come and see the Rolls?' said Claud, winningly.

'Why not?' smiled Betty, smoothing her dress.

*

Over the other side of the room Terry was taking a breather in the company of two abandoned wives. From time to time, one or other craned her neck to see where her husband was, less in the anticipation of his return and more in the hope that he would stay at the bar, drink himself silly, and leave her alone with this charming Mr Eagleton.

Terry had already handed out his card to both ladies, and they sat fingering the little pasteboard billets-doux as he regaled them with the death of Gerald Hennessy.

'And there he was, neat as could be – like that scene in *Heaven Comes Before Hell*.'

'When he accused his wife of adultery.'

'That's right. Pointing his finger, he was, like he was just about to say—'

'*And I thought I had every reason to trust you.*' Jill Ferrers had seen it many times.

'Just like that,' said Terry, and leaned back smiling. Photographers had a way about them which broke all the rules of social convention. Perhaps it was because they carried a certain authority, by reason of their job, which enabled them to ask people they had never met to do things they would not otherwise do. Do it with a smile, and a joke, and they would be eating out of your hand – indeed half of the photographer's art was making people do what you wanted, the technical trickery which went with the snapping of the picture being merely secondary.

Terry had a way with him which made women, especially of a certain age, confess anything.

'Did he dye his hair?' asked Jill's friend Mavis Coryton. 'Surely he did. He must have been forty-eight . . .'

'Forty-seven,' said Jill expertly.

'Forty-seven,' repeated Mavis. 'But you never saw a silver hair on his head. Just look at Ted over there.' She nodded her head in the direction of the bar but her eyes did not turn to take in the vision of Ted Coryton, the town's ironmonger, getting them in. 'He went grey at forty,' she said, and not kindly.

'No,' said Terry. 'He looked in pretty good nick all round, apart from being dead. But you know this acting game—'

he didn't particularly, but then neither did they '—all stress. And they drink a lot too. How's your glasses?'

'Mine's a gin and tonic, thank you, Terry. Large, if you don't mind.'

'Campari,' said the more sophisticated Mavis Coryton, for though she hated its bitterness she felt it gave her a certain polish to be seen with one.

'Coming up,' said Terry, and he was gone.

'You know,' said Jill to Mavis, 'I have in the back of my mind that Gerald Hennessy had some connection down here. Did he go to Blundell's? Exeter Cathedral School? Something like that.'

'I thought he had family down here,' replied Mavis, eager to display equal knowledge of the dear departed hero. Neither had a clue.

Terry, like all photographers, had sliced his way through the queue at the bar and was already making his grinning way back across the dance floor laden down with drinks. He was a winner all right.

'Do you think . . .?' Jill asked Mavis in an undertone as he approached.

'Oh yes,' Mavis said to Jill. 'Most definitely.'

'So why did Gerald Hennessy come to Temple Regis?' they both asked simultaneously when the photographer had settled himself. It had not taken much chit-chat for them to be convinced he knew everything about the case.

'No mention of it at the inquest,' said Jill, who'd been in the courtroom.

'Seems odd he should want to come down here, doesn't it? Temple *Regis*?'

'Shurshay la Fam,' said Terry with an idiotic grin. 'Ask yourself what Marion Lake was doing on the train.'

'Thought so,' said Mavis. She was the more worldly of the two. 'The Grand!'

Just then the town's principal purveyor of hardware goods hove into view, looking suspiciously at Terry who'd picked up his camera and was taking pictures of his wife.

'Just talking about Gerald Hennessy, darling,' said Jill Ferrers, licking her lips as she had seen film stars do just to give them that little extra gloss for the flash-gun. Terry carried on his task oblivious, as all photographers are when faced with danger if their eye is pressed to the viewfinder, to the rising anger in the man standing behind him.

'That's all anybody's talking about,' said Barry, rather nastily. 'Brought some piece of skirt down for the weekend. That'll do the town's reputation a lot of good when it gets out. We're not Brighton, you know!'

'Just like his grandfather,' said Ted Coryton, who strolled up behind his drinking partner and was eager to take his wife home.

'How so?' asked Terry, who was now taking candid snaps of Mary.

'Well, surely you know that Hennessy's grandfather was . . .' but Mr Coryton did not complete this fascinating detail because at that point Ken Dalton, the mayor's sergeant, was praying silence for His Worship who would shortly be making the Loyal Toast.

With the redoubtable Lady Mayoress back by his side, Mr Brough rose and pronounced the words all sensible Temple Regents wanted to hear – that they were loyal to their Queen and wished she would reign for ever. Glasses were raised and quaffed, cheers broke out, and a cascade of balloons wafted from the ceiling on to the dance floor while the band broke into a hot version of 'Chattanooga Choo Choo'.

The noise was deafening but Terry put his mouth to the ear of Ted Coryton. You could see his lips move but not quite hear what was said. However, such was the punctuated delivery of the 'Chattanooga' tune it was possible in the split-second between one 'Choo' and the next to hear Mr Coryton's bellowed reply to what had clearly been a question.

'Bill Pithers,' he shouted. And he nodded.

SEVENTEEN

' 'Ello, Frank,' said Sid. 'Usual?'

Inspector Topham nodded sagely, as if asked for his opinion on Nikita Khrushchev. Sid busied himself fetching down the policeman's pewter mug and jerkily filling it with Portlemouth. The conversation, as most nights here in the private bar of the Grand Hotel, centred around the new football season and Plymouth Argyle's chances for the FA Cup.

Then as usual Frank Topham retired to his corner seat to spend an hour in thought. Miss Dimont and he found it difficult to see eye to eye – reporters were the same the whole world over, he thought bitterly. But Frank Topham, if not inspired, was a diligent man: rightness and properness, instilled in him through those years in the Guards, were his watchword.

Sid polished beer glasses energetically with elbows akimbo, a silent whistle on his lips, while riotous sounds floated down the corridor from the cocktail bar. The inspector sat quite still and stared deep into the dark brown liquid in front of him.

Miss Dimont's angry words at the inquest had left their mark. On the one hand, he sided with Dr Rudkin in his view

that Temple Regis would never flourish with bad publicity –
heaven knows, there were enough rival resorts ready to steal
away the town's bread-and-butter trade, think of Torquay!
But, on the other, he had a duty to the law.

It was true his team, even if they'd first considered it, had
done nothing about the business of Arthur Shrimsley's dog.
But then why would they? From start to finish, it looked like
the drunken old busybody had decided to ignore the safety
warnings on top of Mudford Cliffs and had gone over. Well,
more fool him, thought Topham who'd instilled in his men
the need always to think first before acting. Shrimsley hadn't
thought, he was being his usual nosy know-it-all self going
to take a look at the broken cliff.

It still left the question of the dog. Without it, Shrimsley
had no reason to be up there. Then again, there was the
matter of the piece of cloth – it was gripped pretty tightly
in his fingers. He took out his notebook, but it was more
a gesture of self-encouragement than anything else, for he
neither consulted it nor added to its fund of information.
Inspector Topham was stumped, and no amount of looking
at it this way, or that, helped.

He could not see, as Miss Dimont saw, the connection
between the deaths of Hennessy and Shrimsley and the puzzling absence of Cattermole from the scene. Ray Cattermole
had gone missing before – that old girl of his was forever
crying wolf. He'd probably tootled off to London to seek out
a newer model or maybe to raise some cash, for the theatre
was not doing well, he knew that.

And if there really was foul play, who was it? Hennessy didn't murder Shrimsley any more than Shrimsley murdered Hennessy – it wasn't possible. So who else was there to consider?

That whole business of Prudence Aubrey and Marion Lake was nothing more than a pure domestic drama caused by Gerald Hennessy – and there was nothing suspicious about a heart attack.

The inspector ordered another pint but half an hour later it remained untouched. There was something here, hidden among the debris of the deaths of two men, but he could not see it. It was very depressing.

Finally, Topham picked up his hat and made for the door. Sid knew better than to say more, so confined himself to a soft, ''Night, Frank.'

''Night, Sid.'

He ambled slowly down the corridor towards the side exit but suddenly ahead a group of people burst noisily out of the cocktail bar. Among them was Prudence Aubrey, her eyes alight for the first time since she arrived in Temple Regis.

'Oh, Inspector!' she said, her cheeks pink. 'Just the man!'

'Miss Aubrey.'

'Inspector, I went along to collect Gerald's things this afternoon as you suggested.'

'Yes, madam?' Don't tell me something's missing, thought the inspector.

'Something's missing.'

Here we go, thought Topham, it's always the way. Car

crash, a watch has gone AWOL. Lover's suicide – the letters. Drowned at sea – the wrong amount of small change in deceased's pocket.

'No really, Inspector, something of great sentimental value. His briefcase.'

'Well, I suggest you raise that with the desk sergeant. Give him a full description and he'll go through the effects cupboard – these things sometimes happen.'

Miss Aubrey softly took the inspector's hand and indicated a velvet-covered sofa in an alcove. 'Come with me,' she purred enticingly.

Two martinis, Topham asked himself. Or three?

Whatever the number, they were just about to be augmented. Miss Aubrey stopped Peter Potts as he sailed past and asked for one more, and whatever the inspector was having. Topham hadn't the appetite earlier for his second pint, but curiously now he found his thirst returning.

She really was remarkable to look at, he thought. This evening she had a generously skirted ivory silk dress with what looked like a very large diamond brooch at the shoulder. Her jewellery only just bordered on the right side of discreet, but since she herself presented such a cool and reserved demeanour, it shouted all the more loudly. No wonder men the world over loved this woman!

And, thought Topham, I am sitting next to her *and* I have a pint of Portlemouth in front of me! The blues he had felt earlier started to drift away.

'Now, Inspector,' said Prudence chidingly, teasingly. 'This is something you must inspect!'

'Madam.'

'If there is one thing which joined Gerald and I together more than anything else it was his attaché case. I bought it in Bond Street with my very first film earnings. We both went along to Asprey's and chose it together – I can't *tell* you the cost! That was twenty-five years ago and Gerald took it with him wherever he went – it's old and scruffy now, but, Inspector, *so* becoming!'

'I'm sure the desk sergeant—

'No, no, no!' The martinis were finding their voice. 'No, Inspector, *you* must find it! I asked the sergeant and they turned the place upside down – but here's the thing, a list was made of his possessions and it wasn't even mentioned. I can only assume someone has stolen it, maybe from the train.'

'Was there likely to have been anything *in* the case, madam?' Topham didn't care much, but the Portlemouth tasted very sweet indeed and all of a sudden he was in no rush to go home.

'Well, I bought it for his scripts. But, you know, he had the same kind of photographic memory as Richard Burton – one look and he'd got it. He didn't need to cart scripts round with him. It was one of the most infuriating things about him. It took me for ever to learn my lines – though once I'd got them—' she tossed her head upwards as if to remind Topham of the mentally incontinent Marion Lake '—they stayed with me, come hell or high water.'

Inspector Topham allowed himself a tight smile. He didn't much care for Marion Lake either.

'But even though he didn't need it, Gerald took that case with him everywhere. Mostly he had nothing more in it than his smoked salmon sandwiches and a copy of *Wisden* – he was very keen on cricket,' she added, suddenly sad. 'It means more to me than anything, so you *must* try to recover it.'

'Why would anybody want to steal it, do you think?' asked Topham.

'Who knows? It was very handsome. A memento. Could somebody have been on the train and just whisked it away?'

Topham suddenly jerked to attention. His guardsman's back became ramrod-stiff.

'Um, I must go now, madam,' he said tersely. 'Something to attend to. Need to get back to the office. A pleasure to speak to you again – are you staying long in Temple Regis?'

'Back to London at the weekend. But, Inspector, you promise – you *will* find the case? You have my address, don't you?'

'Yes, madam.'

'And I shall be seeing Colonel ffrench-Blake soon. I'll be telling him how tremendously helpful you have been.'

'Please give him my respects. No man could have a finer commanding officer.'

'Of course, Inspector.'

Topham quick-marched back to the police station. He needed time to think, alone. He let himself into the CID room and sat down heavily in the centre of its empty vacuum.

The prima facie evidence was that Hennessy's briefcase

had been stolen. It had to have been taken from the train – the uniform boys had been their usual efficient selves in cordoning off the carriage and keeping people out once Hennessy's body was discovered, therefore it had to have been taken some time *before* the Riviera Express arrived at Temple Regis. Though the actor apparently died of a heart attack, what had caused that fatal seizure? Was it his too louche lifestyle? Or could it be someone had entered his compartment – maybe he had nodded off to sleep – and tried to steal the case? Had he awoken and grappled with the thief, triggering his own end?

If that were the case, thought Topham, there could be a charge of manslaughter to be answered – for though the subsequent headlines might do further damage to the town, he most certainly could not permit foul play on his patch.

He lifted the telephone and asked the operator for a London number. A male voice answered.

'Inspector Topham of the Temple Regis police here,' he said in unequivocal terms. 'That will be Mr Maltby.'

'Ye-es,' said the voice, both acknowledging and denying the fact in a single elongated syllable. Mr Maltby was the current escort of Marion Lake.

'I have a couple of questions, Mr Maltby.'

The voice at the other end repeated the same ambiguous sound. Mr Maltby was married, and not to Marion Lake.

'When you came down in the train to Temple Regis, you were in the next carriage to Gerald Hennessy I think you told me?'

'Ye-es.'

'And for part of that journey Miss Lake told me she went to sit with her father in his compartment?'

'Mm.'

'You didn't go and join them?'

'No.'

'Was there any reason for that?'

'I think I already explained—'

'That he did not know his daughter was having, hurr-ummm, with a married man? And that it was more diplomatic if you stayed clear, just shook his hand, stayed in the background and so forth?'

'Yes.'

'When did Miss Lake return to you? At what stage in the journey?'

'Some time after the train left Exeter.'

'*Soon* after you left Exeter?'

'Pretty much straight away.' Mr Maltby was beginning to relax – these questions appeared to offer no threat to his marital equilibrium.

'When she came back to the compartment did she, by any chance, have an attaché case with her?'

'What?'

'Small leather case.'

'No.'

'Right. And so there would have been a good twenty minutes when she was back in the compartment with you, then, before you reached Temple Regis?'

'Yes.'

'And you alighted from the train . . .'

'We agreed that Marion would leave the train first. We walked up through the second-class to the front of the train, and got away quick just before that press photographer showed up. Then we grabbed a taxi to take us to the Grand.'

'So you never saw Mr Hennessy after Exeter.'

'I didn't see him after Paddington. I stayed in the compartment.'

'And,' said Topham, 'Miss Lake I think said that her father travelled down alone.'

'He often used railway carriages to rehearse his lines out loud – he was about to go into another film, you know.'

'I know.'

'The first-class section of the train was pretty empty – he had the compartment to himself. So he could practise his lines.'

'The first-class section was down the back end of the train. Anybody from second class would have gone past your window. Did you see anybody who looked like they didn't belong in first?'

'Most of the time I had my eyes on Marion. I think even you would understand that.'

'Thank you, Mr Maltby,' said Topham in a prickly sort of way. 'I see you didn't stay to witness the inquest?'

There was a confused snuffle at the other end. 'I didn't think it wise, given the circs.'

'You might have been able to prevent Prudence Aubrey from attacking Miss Lake.'

'I don't think so, Inspector. I have my reputation to pre-serve.'

Topham did not like this at all, but said nothing. Quite soon he rang off and used the telephone to contact one of his subordinates.

His instructions were terse and to the point: there was at least a twenty-minute gap after the train left Exeter when an assailant or thief could have entered Hennessy's carriage. It was now their job to track that person down.

And, while they were at it, they'd better find out about that blessed dog.

*

On this late summer evening, when Inspector Topham found himself reversing slowly towards the truth, while Betty was out dancing and Terry charming the ladies, Judy Dimont was enjoying a rare night at home. The floral gift from the Mothers' Union was clinging to its last glory in the bay window. She sat at the piano and worked her way through a couple of Chopin waltzes – not without difficulty – then spent some time talking to Mulligatawny. They enjoyed a glass of elderflower champagne in the late sunlight on the terrace (a gift from Mrs Purser across the lane, such a dear), then came inside to enjoy their respective suppers.

This last had been done to the strains of a Michael Hol-liday show on the Light Programme, but as she washed the dishes Miss Dimont found it difficult to concentrate, and switched off the radio. She settled with *The Times* crossword,

Mulligatawny sitting obligingly by her side on the sofa, but even this perennial remedy to distraction and general out-of-sortness failed to work.

She sighed, laid the paper aside, and stared at the mantelpiece. In his shining silver frame, he looked down on her and smiled. It would be his birthday in two days' time.

They had been glorious years – for Auriol, for Judy and for Eric. The work they did together during the War had seen some triumphant moments and though its shadowy nature even now barred her from discussing it in general conversation, Miss Dimont never felt the need. The whole story was held, complete, in her heart and there was little reason to share it with those who'd doubtless misunderstand; for after the War those who were lionised were those whose victories were visible and largely had been conducted in uniform. Auriol had worn a uniform, but her brother and Judy did not; and when war service came up in conversation Judy adopted her reporter's manner – asking questions rather than offering reminiscences. People always had plenty to say about themselves.

It was curious but, given the laws of coincidence, not remarkable that old Rudyard Rhys should turn up again. Back in the days when they all worked together in that tiny cramped room in the basement of the Admiralty, he was *Roger* Rhys, of course – a quite talented sub-lieutenant in the Wavy Navy who came up with some good wheezes to distract and thwart the enemy. The 'Rudyard' came after he became an unofficial spokesman for their group and from there started writing, which led him ultimately to journalism.

Mostly, though, he was known as Rusty Rhys – it seemed to fit.

In those days he rather fancied he would become a novelist eventually, but it was not to be – he lacked the concentration and capacity for the sustained effort it required. He'd always had a slightly awkward nature, which only grew as the years went by, and when she met him ten years after the War's end that element of his personality was uppermost. Technically, he had been a junior figure in an office where both Auriol and Judy held sway; now he was her boss.

It had taken longer for Miss Dimont to find her home in journalism, because for a while after the War she continued plying the trade which had seen so many successes during the conflict. But eventually with the rise of Suez and the Cold War she saw that a new breed was needed to fight the enemy, and that the old rules of 1939–45 no longer applied. Even if her bosses in Whitehall failed to respond with any alacrity to this reality, she could see, or felt she could see, what was coming and Temple Regis was a welcome relief. She loved it here.

Eric's jaunty smile from the mantelpiece encouraged her to search out the elderflower champagne and pour herself another glass. It would have been his forty-ninth birthday, but the tears had all been shed long ago, and now he was simply her constant companion. When she and Auriol met, they talked about Eric and reminded themselves of those silly antics on his motor-bicycle, the elegant clothes he wore, the dramatic figure he cut on the cricket pitch, and that endless ringing laugh like church bells which echoed still down the years. Eric had been one of the War's heroes, but his name was virtually unknown – there were, after all, so many more like him.

'And now there's only you,' she sighed and, as if he instinctively knew this was his moment, Mulligatawny stole sinuously into her lap. She looked down at the noble head and, gently stroking his marmalade ears, added: 'He *was* a bit of a fool, wasn't he? He should never have gone that last time.'

Mulligatawny indicated his agreement by settling deeper into her lap and crossing his paws. He waited patiently while his mistress summoned, and slowly dismissed, her thoughts of long ago.

'You're just as much of a fool as Eric. Up that tree one minute, shooting across the road the next – no acknowledgement of danger, ever. Scrapping with that horrid next-door cat . . .'

Mulligatawny scrunched up his face with pleasure at this compliment, and languidly he washed a paw while Miss Dimont's memory-release took her back to her childhood in faraway Ellezelles, her schooling in East Anglia, her university days and, naturally, her mother. For the redoubtable Madame Dimont was never far from Judy's thoughts, or from her letterbox through which cards, letters, telegrams and other missives of torment never quite ceased to flow. Madame remained safely in East Anglia in order to return home via Harwich regularly to check on her siblings; but though it was a lengthy day's journey from there to south Devon, Judy could never quite be sure when she might receive an unannounced visit.

The moon rose, and through her window she watched the chasing cloudscape, signalling a change in the weather. And maybe much more besides.

EIGHTEEN

Betty was processing the fortnightly dispatches from the village correspondents. These down-to-earth but essential links with the readership were written not by journalists but by local people who were quite as clever – often far more than – the newspaper staff to whom they submitted their weekly gleanings.

Only problem is, thought Betty snootily, as she fed in the copy-paper to her typewriter, they don't know a story when they see one.

Others might argue that the correspondents knew all too well what a story was – the vicar berating his flock for their poor attendance record, the parish council chairman falling down in the pub (again), the carnival queen and the undue influence her mother brought to bear on the vote – but they didn't want to see it in the paper. The rules which Dr Rudkin applied to wiping clean Temple Regis' muddy escutcheon were equally practised in the many small villages which surrounded the town.

So Betty, who was less than generous about being made to handle these weekly slices of village life, looked at the handsomely handwritten account of the recent meeting of Silverham WI on her desk with some disdain before shovelling more paper into her typewriter for a quick rewrite.

'We may have met on a wet and windy night,' went the lively account, 'But spirits were soon lifted when members saw the speaker for the evening, Jackie Ensor, behind a table laden with all types of greenery, flowers, robins and all.

'With Christmas just over the horizon, we were shown how to make a door wreath from a traditional wire frame and an oasis ring. Also table decorations, large and small, a time-consuming swag, and to finish a lovely hand-tied bouquet. All were made to perfection and made us feel we really must have a go this year!'

Terry sauntered over and they compared notes from last night.

'Lively, wasn't it?' said Terry. And rather more so than Betty knew, because after she slid out of the door with Mr Hannaford, there'd been a bit of a dust-up.

'Dunno what the fuss was about,' he complained.

Betty was listening while typing up the Bedlington Harbour Boat Club report – 'There are a few places left on next week's course, "Know your local waters", to help you understand charts and tides.'

'What happened, Ter?'

'I thought I might do a picture feature on Jill Ferrers and Mavis Coryton – fashionable coronation ball wives – but their husbands took exception. Specially old Ferrers when I asked Jill to get up on the table and raise her skirt a bit.'

'Mutton dressed as lamb,' gritted Betty, pencil between her teeth as she wrestled more copy-paper into her typewriter. She was now writing up Exbridge Flower Club – 'Fiona started her demonstration using an oval-shaped dish to display a large array of twisted willow, senecio, violet irises, purple and yellow tulips. A lovely evening and Janet Eccles gave the vote of thanks.'

'Old Barry Ferrers wanted to take it outside. He'd been at the bar for the best part of an hour and probably would have tripped over his shoelaces on the way out. Still, it was *nasty*,' added Terry, sublimely unaware of his part as *agent provocateur* in this disturbance.

'Heskton Natural History Society,' rattled Betty furiously, nodding her acknowledgement. 'Our next meeting is all about our lovely local River Avon. It looks idyllic as it tumbles down from Dartmoor to the sea. But its biological condition is not as good as it should be.'

'Done your ball report?' asked Terry, sensing Betty hadn't.

'*Not yet*,' hissed Betty, for though it was mid-morning she had yet to wrestle the cocktail-stained notes she made last night from her purse. The evening had turned out to be much longer than anticipated, and she was not quite herself.

'Stowchurch Sorority,' she hammered. 'Dora Freeman told us she began composing music at the tender

age of nine. From the age of four, she yearned to
have piano lessons but her mother refused until
she had learnt how to read. She started by playing sixteen short pieces inspired by her life in
Devon, followed by some lengthier compositions.
Members were grateful for the teas supplied by
Mesdames Smith, Turner, and Babcary.'

'Just wondered what your intro would be,' said Terry,
leisurely enjoying his mug of tea.

'"Coronation Crowns",' said Betty peremptorily. 'Those
women who wore tiaras. That's a first.'

'Ur,' said Terry who wanted to push the pics of his over-
excitable matrons.

'Dartmoor Ramblers,' typed Betty distractedly, for her
thoughts were now on Mr Hannaford and his Rolls-Royce.
'Eight miles and grade is strenuous. Bring packed
lunch.'

'Got time to come over to the darkroom and have a look
at what I've got?' Terry, like Miss Dimont, never left a job
overnight and could not rest until his film had been through
the bath and the prints had come off the dryer.

'Not just now, Terry. Got to write up the ball before old
Rudyard comes round looking for copy.'

Terry, who had nothing much to do, went to fetch them
both some more tea then sat down in Judy Dimont's chair
opposite, reckoning he could persuade Betty to change her
mind about Mesdames Ferrers and Coryton.

Betty sat for a moment, willing herself to sum up the spirit of last night. Like all journalists she found the longer you left it, the harder it is to write, and what with her slightly aching head she was finding it difficult to construct the first sentence.

'Interesting what old Ferrers had to say,' said Terry, for his was not a trade which required inspiration. He did not mind interrupting a train of thought.

'What,' said Betty crossly. It wasn't a question.

'That Gerald Hennessy. Apparently the grandson of Bill Pithers.'

'Oh yes,' said Betty. 'We were talking about him last night. Claud Hannaford got left his Rolls-Royce.'

'That horrid pink thing?'

'It's very comfortable inside,' said Betty, smirking proprietorially.

'Well Hennessy . . .'

'Apparently he left loads of money, Bill Pithers. Squillions.'

'Really,' said Terry. 'Because Gerald Hennessy—'

'Hold on,' interrupted Betty, suddenly struck by inspiration. She began to type: 'The Coronation Ball had, apparently, reached new heights of style with the adoption of tiaras as female headgear.'

No, that didn't sound right. She pulled out the copy-paper, threaded in a replacement, and started again. 'The Coronation Ball . . .'

'Well, that's interesting,' said Terry crossly to himself as he got up and walked away. Nobody ever listened! Hennessy not only came from around here, but he had been left a small fortune by the most disreputable person Temple Regis ever had the misfortune to welcome into its fold. As information went, it was worth a mint, and you never knew when it might come in handy.

This is how newspapers work. People who aren't paid to find things out, find them out, but don't necessarily share them. It would be of interest to Miss Dimont that both Betty and Terry had gleaned some remarkable information at the coronation ball last night, coming as it did from different directions, but each was too busy paddling their own canoe to pass on to her what they'd learnt. Terry had told Betty and Betty had told Terry, and there the matter rested. In limbo.

Betty battled on with her report and barely noticed when Judy sat down opposite. The paper debris created by her uninspiring task had spread like molten lava across the desk to engulf most of the available space between the two reporters, but Miss Dimont did not mind. Instead she did her best to tidy things up without in any way wishing to make her gestures seem reproving. Long ago she'd come to the realisation that Betty was an untidy individual, it was something you learned to live with – the borrowed pencils which were never returned, the shorthand notebooks in which she would find Betty's notes when she couldn't find her own pad, the purloined pairs of gloves.

In her orderly way, Miss Dimont scooped up the well-bred communications from the Silverham WI, the Bedlington Harbour Boat Club, the Exbridge Flower Club and the rest and put them neatly into a folder. As she was separating the envelopes to throw in the waste-paper basket she found one which remained unopened and clearly had missed the 'From Our Village Correspondents' column for this week (apologies, shortage of space, was the usual cry when such a report went missing, which happened quite often).

The missing dispatch was from the Arburton Golf Club, a lengthy account of the annual general meeting and election of officers – an arduous narrative which included the name of just about everybody who had any association with the club, the sport, the village – indeed, the whole county. Just the sort of report which bred ill will on both sides, for Rudyard Rhys would never allow more than four paragraphs on any given topic and here was a full page; severe editing would reduce the mind-numbing effect of this roll-call of the great and good, but there'd be Complaints because of the severe pruning. More diplomatic, by far, to cry 'shortage of space'!

Miss Dimont was nonetheless diligently shuffling the paper into the folder when her eye spotted something which caused her quickly to haul it out again. There, buried in the indigestible account of the affairs of Arburton GC, was the name Hennessy.

She looked closer.

'There were cheers when it was announced that Mr Gerald Hennessy had agreed to become Life President of the Club.' That was all.

The Gerald Hennessy? If so, when was this written? And did this lost message contain the so far unexplained reason why he had come to Temple Regis?

'Penny for them,' said Terry who'd wandered back – he

really had nothing to do this morning, did he? Photographers rarely understood one needed time just to think – just because one wasn't writing, or phoning, or collecting up green wedding forms, didn't mean you weren't working.

'Hennessy,' said Miss Dimont half under her breath, but Terry was more interested in tackling Betty over the lively Mesdames and their lifted skirts. However, Betty had disappeared into that hinterland which can never be invaded – when a writer starts to write, nothing must breach the sacred moment – and instead he had to listen to Judy.

'This is odd,' she said. 'Some time before he died – but only a week or so, given the date of this letter – he'd agreed to become Life President of the golf club.'

'Pithers,' said Terry knowingly. It was inordinately frustrating to Judy that he always seemed to know more than she – even if he didn't know what to do with it.

'Tell me,' sighed Miss D, flopping back in her chair.

'Bill Pithers bought himself honorary presidency of the club – that's why they couldn't chuck him out when he behaved so badly – and when he died, obviously he told them who was next in line. His grandson.'

'Grandson?'

'He left Gerald Hennessy a stack of money *and* the presidency of the golf club. Heaven knows why Gerry should want to take it up, but obviously he felt the need.'

Terry then took a minute or two to sum up last night's accumulated evidence. He left out the bust-up with the two fashionable ladies of Temple Regis, but was less sparing in his account of Betty and Mr Hannaford.

'But I thought Derek . . .' said Miss Dimont, marvelling at Betty's sudden defection to the older man.

'Nuh. He sent a telegram.'

Both looked pityingly on Betty, now over at the subs' table, still lost in her world of the coronation ball. Though she looked tired, there was no sense of loss or disjointure in her life – that had been yesterday. Today was today – there was no looking back for Betty.

Terry drifted away and Miss Dimont typed out a handful of NIBs – news in brief paragraphs – short items from the courts, council, public relations handouts and other vital news resources. Her favourite this morning was about the repositioning of a drain cover halfway down Denmark Street. Although the Mothers' Union skeleton hunt was, in its way, a bit of a corker.

While she typed, she brooded. If Gerald had inherited a fortune, why had Prudence Aubrey not told her? If he was coming down to claim his life presidency, why didn't she mention it? Were things worse between them than she'd actually confessed? Or was Prudence Aubrey, how could one put this, a bit of a liar?

She lifted the phone and asked the operator for the Grand Hotel. Miss Aubrey, who had parted with her on such good terms, no longer seemed so keen to talk.

'The golf club?' pressed Miss Dimont.

'He never told me.'

'But he must have mentioned his inheritance. I gather it might be as much as a million.'

'He might have.'

'Look, Miss Aubrey, I feel you are telling me things which don't always quite add up. And at the same time, not telling me quite a lot.' This last was said with some asperity.

'I'm an actress,' said Prudence shortly, as if that were some kind of explanation.

'Your husband died. That's very sad, but as I gather from you, the marriage was over. There's some evidence which points towards . . . well, not as the coroner summed up. Not accidental death.'

'No,' said the actress, not sounding in the least surprised. 'Something was going on, I'll grant you that. He was talking to that man Shrimsley – the one who died, I do know that.'

'Why didn't you mention that before?' asked Miss Dimont, confused and not a little angered by the illogicality of Prudence's behaviour and her propensity to tell only fragments of the truth at any given time.

'*Because*,' replied the actress heatedly, 'it was that rat who was going to write Gerald's memoirs. Shrimsley was a ghostwriter – what a slovenly job – and he'd written articles for Gerald over the years when some editor would ring up and commission him to write about life in the movies, that sort of thing. They knew each other in the West End – oh, you knew that.'

She paused.

'I told you about Gerald wanting to change. The inheritance finally decided it. He had enough money to take the gamble and reconstruct himself as an actor for today – not like those has-beens Gielgud and Richardson, so stuck in the past. His memoirs were to be a reinvention for the next generation and that included telling every story against himself and – as I said before – some against me, too. He wanted to show how I was old school and he was new wave. And how as a result my career had hit the rocks.'

There was real anger in her voice. And understandably, thought Judy Dimont, but why not come clean in the first place?

'Why didn't you tell me this when we met?'

'There's more to it than that.'

'Did you try and stop him in any way?'

'Yes. I threatened to go to the papers. I threatened to tell them all about his young friends and his outré life. He was drugging, you know.'

Miss Dimont did not know, and actually did not want to know. Though the layers were beginning to peel away, she was still at heart a fan of Gerald Hennessy and could not quite believe what she was hearing.

'It's a horrid word, Miss Aubrey, but in a sense you have to admit you were blackmailing him.'

'On the contrary,' came the sharp reply, 'he was blackmailing me.'

Miss Dimont drew her breath in sharply. She said, 'The reason why I use that nasty word is that Shrimsley was encouraging Raymond Cattermole to instigate some sort of blackmail campaign against someone, I don't know who. Did Cattermole try it on with you?'

'No, as I said the other day, I had more on him than he had on me.'

'Then he must have been attempting to blackmail Gerald.'

'More than likely,' came the reply. 'Lots of fertile ground there.' You could tell Miss Aubrey was no longer interested.

However she had a last word for the reporter: 'I have to say, Miss Dimont, your policemen aren't being terrifically efficient.'

'Well, this is a rather complex state of affairs.'

'No, I mean about the attaché case,' said the actress.

'What attaché case?'

The widow told the reporter of her recent conversation with Inspector Topham. 'Somebody came along and pinched it. He doesn't seem to care very much. But it's odd, isn't it, that someone should sneak down the train and walk over a dead body to help themselves to a leather case?'

'There wasn't anything in it?'

'Usually he just kept his sandwiches in it.'

Miss Dimont remembered the paper she'd tidied away. Had it been to wrap his sandwiches in? She must unearth it and take a look.

'Anything else in the case? Letters, perhaps? Maybe some ideas about this book he was going to write with Shrimsley?'

'I have no idea,' said Prudence in a jaded voice. 'To be honest, I am getting over the shock of Gerald dying and now feeling rather angry that all this nonsense is going on around him.'

'Can I ask, will he have left you any money?'

'We never had any. The house we live in is beautiful but is on a Crown lease. We had plenty of clothes, and I have some jewellery but apart from that . . .'

'Where, do you think, his inheritance from Mr Pithers will go?'

'It should come to me, of course, his widow. But he was a bit strange towards the end – it wouldn't surprise me in the slightest to discover he'd left it to that . . . that . . .'

'Miss Lake, you mean, his daughter?'

'For heaven's sake, she had all our money while she was growing up,' snapped Prudence Aubrey. 'He paid for everything. I . . . now . . . discover,' she added bitterly.

'Where do you think he spent the night before he died?' The question had been asked so many times before, but now it seemed more important than ever.

'I literally have no idea. There were so many young friends.'

'Had he often stayed away before? When you had rows?'

'A couple of times.'

'And where did he go then?'

'Well, his club usually. Though once he went to stay with his cousin – she lives somewhere off Piccadilly.'

Just then Miss Dimont heard a thunderous bellow and, looking up, saw the red-faced apparition of Rudyard Rhys thrusting down the corridor from his office into the newsroom. He was waving in his hand two ten-by-eight prints and he was roaring Terry's name.

True you could see the stocking-tops of Mesdames Ferrers and Coryton but really, so what?

Just that Mr Ferrers had been into the office and made clear his opinion, in no uncertain terms, on the question of press ethics and the exploitation of innocent parties for financial gain. The words pouring from the editor's mouth were not what a lady liked to hear, especially in an office.

Miss Dimont could only rise above.

NINETEEN

Temple Regis was relishing its brush with fame. While Prudence Aubrey was downing cocktails in the Palm Court of the Grand, just as lively a consumption was taking place down at the snug bar of the Fortescue, where the death of Gerald Hennessy and the presence in town of two such dazzling stars as Prudence Aubrey and Marion Lake had caused a temporary suspension in the ongoing debate on whither Plymouth Argyle.

'at Mary-un.'

'She brite.'

'Werm coddit.'

'Doo more 'ere, Jethro, quick aboudit.'

As a consequence of these celebrations few Temple Regents would have noted the arrival on the late train of a sharp-suited, middle-aged man with a pencil moustache and expensive luggage. His arrival at the Grand went just as unremarked, and the transfer to his suite was achieved with the minimum of fuss and the maximum of unctuousness. Hartley Radford believed in the liberal distribution of pound notes to ease his passage through life, but then he'd accumulated so many of them he could afford to shed a few.

In fact it was remarkable how rich he had become, given that he did little more than sit in an office all day and talk into the telephone. Occasionally he might go out to lunch, in the evening perhaps the occasional theatre; but on the whole life asked little of him and as a consequence he gave little back. His clients might argue these days he was niggardly with his time, his advice, his condolences, his encouragement. And they had a point – for the gifts once showered liberally upon them were now held in reserve for the newest, the brightest talent swimming towards him from just over the horizon.

Temple Regis, had it known who'd slipped so sinuously from station to taxi and thence into the Grand, would have gladly laid down a path of palm leaves to welcome and celebrate this man; for though his name was unknown to them, he knew more famous people than most famous people did. Hartley Radford was not only a theatrical agent, he was *the* theatrical agent. A curt word from him on the telephone could send even the most eminent star of film or stage scurrying down to the Imperial, Scunthorpe, to play second fiddle to a pair of unicycling costermongers, such was his power.

Hartley Radford had easily accumulated power and contacts because he instinctively understood the nature of celebrity – its insecurity, its narcissism, its greed and all-consuming envy – and with effortless alchemy he was capable of transforming these negative forces into that unique product called stardom. He was Gerald Hennessy's agent, and he was Marion Lake's agent. He was no longer Prudence Aubrey's.

A limp hand lifted the telephone. 'What is the oldest champagne you have,' he intoned, the words more an instruction than an enquiry. The response evidently did not fill him with hope, but he ordered a magnum before calling Marion Lake's suite and issuing a softly spoken invitation.

The actress was there in a moment, and the murky business of her recently revealed parentage was discussed at some length. Hartley Radford smelt money in this extraordinary revelation, but to his client his tone was one of hurt and surprise.

'That you . . . and Gerry . . . should never think to tell me . . . Marion, I really am *saddened* by this . . .'

Arguably the most desired woman in the land knelt on the floor in front of her agent. 'Hartley, I am *so* sorry,' she whispered tearfully, her delivery not a million miles from that line which stole so many hearts in *Don't Call Me Baby*. 'I . . . had . . . no . . . idea . . .' and, with that, her platinum blonde locks fell forward abruptly and she began to sob.

Radford, battle-hardened to such absurdity, had his mind focused on the path ahead. Crisply he issued instructions to his protégée and sent her packing. The glass of champagne he had poured her remained untouched on a side table.

*

The matter of the attaché case seemed so trivial and yet at the same time so important. With the whiff of suspicion hanging over two, if not three, deaths in Temple Regis yet with no firm evidence to point to foul play, its absence assumed an undue prominence in the minds of both Prudence Aubrey and Inspector Topham, and now Miss Dimont. What lay within its battered but urbane exterior most likely held the clue to . . . who knows what? But that it must be found became the focal point of their thinking.

Miss Dimont was having her lunch in the Signal Box Café – the ham, egg and chips were always terribly good – when in came two of those anonymous men who strode each morning into the CID room down at the police station. Nobody knew their names and it would be difficult to recall what they looked like, which probably served them well as agents of the State, but their demeanour was cold and brittle. They engaged Lovely Mary, the proprietress, in purposeful conversation and from where she sat by the window Miss Dimont could see them pointing back towards the station and Platform 1.

One of them made notes while Lovely Mary pointed and gesticulated. The reporter could see her offering the detectives a cup of tea but they swept away, shaking their heads, each face an inscrutable mask.

It may have been her lunch hour but Judy Dimont was never off-duty.

'What was that all about, Lovely?'

'Bluddy buggerrs,' said Mary, not in a lovely way.

'What's that?'

'Tole me the licence sign on my door was out of date and I could be prosecuted.'

'They came here, from the police station, two of them? To threaten you with prosecution? Over a sign? When did it expire?' Here were the makings of a story, she thought, police making threatening noises to an innocent café owner whose ham and eggs were quite exceptional while murderers were on the loose and could strike again at any moment.

'Lars week,' said Lovely Mary. 'I offerum a cuppa tea but they say no.'

It seemed unreasonable. Inspector Topham had a well-paid and, by the look of them, well-nourished team of underlings who surely had better things to do than bully Lovely.

'But I tole 'em about that case anyways,' said Mary, for at heart she was a magnanimous soul who often deducted ha'pennies from Miss Dimont's bill because she liked her face. 'I tole 'em about that young lad.'

'Oh,' said Miss Dim, pushing her spectacles up her convex nose as dawn slowly broke. 'Oh! What case would that be? An . . . attaché case by any chance?'

Lovely Mary confirmed that this indeed was so. She liked Miss Dim so much she presented the reporter with the full evidence she had offered Inspector Topham's surly henchmen.

Shortly after the late Gerald Hennessy arrived at Temple Regis station, she said, a young man had come into the Signal Box, ordered a cup of tea, sat down and opened a small case.

'Not much inside, just a yellow book,' said Mary. ''Ere, you wanoo have a look? I forgot to show it to they police.' And from under the counter she produced a small volume bearing the name *Wisden* on its cover.

'Summat to do with cricket,' she added obligingly.

'What happened next?' asked Miss Dim.

The young man, apparently, had shut up the case, paid for his tea, and scarpered. He was very polite but looked poor. 'I was going to give 'im some toast but 'e went,' said Mary. 'Nice boy.'

But *was* he a nice boy, Miss Dim asked herself as she walked back to the office. One read so often of angel-faced killers. If he had his hands on Gerald Hennessy's missing case, he can only have got it by stealing it from the first-class compartment on the train – there simply wasn't time for it to have changed hands because he came into the Signal Box only moments after the Riviera Express had steamed to a halt.

Hennessy, it had been established, was alone in his compartment. Had the young man entered, threatened him, struggled with him, caused the heart attack, nabbed the case and run off? Was the tracery in the dust of the letters 'M . . . U . . . R . . .' the actor's message that he'd been murdered? In the absence of other evidence, at least this was a fresh line of inquiry.

Just as she reached the front door of the *Express* she saw across the street a distracted-looking Inspector Topham, talking to the two shadowy figures who'd quizzed Lovely Mary only minutes before. Miss Dim purposefully crossed the road as the anonymous pair melted away.

'Just a moment, Inspector.'

Topham did not care for her tone. If his service in the Guards had taught him anything, it was about position. In his eyes, a detective inspector of police ranked higher than a mere reporter on a local rag.

'Nothing to say,' he said. 'When there is, I'll let you know. Or you can *ask Sergeant Gull*.' The Inspector did not approve of the officially sanctioned leakage of police information to nosy reporters. He did not approve of Sergeant Gull chit-chatting to the press every morning, for he was of the firm belief that knowledge is power and the withholding of knowledge made one more powerful still. And he did not like Miss Dimont, for she made him feel decidedly uncomfortable.

'Correct me if I'm wrong, Inspector, but do we now have a murder inquiry?'

Topham stared down at her. 'I correct you,' he uttered stiffly. 'What are you talking about?'

'Inspector, there is something not quite right about the deaths of Gerald Hennessy and Arthur Shrimsley. Despite Dr Rudkin's findings, this story won't go away. Now we have a young man on the run with an attaché case belonging to Mr Hennessy, which he quite clearly stole from the compartment. Did he also bring about Mr Hennessy's death?

'*And*,' she went on, 'what about Mr Shrimsley's dog, Inspector? He didn't *have* a dog. What on earth was he doing walking a dog on Mudford Cliffs, miles from his home, and what happened to the dog?'

The inspector's body gave every sign that he was about to break into a parade-ground quick march, to get away from this nonsense. Miss Dimont stepped in front of him and looked up.

'And just explain to me that if it wasn't a letter in Mr Shrimsley's hand, what he was doing holding a piece of cloth, Inspector? And, while we're about it, what progress have you made in finding Mr Cattermole?'

Have I overstepped the mark? she asked herself. On the one hand, it was right to ask these questions – her job expected it of her – on the other, she could see the angry bafflement in Topham's eyes. He was a straightforward, decent, honest fellow, but what this investigation clearly needed was someone who could match fire with fire, someone whose mind tended towards the criminal. Topham was just too upright a fellow for the job.

From Topham's point of view, these questions unnecessarily raked over old coals. Hadn't the inquest disposed of these two deaths? Hadn't the disappearance of Cattermole more to do with the fact he couldn't bear living with that old Gaiety Girl any more and had found a younger companion? That left only the attaché case, which was quite simply an opportunistic theft: young man goes past first-class compartment, sees Hennessy asleep (or dead), nips in and takes the case.

The inspector, despite having a good war, was feeling his age. He suddenly wanted to go home to Mrs Topham, always a comfort in troubling times. Theirs may not have been the most demonstrative of marriages, but she gave him strength. Miss Dimont, he found, was too daunting an adversary.

'Nothing more to be—' he started.

'Two deaths, Inspector. One missing person. A chap on

the run with a vital piece of evidence.' Her tone was firm, her point incontrovertible.

'Did you ever think of becoming a detective?' asked Topham acidly, jutting his chin forward, his defences running low.

If only you knew, thought Miss Dim, that while you were in the desert bravely winning your Military Medal I was . . .

But she let the thought go, and parted from the policeman with as much cordiality as she could muster.

Back in the office, she looked for Athene but soothing Miss Madrigale was evidently elsewhere, engaged in necessary converse with the spirits. Instead she had to make do with Betty, who was filing her nails and reading a magazine.

'Have you had any dealings with Topham?' asked Miss Dimont, more as a conversational opener so that she might air her despair about his inadequacy.

'Lovely man,' said Betty warmly, patting her hair. 'Bit of a war hero. Just the sort to have in the police force. He was very kind to me when I . . .'

Judy stopped listening. If it wore trousers and didn't send her telegrams, it was OK with Betty – no point in further discussion. Topham probably once bought Betty a cup of tea, that's all it took. She would have to wrestle alone with her conscience on this one.

In a post-war world, which even a decade and a half after peace this still was, conflicting forces were at play in Temple Regis. There were bad people – the fat-rendering Bill Pithers sprang to mind, and there were others like him – and then there were those who wanted to paper over the cracks and assert that yes, there was honey still for tea. Civic pride was ever-present, wherever you turned. You only had to see old Miss Pleram with her ancient blunt secateurs, walking down the street and snipping odd outgrowths from hedges and bushes, picking up the discarded toffee papers, leaving her apple crop outside her front door for passers-by to help themselves. People wanted life to be as it once was; murder had no part in this healing process.

Rudkin, Topham, and the others were working towards a better future, to a time when Temple Regis would be acknowledged internationally for the warmth of its sunshine and of its welcome. For that to transpire, there could be no blots on the town's escutcheon. When Samuel Brough, the mayor, walked behind his tailcoated sergeant to St Margaret's Church each autumn to rededicate the town to goodness and prosperity, he wanted to do it with head held high.

Miss Dimont saw it all and sympathised, for she loved Temple Regis too – who did not? But you could not excuse wrongdoing – wasn't that also what the War had been about? To preserve the reputation of this place at the expense of justice, which is what these people seemed to want to do, seemed a dangerous step – for what other misdeeds would be covered up in the interests of Temple Regis' future prosperity?

And then again, if she was right, there was a killer on the loose. Unless action was taken he could strike again. Something needed to be done and if the police wouldn't . . .

There was sometimes a recklessness about Miss Dimont

– anybody who'd been privy to the business of the Conservative Winter Ball could attest to that – and there were few
who could rein her in. Curiously, one who could was Terry
Eagleton. Though they were oil and water – the thinking
versus the instinctive – she recognised in the photographer
qualities she herself lacked.

Terry was talking to the pretty girl in reception. She could
never remember anybody's name, which Miss Dim found
irritating, but Terry didn't seem to mind.

'Terry, may we speak? Come to the Fort?' Reluctantly the
photographer detached his gaze and picked up his camera
bag.

The snug bar at the Cap'n Fortescue was deserted. Miss
Dimont did not waste words.

'. . . you'd almost think it a conspiracy. Two unexplained
deaths and they want to bury any questions along with the
bodies. And Inspector Topham! Do you know, now he's wasting his time – and that of his men – chasing some young lad
who pinched Gerald Hennessy's attaché case from the train.

'Not,' she snarled, 'because maybe he caused Hennessy's
death – I don't know how, but he *could* have done – but the
retrieval of stolen property seems to concern the inspector
more than any number of suspicious deaths.'

'He's very sweet on Prudence Aubrey,' said a laconic Terry,
sipping his cider.

'Well, he shouldn't be,' snapped Miss Dim. 'There's something very strange about her. She told me she felt like killing

him – and the way she blows hot and cold, sweet to me one minute and at daggers drawn the next . . .'

'Actress,' said Terry, as if he knew.

'Topham seems to be on a personal errand to get back her husband's attaché case instead of concentrating on the job in hand.'

Terry looked at her steadily. 'Is that like a briefcase? This attaché case?'

Miss Dim blinked. Really, photographers, did they know nothing at all? Of the near-million words in the English language, how many did they ever deploy in daily conversation? How many did their brains hold in reserve for special occasions? Did they write poetry ever – come to that, did they ever *read* it?

She could do no more than nod. Words, of which Miss Dimont had many at her disposal, failed her.

There was a pause.

'Barry Shaldon,' said Terry.

Miss Dimont looked at him. 'What?'

'Barry Shaldon. The chap with the whatever-you-call-it case.'

'What do you mean?' demanded Miss Dim heatedly.

'Saw him getting off the train when we were on the platform. Nice chap, bit sad really.'

The reporter almost knocked her glass of ginger beer over. It was impossible. A photographer who didn't know what an attaché case was, but could name a murder suspect – just like that. Impossible!

'Terry,' she said slowly, 'you realise we're talking about a possible murderer. We've been going round in circles trying to get to the bottom of these two mysterious deaths. Why on earth didn't you . . .?'

At that Terry took umbrage. 'If you'd said *briefcase*,' he said. 'If you'd used plain English. If you'd told me what's in that complicated mind of yours instead of wandering round the houses. If you'd done any of *that* I could have told you. Barry Shaldon.'

'Who is he?'

'Garage mechanic. When he's working. He fixed the timing chain sprocket on the Minor the other day. But he's a bit strange, lives with his aunt and uncle – his parents were killed in the War. Army lorry went over them in the blackout. Barry too.'

'How do you know all this?' asked Miss Dimont in bewilderment. 'How do you know it was him with the att— er, briefcase?'

'I recognised him as he got off the train, didn't I? Now I see why he didn't want to know me – he'd just nicked that case.'

Miss Dimont threw down the remains of her ginger beer.

'Let's go and pay a call on your Mr Shaldon,' she said.

TWENTY

In September, when the holidaymakers had gone but the weather was still wonderful, the townsfolk of Temple Regis took their *passeggiata* down through the greensward, past the bandstand, and out on to the seafront. It was remarkable how many familiar faces you could see, stopping at Beryl's for a glass of lemonade or an ice, nodding to each other. The town stopped work at 5.30 prompt and there were still a good couple of hours before the purple and grey crept up to claim the daylight.

Betty was having a cup of tea with Claud Hannaford. Neither was quite as the other remembered from the Coronation Ball, for daylight has a way of telling truths that are sometimes best left unsaid. Claud sat urbanely on his chair wishing it was cocktail time while Betty was noticing that his hand shook ever so slightly when he reached for his cup. He's older than I thought, she said to herself. Not so pretty when she's wearing her work clothes, observed Claud.

Still, whatever occurred in the cerise Rolls-Royce had been the beginning of something which neither, for their different reasons, wanted to let go just yet.

'We might stroll on to the Grand for a drink,' said Claud by way of conversation.

'Oh,' said Betty, colouring. 'I've got a . . . it's the Council of Social Services meeting at seven.' Implicit in this response were two contiguous messages – that she did not drink alcohol while she was still working (a good girl) but if he cared to wait until the job was done, she'd be gasping for a Babycham (but not all the time).

'Let's have another cup,' said Claud, who understood her meaning if he could be bothered to. You could tell this wasn't going well.

Betty struggled to keep the conversation afloat as Beryl and her sluggish daughter slowly worked their way round the seafront tables taking orders.

'Tell me more about Bill Pithers,' she said, looking out to sea. Claud had banged on about the old crook leaving him his Rolls, he enjoyed talking about that. Keep 'em talking, Betty had learnt long ago, it keeps 'em happy.

'He was very proud that Gerry Hennessy was his grandson, but long ago Gerry put a stop to him boasting about it. He told him it was bad for business. Fat rendering and film stars don't exactly make ideal bedfellows,' said Claud, waggling his eyebrows. Betty simpered.

'It's odd really. Old Bill took orders from nobody – he was rude, he was overbearing, he'd steal your last shilling if you left it on the counter. He was rough and – well, you know about the women,' said Claud, and Betty nodded.

'I think, though, that he thought in death their names

should be linked – which is why he gave the presidency of the golf club to Hennessy – so that everyone in Temple Regis would know he was Gerry's grandfather. And what could Gerry do but accept? For all I know, when Bill left him his millions, maybe he made it a condition of acceptance that Gerry would take on the club as well.'

That had got him going again. He was quite lively when you got him on song.

'You said there were two grandchildren,' said Betty, smiling engagingly. 'Who was the other one?'

Just then Beryl's surly daughter, a recalcitrant recruit to the family business, dropped the contents of a hot cup of tea into Betty's lap and an evening laden with promise evaporated in an instant.

*

Terry and Judy were sitting on a bench high above the town in Westville, a clutch of small Edwardian cottages which marked the civic boundary. From this standpoint they could view the swoop and rise of Temple Regis' elegant contours and its multi-coloured roofs melting into the green and blue of the landscape and sky, as if nature were trying to steal back the land robbed by centuries of slow urbanisation. Beyond lay the bleached-gold wheat fields awaiting their harvesting, while below, away from the town, lay a broad valley studded with pink sheep, their fleeces dyed by the rich red earth beneath their feet. In the clear still air you could hear the bell of St

Margaret's chime the hour, a message which at this distance sounded both protective and devout.

Terry was noisily sucking a toffee. 'Won't be much longer,' he said.

'That's all right,' replied Judy. 'It's heavenly up here.'

As if in agreement, Terry picked up his camera, selected f8 at 1/125th, and focused on the spire of St Margaret's below. He never wasted film, and had got what he wanted in two shots. Then slowly he turned the lens on Judy Dimont, who was looking quite beautiful in the evening sunlight. She smiled, pushed back her corkscrew hair, and Terry pressed the shutter. In the shining evening light, time stood still for a moment.

Slowly into view meandered a lost-looking young man, his eyes cast down to his feet, his demeanour one of world-weariness and despair. He was tall, handsome in a rough-cut sort of way, and athletic. He walked as though a part of him was missing.

'Our murderer,' whispered Miss Dimont.

'Hello, Barry,' called Terry, unimpressed, but for a moment the young man did not respond. Then, as he continued towards them, he suddenly looked up. He blinked and then said, 'Mr Eagleton. How's the Minor?'

Terry nodded approvingly towards the car, parked on the opposite side of the road. 'Your mum and dad said you were on your way back from Exeter.'

'Been to see about a job.'

'This is Miss Dimont, she works with me at the *Express*.'

'Two Riviera Expresses,' said Barry quite slowly, unwinding the long scarf which seemed superfluous on such a warm day. 'The train, and the newspaper. That seems strange.'

'Have you just come back on the Express now,' said Miss Dimont, catching the moment, 'from Exeter?'

'I love it. I'd be able to go on it every day if I had a job in Exeter.'

The reporter chose her words carefully. 'Did you go up to Exeter last week?'

'Most weeks I go up. I'm trying to find a job. There are more jobs up there. Only part-time work at the garage here.'

Miss Dimont felt her heart soften as she looked at this handsome but broken young man, coming home for his tea to the two loving guardians he called his mum and dad. She looked into his eyes in the hope of catching some information as to his character: could this sad and disconnected individual, who clearly had little chance ever of leading a fully independent life, have had a hand in ending the life of Gerald Hennessy? It seemed so unlikely, but she must be sure.

'Do you remember last week, on the train, going into the first-class compartments?'

'I do that once the guard's been round and punched my ticket. After Exeter he doesn't come round again. The seats are more comfortable.'

'Do you remember the day when there was a bit of a fuss?'

Barry shot a hostile look at Miss Dimont. He didn't say anything.

She tried again. 'A man on the train died.'

'They took the train out of service,' said Barry helpfully. 'Shunted the first-class round into the sidings. The carriages stayed there until 3.23 p.m. the next day. Then went back up the upline. The police . . .'

'On the train, Barry. When you were on the train, did you see the dead man? Did you go into his compartment?'

The young man started angrily. Some native instinct warned him he was under threat. '*What'sitmatterwhat'sitm atterwhat'sitmatter?*' he stuttered, and he stepped forward urgently, moving his shoulders around like a boxer warming up.

'You took his, ah, briefcase,' said Judy Dimont, with just a trace of imperiousness. 'We know you did. What did you do to him, to Gerald Hennessy? Did you fight with him? Did you knock him about so you could steal his case?'

'Naaaaaaaaggghhhhh!' shouted the young man, and launched himself at his inquisitor. He clamped his muscular hands on her shoulders and started to shake them very hard indeed. Miss Dimont's glasses fell off and a look of terror gripped her features.

Terry was quick and efficient. 'That's enough, mate,' he barked, and punched Barry underneath his outstretched arms. That was all it took, and the attack was over in less time than it takes to tell. Barry flopped down on the bench and began to sob.

Miss Dimont sat down next to him, for she was very shocked and her legs did not feel too sturdy at that moment.

Terry picked up her spectacles, took out his lens cloth and gave them a gentle polish, and put them back on her nose.

She turned to Barry. In those brief, violent, few seconds she had deduced what had happened.

'He was dead, wasn't he? You saw him when you went into first class and he was dead? You thought he wouldn't mind if you took his case?'

Barry was still crying. 'Never seen anyone dead before,' he said, and burst into angry shudders of remorse. 'Apart from my mum and dad. They were dead. They're still dead. I want them back, but they won't come.'

'But you took his case?'

'I dunno why. I was angry because he'd only just died, and Mum and Dad had been dead for years and years. I wanted to punish him for . . . only just . . . dying.'

'So you took the case?' Miss Dimont had taken his hand.

'I've never stolen anything,' sobbed Barry. 'I was just . . . *so* angry.'

'It's all right,' said Miss Dimont, and squeezed his hand. 'You went into Lovely Mary's – the Signal Box Café – and had a cup of tea. I would have wanted a cup of tea after that.'

'She was very nice to me. Said I could have a slice of toast for nothing with my tea, but I couldn't eat nothing.'

'What did you do with the case?'

'In the coal cellar.'

'Here?'

Barry nodded. At that point Terry took over, leaned forward and said quite quietly, 'Let's go and find it, Barry, shall we?' and the pair wandered off together.

In her time Miss Dimont had seen many tragic cases of personal loss, and long ago had come to the conclusion there can be no greater damage done than to those who are orphaned in childhood; they have lost, and nothing can ever be done to ease their wretched pain. She composed herself, for the whole episode had been quite upsetting, and reached into her raffia bag for a handkerchief.

Terry was back within a minute. 'I let him go indoors,' he said. 'No point in upsetting him further – that one's got an ugly streak, you can see. Is this what you were looking for?'

Hanging in his outstretched fingers was, Miss Dimont felt sure, the key to the mysterious deaths of Gerald Hennessy and Arthur Shrimsley. A beige and tan object in soft leather with faded gilt locks, weathered handsomely by the years, the sort of item one might find equally at home in Mayfair or Monte Carlo – not in a Devon coal-hole covered with black dust.

Miss Dimont wiped her eyes, for she had been as upset by the tragedy of handsome Barry Shaldon as much as his attack on her, and she placed the case upon her lap. Its locks burst obligingly open at a touch of a finger, and she lifted the lid in a horror of anticipation.

It was empty.

Not quite empty, for there were some breadcrumbs and a couple of what appeared to be minuscule red balls the size of a large pinhead rolling around inside, and in a folder there was what turned out to be a script. But when Miss Dimont read swiftly through its contents, hungry for clues, it offered nothing more than a selection of the lines Hennessey was due to deliver in his next film. In the present context, they seemed banal.

Terry could sense her disappointment. 'Quick one in the Fort?' he said.

'No,' said Miss Dimont, 'the Grand!'

Reporter and photographer tumbled into the Minor, and as it rolled downhill towards town an earnest debate took place over the case's future. Terry was all for handing it over to the police, Miss Dimont for using it as a lever to get more information out of the mercurial Miss Aubrey. Since Judy had promised to buy the drinks, she won the point and in a few moments they were walking through the hotel's imposing portico and out on to the sun-splashed terrace.

'Hello, Peter.' Miss Dimont smiled at her favourite waiter. 'Give us two cocktails – any kind you like. And, is Miss Aubrey in the hotel still?'

'Yes.' Potts nodded. 'In the bar.'

'Would you give her this note?' She scribbled in her reporter's notebook, tore out the page and handed it over.

It took the film star less than a minute to arrive, preceded (but only just) by a quick-marching Peter Potts bearing on a salver her half-consumed martini.

'You found Gerry's case?' Miss Aubrey trilled. 'I am *so* grateful – so grateful. It means so very much to –'

'Won't you sit down?' said Miss Dim. Her voice appeared to have been chilled by the ice in her cocktail, in fact it sounded positively frosty. Miss Aubrey plonked down rather heavily on a chair; evidently Peter Potts had been working zealously on her behalf for some time.

The actress looked up, then blinked. 'But how come *you* have Gerry's case? I thought Inspector Topham—?'

'It was stolen by a very unhappy young man,' said Miss Dimont, primly shaking her head as murmurs of arrest and imprisonment bubbled to the actress's lips. 'It is unharmed and intact and that I hope will be an end of the matter.'

Prudence Aubrey, through a slight haze, got the message. She took the case in her hands and stroked it gently.

'It's a . . . talisman,' she said. 'A token of a happy time. When Gerry and I were young, when we had stardom in front of us and ambition at our elbow. We were beautiful people, we were in love, we were . . . *wanted*.

'"Murgs," he used to say – that was his name for me – "Murgs, together we will go to the top." And the rest didn't matter – the fact we never had any money, we had no children, not even really a home we could call our own. Acting has a way of displacing conventional priorities but it happens so gradually that you don't realise you are drifting away from the shore. Then one day you wake to find yourself in the middle of the river, with no oars, and the rocks up ahead.'

She clutched the case. 'That moment came when I heard Gerry was dead,' she said. 'I woke up to the fact that I had moved far, far away from the real world, but now it was marching towards me and shouting that it was going to take me back.'

A large tear welled in the corner of one eye and slid elegantly down her cheek. It was a good performance. Miss Dimont paused, appropriately, then started her questioning again.

'Are you surprised that Gerald died of a heart attack?'

'Yes and no. He has always been pretty fit – his job required it – but, of course, the drink . . . and recently he'd started taking pills.'

'So that could have been it? Too many pills?'

'You heard what the pathologist said. It was a heart attack. If he'd been taking pills there presumably would have been some evidence.'

'You see,' said Miss Dimont, 'although my job is a reporter, I have had some past experience in . . .' She left the sentence unfinished. Miss Aubrey, looking at her interlocutor as if for the first time, suddenly saw a different woman. It caused her to choose her words with care. 'Had he had any illness, Gerald?'

Miss Aubrey thought about that. She did not immediately answer. Then slowly she answered, 'Well, I don't suppose it matters now. We never talked about it during his lifetime because nobody wants to hire an ill actor – even one with a reputation like Gerald's. In films, you know, the insurance . . . so costly. So you keep quiet.'

Miss Dimont leaned forward. 'But . . .?'

'About five years ago, Gerry keeled over and nearly died. It was horrifying – we were having dinner and he suddenly went red, then purple, in the face, he was sick, and then slid under the table. The ambulance was called and he was in hospital within fifteen minutes. If they'd been any longer he would have been dead.'

'What was it?' asked Miss Dimont.

'Anaphylactic shock, I think they called it. Gerald had developed an allergy to caviar – well, all fish eggs really, roe and suchlike, but on this particular evening we'd had some caviar. Still hard to come by, even in this day and age, but it was that sort of restaurant.

'It was horrible to see, and the worst of it was that nobody at the hospital knew what to do – they couldn't work out what was wrong with him. They pumped him full of some drug – epinephrine? I don't know – and slowly he recovered. It's ironic that if anybody had lived the champagne-and-caviar way of life it was Gerry. But that put an end to it.'

A slow realisation was forming in Miss Dimont's mind. But Prudence Aubrey was rambling on. 'Funny thing was, Gerry was never that keen on champagne. So all that guff in the newspapers about champagne and caviar – it was all nonsense. By the end he didn't take either. Of course he kept up the legend, never told a soul he couldn't eat caviar. I mean, what would *that* have done to his reputation?'

'It's a very strange malady,' said Miss Dimont, thoughtfully. 'Was there no warning?'

'Well, he'd been unwell a couple of times after eating caviar but we never made the connection – we thought it must be food poisoning. Then one night we were having dinner in the Russian Tea Room in New York. Django Reinhardt was playing. We ordered the full Russian menu but Gerry disappeared after the first course and didn't come back until after the band had finished – he'd spent the evening in the bathroom, poor lamb. Missed the entire performance. And still the penny didn't drop.'

Miss Dimont's voice was so low it could barely be heard above the clatter on the Grand Hotel's terrace.

'And so, if someone had wanted to murder Gerald,' she said very slowly, and as she did so she leaned forward and took back the attaché case from Prudence Aubrey's lap, 'they could do it by feeding him caviar.'

The actress went white. 'Well, no . . . no . . .' she stuttered. 'No – Gerry wouldn't touch anything which contained even the merest hint of fish eggs! It's an allergy which only gets worse as time goes on – he knew after that hospital trip he could die.'

Miss Dimont lifted the worn leather case on to her lap and snapped it open.

'Salmon eggs,' said Miss Dimont bleakly. 'Red caviar.'

She looked over the attaché case lid at Prudence Aubrey. 'That's what killed your husband.'

Like poor Gerald, his widow had to be helped up from under the table. She had fainted.

TWENTY-ONE

Frank Topham had taken his leave of Sid with the customary exchange of monosyllables, and only by chance emerged from the bar of the Grand on to the terrace via its garden door. If he'd gone out his usual way, through the Palm Court, things might have turned out differently.

Instead he turned the corner to find Peter Potts, Miss Dimont and that photographer fellow struggling under a table to retrieve the inert body of a woman who, as he approached, he identified as Prudence Aubrey.

In keeping with the hotel's famed discretion the fuss was being kept to a minimum by Peter, who'd swiftly called a colleague to place a couple of screens around the table; but Topham's eyes had already taken in the scene and, just as quickly, seen and identified the missing attaché case.

'How'd that get here?' he demanded pugnaciously.

Miss Dimont, helping the actress into a chair, left the answer to that question with Terry, who gave a vague account of the past two hours' activities without identifying Barry Shaldon or even which part of town they'd visited.

It infuriated Topham, who pictured the scene back in the

CID room when he explained that, once again, his investigation had been bested by that owlish-looking reporter on the local rag. He could hear the cooing chorus of 'Not *again*, Stanley!' and it chilled his blood.

'That,' he said in midnight tones, 'is evidence in what may be a murder inquiry.' Miss Dimont shot him a triumphant look. 'Give it to me. Now.'

Nobody raised a finger, so Topham helped himself. Prudence Aubrey was coming round with the aid of a table napkin dipped into an ice bucket.

'Inspector,' she said weakly. 'I shall be telling Colonel ffrench-Blake what a miracle worker you are. Gerry's attaché case . . . so glad . . .'

The faint, the accumulated cocktails, and frankly the shock of all that had taken place in the past few days had rendered her helpless to comprehend who had done what, thought Topham, but he was mollified to think this might end with a commendation to the CO. But such was the fluster caused by this small group trying hard not to create a scene he realised he would get little more from reporter or actress so, taking up the prized piece of evidence, he turned to walk away.

'It will be returned to you tomorrow,' he promised Miss Aubrey, 'and please don't hesitate to pass on warmest regards to the colonel.'

The actress sighed, threw a mournful look at the departing case (in the stage version of *Brief Encounter* she'd delivered a similar moue to departing Alec Harvey) and looked round vaguely for her cocktail glass.

Miss Dimont had waited patiently for the hubbub to subside but now turned again to Prudence.

'May I just ask you a couple more questions?' she said, rather more a statement than a question.

'I seem to have lost my drink.'

'Have some water,' said Miss Dimont, firmly. The actress suddenly looked anxious.

'Inspector Topham now has the case and will no doubt be having its contents analysed,' she said. 'But unless I'm much mistaken the cause of Gerald's death is in there, for all to see.

'We can take it that he did not want to kill himself with caviar. Therefore, we may conclude from the breadcrumbs that it was put in a sandwich by someone else – someone who wanted him dead.'

Miss Aubrey went white.

'You have said yourself,' went on Miss Dimont, gently but firmly, 'that you wanted to kill your husband. He had been unfaithful, he was preparing to leave the marital home. He had come into a substantial amount of money which he was not prepared to share with you. He had changed from a loveable national figure into something of a monster. He was going to write his memoirs, which might do something to refresh his image, but would cause your own reputation – at a difficult juncture in your career – nothing but damage.'

Miss Aubrey gripped the tablecloth and stared fixedly at Miss Dimont. From a wilting soubrette she had suddenly transformed into a tigress at bay, but the reporter seemed not to notice.

'Gerald was coming down here to claim his fortune – and he was doing so in the company of a woman you thought was his mistress,' she went on.

'Or, did you know? Did you know that Marion Lake was in fact his daughter? That he had something you could never have – apart from the fame and the continued glory – that he had a child? Had you discovered that? Is that what made you plan to kill him?'

Miss Aubrey stood up jerkily and threw the contents of her water glass in Judy Dimont's face.

'Youuuuuuuu,' she hissed, 'youuuuu . . . you don't know what you're talking about! You have no idea!' Her face was bunched up, its natural prettiness all but overcome by a sudden mad-eyed pallor. The water glass in her hand now became a weapon, shoved threateningly across the table towards the reporter, who was dabbing her face with a napkin.

Terry and Peter Potts, caught off-guard, moved belatedly to protect Miss Dimont, who was clearly in danger. The water glass remained just inches away from her face until Terry gently grasped the actress's wrist and at the same moment relieved her of the glass and pushed her back into her chair.

'You see,' said Miss Dimont, wiping her spectacles and returning them to their rightful place, 'only you could know about Gerald's allergy – you said as much yourself. It would be damaging to his career if it were known he suffered such a terrible weakness, both from a publicity point of view, but also because of the insurance. You kept it a secret between yourselves – you told me so just now.'

Terry had his hand on the actress's shoulder, a heavy reminder that he was Miss Dimont's protector. Peter Potts stood sturdily by the reporter's side. There could be no renewal of her attack, yet she sat like coiled steel, an eerily frightening presence in the gathering dusk.

'Who then had the knowledge, the motive and the means to kill your husband – apart from you?'

'Who do you think you are, asking all these questions?' demanded the actress. 'What are you? Just some jumped-up reporter from a local rag who—'

'Well,' said Miss Dimont, 'we can always ask Inspector Topham to come back. Given the circumstances, I think you'd find his questions were very similar to mine.' Or they should be, added Miss Dimont silently.

She continued. 'When he went on his rail trips, he used to take his script with him to rehearse in the compartment.'

'Yes, I already told you that.'

'Would he take anything with him to eat, or did he use the dining car?'

'He liked to get into the part and didn't want the distraction of people bothering him, so he'd have a sandwich in the compartment.'

'What sort of sandwich?'

'Well, usually smoked salmon. If I could get it. Not always easy, even now.' She bit at a fingernail.

Miss Dimont considered this. 'So it would be terribly easy,

wouldn't it, to fold a layer of salmon caviar into the sandwich without his noticing as he took a bite?'

'What do you mean?'

'Well, he wouldn't be able to tell, would he? The taste of the salmon eggs would be lost in the flavour of the smoked salmon. And how would he know the eggs were there – you don't open a sandwich to inspect its contents before eating, do you?'

'Listen, I don't know why you think—' said Prudence Aubrey, now very angry indeed.

'Who else?' asked Miss Dimont, pressing hard. 'Who else could it be but you? Who else knew about his fatal allergy?'

'Only members of his family, I suppose.'

'But he hasn't got any family . . . apart from his daughter. Marion Lake.'

'Then,' said Prudence Aubrey, rising magnificently from the table, 'I suggest you go and talk to Marion Lake! She saw Gerald far more recently than I. She was on the train with him, for heaven's sake!' She was gathering strength as she spoke. 'Remember Gerald did not spend that last night with me.'

'We only have your word for—'

'In this case, my word is good enough,' snapped the actress. 'And if you're looking for – whaddyou call it – motive, then think about this. Marion Lake was abandoned by her father before she was born. She had a difficult time with her stepfather, who constantly sneered about her not being his. Sometimes the money Gerald was supposed to send – well, we existed on very little in the early years of our marriage and he didn't always send the right amount, and sometimes not at all.'

'So you *did* know about Marion Lake.'

'Let's say I guessed. I didn't know who she was, of course. I didn't know that until you told me in the courthouse.'

'But why would she want to kill a father with whom she'd only just been reunited?'

'How should I know?' said the actress. 'Rejection? I don't know. All I know is, I wasn't with Gerald for thirty-six hours before he died. She was.'

And with that Miss Aubrey swept magnificently off the terrace and up to her suite.

*

It was not that Betty Featherstone was ungrateful, but somehow she expected better of Rudyard Rhys. Truth be told, the byline queen of the *Riviera Express* was upset to find in the engagements diary her initials pencilled against the annual meeting of the Regis & Bedlington Bowls Club.

For a start it was in Bedlington, which was a nuisance to get to. In addition, though local newspapers, especially in this part of the world, left no stone unturned in trying to squeeze a story out of a non-event, it could hardly be said that the AGM of the bowls club was likely to get her a Page One story. She had been almost inclined to do a pick-up – calling the club secretary next morning to glean what miserable nuggets of information had dribbled out during the no doubt dreary (and lengthy) meeting, but Rudyard Rhys was very particular about pick-ups.

Everyone in local journalism had heard the story of the theatre critic who couldn't be bothered to attend a performance of *HMS Pinafore* given by the Young Farmers and so wrote his review from the programme without hearing that the theatre had burned down. That was most decidedly *not* going to happen on Mr Rhys' patch, and so to Bedlington poor Betty duly went.

In fact, if she'd bothered to read the note left on her desk by the editor – submerged in the tidal wave of detritus Betty so inexplicably accumulated each day – she would have learned that this was to be the most momentous AGM in the club's seventy-year history.

She awoke to that possibility an hour into the meeting when the chairman passed on to Any Other Business.

'The proposal,' he intoned, 'is that lady members should be allowed access to the clubhouse.'

Gales of laughter greeted this seemingly innocuous notion, and the chairman sat down while the gentlemen members made merry at the very thought. For in Temple Regis and Bedlington, as in many other parts of the British Isles, lady members had yet to attain equal status in any number of spheres of leisure. This despite their universally being granted the vote in 1928 and having shown they could do the work of a man in both world wars.

The hilarity went on for some time before the chairman rose again. 'This is a serious proposal,' he said with mock gravitas, 'put forward by Mesdames Tuck and Hay. I will read you an extract from Mrs Tuck's letter.

'"We on the Ladies' Committee have at all times striven to maintain the reputation of this Club, but our job is made the harder by gentlemen members refusing to grant us equal status. We are expected to provide the teas at club matches, but have to ask permission to enter the clubhouse to get water for the kettles. The kitchen is a separate building with no washing-up facilities and lady members have to take home the dirty plates and cups. Then there is the question of other facilities . . ."'

'Oh dear what can the matter be?' yodelled a voice from the back of the hall. 'Two old ladies got locked in the lavatory . . .'

Explosions of mirth halted the proceedings, and Betty felt quite uncomfortable. On the one hand she expected men to open doors for her and to pay for dinner, but really, didn't the women have a point? Slowly it dawned upon her that there might be a page one story here after all.

The womenfolk of Regis & Bedlington BC were ahead of her. As Betty turned over a page of her notebook and sucked on her pencil, Mesdames Glenda Tuck and Nancy Hay unexpectedly strode up the room and took the stage.

'Ladies of this club,' intoned Mrs Hay in a commanding manner, 'are we all agreed?' She was answered by a thrilling cheer from the water-starved section of the membership.

'Then,' she said, 'this is to give the AGM formal notice that the ladies of Regis & Bedlington have resigned their membership. There really is no need for further explanation, but since some gentlemen are unable to grasp the virtues of equality, I will make it plain.

'We have consistently won all our matches at both home and away games. The gentlemen . . .' She let the rest of the sentence hang in the air, for the old gentlemen were not so good on the mat.

'We have washed and ironed the gentlemen members' flannels. We have made their tea. We have taken home their dirty crockery. We have never so much as been allowed to wash our hands or even . . .' Again she left the words unsaid, for lady bowls members were above talking about facilities.

'We have given more than our fair share to this club, but gentlemen members' attitudes remain patronising and dismissive. So we resign.'

'Oo's going to make the tea?' called out one wag in a mock-wavering voice.

Mrs Hay pressed on. 'The ladies' committee has spoken to Lord Mount Regis and he has agreed to our creating a new green at Linhay Mead. He recognises that the women's team has a greater chance of bringing home silver from the national championships than the men ever would.'

There was a stunned silence. 'In addition, Lord Mount Regis has indicated to us that he is reviewing the lease currently coming to an end on this clubhouse, and has told us that he now has other uses in mind for the site. He is constantly being plagued to provide new and better housing for his estate tenants.'

The silence which followed these very reasonable words went on for some time. And then pandemonium broke loose – the hilarity of a few moments ago replaced by angry shouts, waving fists and red faces. Most of the gentlemen members had spent an hour in the bar before the AGM and were confused and uncomprehending. Some shouted things at their wives they would come to regret once they got home.

In sporting parlance, Betty was slow to collect the ball, but once she had it she knew what to do with it. As the meeting broke up in disarray, she hastened to the side of Mesdames Tuck and Hay and interviewed them vigorously about their plans to close down their husbands' club and form their own. This was Page One stuff all right!

TWENTY-TWO

Such is the nature of journalism that two reporters on the same newspaper can gather between them the components of an explosive story – one the bearer of the nitro, the other the glycerine – yet the two never come together.

Betty had the answer to the death of Gerald Hennessy, but did not know it. Judy Dimont had all the clues, but without Betty's one important part of the jigsaw, could never solve the mystery. Meanwhile Inspector Topham . . . though working earnestly, he seemed to have no clues at all.

The nitro and the glycerine passed each other on the hill just out of Bedlington. Betty was returning to town beside herself with delight at the scoop she was clutching to her bosom. Judy was being driven by Auriol Hedley to spend the night at her seafront cottage. Neither reporter saw the other, and as a consequence there was no explosion.

'I have some delicious Burgundy,' Auriol was saying to her old friend. 'Just what you need to soothe your nerves. What a day, Judy!'

'Thank you for coming to rescue me,' came the muted reply. 'In the end I don't think that young man meant to do me any harm, he was just frightened and confused. He thought we might have him taken away. But you know, Auriol,' she said, 'no jail cell could rectify the damage done to that poor thing. The safest place for him is where he is, with his adoptive parents.'

'I wonder what will happen to him when they die,' answered Auriol absently, but her thoughts were already on the greater threat of Prudence Aubrey.

'She was much more of a danger,' said Judy, her thoughts running parallel. 'There's something not right about her and you know, in spite of her denials, I can't help feeling she had a hand in Hennessy's death.'

'Let's wait till we get home,' said Auriol, shifting into a lower gear as they came down the steep hill into Bedlington.

The light had almost gone, but as they stepped out of the car a last ray defiantly clung on, striking the rim of the cliffs which rose darkly over Bedlington harbour. Miss Dimont looked up and remembered the sprawled body of Arthur Shrimsley, a man all but forgotten in the pursuit of Gerald Hennessy's murderer – she hadn't been able to make any headway there. A cold wind blew in from the sea as they walked up the garden path.

'Much better here with me,' said Auriol kindly, as she turned on the lamps in her tiny cottage and made for the kitchen. 'Cheese omelette?'

'That would be lovely.'

'You know,' Auriol went on, as she opened the wine, 'it's all most *irregular*. I think we can find our way to Hennessy's murderer, but the more that path seems certain, the more obscure becomes the death of that other man.'

'Shrimsley.'

'And the missing theatre chap.'

'Cattermole. There's got to be a connection, but I just can't find it.'

'Let's take it apart, piece by piece, just like we did in the old days,' she said, and both women glanced up briefly at the photograph of Eric Hedley on the mantlepiece. 'Who, in the end, do you suspect? And why?'

Miss Dimont sipped her wine and thought. 'You know, Terry is marvellous,' she said eventually. 'He's incredibly irritating. He seems to know everything without ever having learned anything – that's so maddening! But he *is* a perfectionist.'

'Eric was a bit like that.'

'Yes.' There was a pause between them.

'Go on.'

'Even when he was confronted with a dead body, Terry made sure his light and aperture were spot on. The night Gerald died he showed me the photos he'd taken of the body. Rudyard was never going to print them, but they did show one extraordinary thing. He had written in the dust on the window the letters M . . . U . . . R . . .'

'Murder,' said Auriol drily. She didn't believe it for one second.

'No,' said her friend, 'no. It could easily be the first three letters of his pet name for his wife. He called Prudence

"Murgs" because one of her names is Murgatroyd. Don't you see?'

'It could still be murder.' Auriol could be irritating like that. They'd had a few up-and-downers back in the old Admiralty days when she would vaporise some brilliant idea of Judy's with her down-to-earth practicality, then turn the proposition back upside down – just for the hell of it. 'More likely "murder" than "Murgs", and frankly neither seems very likely to me.'

This was not the way to make progress.

'You asked me,' snipped Miss Dimont, pushing her spectacles up her nose, 'what I thought. This is what I think. I think Prudence Aubrey is mentally unbalanced, I think she is probably capable of being two different people – one who loves her husband, and one who is an animal that will fight and kill to preserve her professional reputation. I have witnessed those mood swings and they are quite frightening.

'Gerry Hennessy was about to leave her for a new life, expose her washed-up career, and who knows – maybe there was another woman involved as well, it wouldn't be surprising knowing what we know now. She had to stop him in his tracks. Only she knew about his allergy to caviar.'

'No,' countered Auriol. 'You told me on the way here, members of his family as well.'

'He *had* no family. Both his parents are dead and he has no brother or sister. The only other person related to him is Marion Lake, and the way Prudence was so ready to point the finger at Marion, the more I suspect her. We don't *know* that Marion knew about the caviar, but we do know that Prudence did.'

Auriol lit the fire and they talked on as its embers burned low. Progress may or may not have been made that night, but eventually the talk went back, as it always did, to the old days. There was much fun to be had at the expense of Rusty Rhys and his erratic contribution to the war effort, but inevitably, as the evening wore on and a glass of Armagnac soothed away the terrors of the day, their conversation turned to the absent Eric Hedley.

It was as if he were in the room with them still.

'How would it be, if he were still alive?'

'We'd all be living here, I'd be running the café and you would be reporting for the *Riviera Express*. Eric would – well, he'd be married to you for a start.'

'I don't know,' said Judy, 'I don't know . . . It always had to be adventure for him – you remember his plan to sail to the Falkland Islands when the War was over.'

'To finally solve those murders – Mathew Brisbane and the others. But everyone knew that Rivero, or whatever his name was, was to blame. We heard that story so many times the record had worn thin.'

'He wanted to be sure – was Rivero a national hero, or was he a criminal? The two, as we know, Auriol, are so closely linked.'

'A long way to go to solve something which happened over a hundred years ago. The effect of which has no importance to this country at all.'

'But that was Eric,' said Judy Dimont, and they both smiled.

'He gave you the taste for investigation, though,' said Auriol, putting the cork back in the Armagnac bottle.

Miss Dimont knitted her brow and thought back to those subterranean days and nights in the old Admiralty building. 'I think it was when we thought we had sight of those contemptible men who betrayed our side.'

'Stanley, Homer, Hicks and Johnson.' The traitors' names slid like serpents from Auriol's mouth.

'Well, Eric was right about two of them. Sooner or later we'll know about the others. *And* all the rest.'

With that, the two women rolled up their memories like a groundsheet, extinguished the lights and said goodnight. Miss Dim gave one last glance at the photograph on the mantlepiece, but her last thoughts before sleep were for Mulligatawny, fed and put to bed by her lovely neighbour opposite, Mrs Purser. She wished him pleasant dreams and good mouse-hunting.

*

Betty was in the office bright and early. Her path just happened to take her past the editor's door and she popped her head in.

'Morning, Mr Rhys.'

'Rrrr.'

'I think I've got the splash for you, Mr Rhys.'

'Rrr-rr.'

'The bowls club last night. You can't believe what happened!'

'The womenfolk walked out,' said the editor, without raising his eyes from the page-proof he was reading.

'Oh!' squeaked Betty, perplexed. 'How did you—'

'*If you had bothered*, Miss Featherstone, to read my memo to you,' snarled Rhys, 'you would have known that in advance. Clearly you do not believe in reading missives sent by your editor.'

Betty glanced guiltily over her shoulder to her desk in the corner of the newsroom, covered in its usual slurry of paper and office debris. But she knew her editor's moods.

'Bet you didn't get the next bit, though,' she chirped. 'The women are setting up their own club, yes, but they're closing the men's club down!'

Rudyard Rhys picked up his gnarled briar pipe, inspected it suspiciously, and paused weightily.

'Make it the splash, then,' he conceded grumpily, and Betty skipped away to excavate her typewriter from the chaos.

Just then Terry popped his head round the door. Mr Rhys was always more circumspect in his dealings with photographers for they are, indeed, a race apart. One could never be sure they ever read the newspaper they worked for, yet by some strange osmotic process they acquired every last detail – usually, it was Rhys's opinion, by sitting round with cups of tea grilling the pretty secretaries and sub-editors for information about their private lives and having to absorb, *inter alia*, the daily gleanings of the newspaper.

'Miss Dim been in yet?' said Terry.

'In court this morning,' said Rhys curtly, resuming his proof-reading.

'Just to let you know then, the Hennessy story. It's murder now.'

A stricken look crossed the editor's face. 'Ohhh . . . rrr-rrr,' he groaned, as though a loved one had just passed away. 'Don't tell me . . .'

This utterance, it was understood between the two men, was merely a staying rhetorical device. Mr Rhys was not so incompetent he would turn his back on a story of such magnitude, he *did* want to be told; but his agile mind already stretched ahead to the complications of the *Express* breaking such a piece of news – the national press descending, the scrutiny of his own conduct of the story, the anger of the city fathers who forbade him, whenever they met, to write anything which damaged the reputation of gorgeous Temple Regis.

Murder. He saw the barbed-wire hurdles ahead, and he shrank from their challenge. At the same moment, he calculated he would now have to put the bowls club story on page three and face the intimidating tears of Betty Featherstone.

'Go on, then,' he said. His words chilled to frost as they left his lips. Was it the Greeks who killed the messenger? No, recalled Rhys, it was Tigranes, Emperor of Armenia who, not best pleased that the Roman commander Lucullus was coming to give him a drubbing, chopped the head off the poor messenger who brought him the necessary intelligence.

Terry was in less danger, but only because he was a photographer.

'Murdered by caviar,' he said, negligently lolling against the doorpost.

'What?'

'Never heard of it?'

'*Caviar?*' roared Rhys.

'You know,' said Terry, encouragingly. 'Fish eggs. Someone put the caviar in his sandwiches. He was allergic. Gave him a heart attack. No question, it's murder.'

'Why isn't Miss Dimont here to tell me this?'

'She's hoping to see Marion Lake during the lunch break.'

The editor looked imploringly at his photographer. It was easy to read the question in his eyes.

'Suspect,' said Terry. 'It's either her or Prudence Aubrey that did it. Miss Dim will make up her mind once she's spoken to Marion.'

Despair bathed Rhys's craggy countenance. 'And what are the police doing about—'

'No idea,' said Terry brightly. 'Not much. Time old Topham retired, I reckon. Too interested in the briefcase.'

Rudyard Rhys had not heard about the briefcase, and did not want to. 'Well, we'll need to see what they have to say about it all.'

'She'll be back after lunch,' said Terry, and wandered off to collect his cameras. It was the Townswomen's Guild annual flower show in an hour, he always got a nice cup of tea. The editor sank his head in his hands.

While this conversation was going on, the chief reporter of the *Riviera Gazette* was settling herself into the well-worn press bench in Temple Regis Magistrates' Court. Today there were representatives of the *Western Daily Press* and the *Torquay Times* alongside her – crumpled journeyman scriveners called in when there was a case which might interest their readership. The unfortunate dust-up on the seafront between some ton-up boys from Exeter who had roared into town on their motorbikes and their sworn enemies, the Torquay Teddy Boys, was just the sort of thing to give their front pages some pep.

Waiting to go into the dock were an ill-assorted group of youths, some wearing leather and others in impossibly tight trousers and strange jackets, all with their hair arranged in impossibly greased folds. They looked rather gorgeous in their lanky, ill-disciplined way, thought Miss Dimont – frightening yet curiously appealing at the same time. It must have been the same when the Vikings invaded – handsome warriors dressed to kill, both literally and metaphorically. She allowed her gaze to linger.

'Budge up,' said Kathy Greenway, a hurrumphing old dear long past retirement who got called out for specials like this. She had a superb shorthand note but her asthma sometimes made the proceedings difficult to hear.

'Your turn to get the charge sheet,' said Miss Dim, for she hated being snubbed by Mr Thurlestone the magistrates' clerk.

'Got it,' chirruped Barry Bowles, as he slid in beside them.

Barry had made it big on the *Biggleswade Chronicle* before coming down to Devon. Nobody was quite sure what had happened, but now he spent most of his time ferrying people round the harbour and only took his notebook and pen out for specials. There was something unnerving in Barry's gaze and Miss Dimont preferred not to sit next to him when he came into court.

'Look at them,' wheezed Mrs Greenway. 'Teddy boys, motor bikers – disgusting! And here in Temple Regis! If they want to kill each other with their flick-knives and bicycle chains why don't they do it in their own towns?'

Miss Dimont could see that one of the accursed tribe had been obliged to sit down. He was shaking like a leaf and clearly very nervous indeed, as if the charge of causing an affray carried with it the death sentence.

'All rise,' Mr Thurlestone barked nastily. 'The court is in session.'

In swept the Hon. Mrs Marchbank, looking quite wonderful this morning in tweed suit, pearls and maroon velvet beret perched, not too saucily, on one side of her head. She was accompanied by two elderly aldermen who you could tell were already looking forward to their lunch at the golf club.

Mr Thurlestone adjusted his disreputable wig and launched into the charges against these youths. Miss Dimont settled back, her pen at rest. While this outrageous display of martial arts on Temple Regis' seafront may be of interest to the readers of the *Daily Press* and *Torquay Times*, it would rate no more than a filler-par or NIB in the *Riviera Express*, for

Rudyard Rhys had no wish to invite more larrikins from foreign parts to come and overturn the litter bins around the bandstand, or lift up the skirts of the waitresses at Beryl's. Writing about such affairs, he believed, only encouraged them.

And so the morning passed in something of a daze. A good supper and an excellent night's sleep at Auriol's had erased the unpleasantness of her two confrontations yesterday, and Miss Dimont used the time to go over what Prudence Aubrey had said last night. As Terry had announced to the editor, once she'd seen Marion Lake she would make up her mind which woman to believe. Only then would she share her findings with Inspector Topham and her readers (though not necessarily in that order).

She emerged from her reverie to hear Mrs March delivering her magisterial findings together with a customary dash of hometown homily. The aristocratic custodian of the town's reputation spared the young men no quarter.

'You will each go to jail for three months. Take them down.'

Consternation broke out. Some of the hooligans' parents had accompanied their sons into court and their shouts and scuffles erupted in the gallery. The solicitors brought in at some expense to defend Devon's gilded youth and safeguard their liberty looked at each other and scratched their heads. On the whole, the young men took their fate reasonably well, though the blond chap Miss Dimont had spotted before looked as though he was about to be sick.

Mr Thurlestone rose swiftly and turned to speak to Mrs Marchbank, but she had already pushed back her heavy oak chair and was striding towards the door. The rosy-cheeked aldermen shuffled behind, eager for their pre-prandial gin and tonics.

The two other reporters in the bench looked at each other with surprise and delight. They had their story – jail all round for the ton-up boys! But Miss Dimont saw it differently.

'She can't do that,' she said, quite determinedly. And elbowing past her fellow-scribes, she strode purposefully towards the Bench.

TWENTY-THREE

Mr Thurlestone seemed strangely diminished without his wig. He was taking off his lawyer's gown and tabs and looked startled to see Miss Dimont's face at the door. In court Mr Thurlestone was king but here in his little rabbit-hutch of an office, in déshabille, he seemed unmanned.

'Yes?' he said, hesitantly.

'Mr Thurlestone, what has happened in your court is not allowable.' Miss Dimont saw no point in beating around the bush. 'Mrs Marchbank has passed a sentence which is as astonishing as it is plain wrong. These are all first-time offenders!'

You could see from Mr Thurlestone's corrugated brow that he knew it was so.

'However much of a nuisance it is to have Teddy boys coming to disturb the peace in Temple Regis, you cannot allow—'

The lawyer limply rallied. 'Her Honourable Worship is a lady of very firm opinions. She has many years of experience as a magistrate and Chairman of the Bench. And in any event in this decision she had the support of her fellow magistrates.'

'Those two old boys were barely awake. It's time they introduced a retirement age.'

Miss Dimont's coruscations, it must be noted, were as audacious and misplaced as Mrs March's draconian ruling – for journalists have no part in the legal process, they merely report it. But in the past she had seen the court clerk argue successfully against overly harsh sentences and wondered why he had not done so on this occasion. True, the Ton-Up boys and Teds had made a terrible nuisance of themselves on the seafront and seriously upset the local populus, but their crimes amounted to little more than an overenthusiastic exchange of opinions. A suitable punishment might be probation or suspended sentence, but jail – never.

'I wonder what the readers will make of today's ruling,' she said pointedly, meaning the injustice of it all.

'They'll be delighted,' snapped Mr Thurlestone. And he was right – Temple Regents didn't concern themselves with finer points of the law, what they minded was hooligans riding into town and staging a vulgar brawl.

Miss Dimont felt there was nothing more she could do. If the defence solicitors couldn't be bothered to save their clients from a spell behind bars, who was she to interfere? She turned impatiently to leave, but just then Mrs Marchbank's head popped round the door.

'Mr Thurlestone,' the magistrate began commandingly, before her gaze fell on Miss Dimont.

'What are you doing here?' she demanded imperiously. Clearly the place for reporters in court was on the press benches – nowhere else. She turned her head away from the offending intruder and started to speak again to her clerk, but Miss Dimont, unmoved by this aristocratic snub, decided to answer her enquiry.

'I was pointing out to Mr Thurlestone that these are not jailable offences,' she said, standing on tiptoe as if to emphasise the point – in her court shoes Mrs March was several inches taller. 'All of those young men will be released on appeal.'

'What do *you* know about—' blurted Mrs March before realising the ridiculousness of her question, for Miss Dimont was in court quite as often as she. Neither had had formal training, but both had a considerable working knowledge of the legal system.

'They'll all be out in a few days. It makes the whole process a laughing stock.'

'I really can't discuss such matters with – *you*,' snapped Mrs March, though her hand reached up to straighten her velvet beret in what was clearly a nervous motion. Her clear blue eyes, so beloved of the ancient town councillors she beguilingly patronised, narrowed sharply.

Later, as Miss Dimont tried to piece together her recollections of what happened next, she found it hard to remember at which point Mrs Marchbank completely lost her temper. Maybe it was during the reporter's cool roll-call of the many who had been sent to jail in recent months by the Chief Magistrate. Maybe it was her subsequent analysis of the necessity for the magistrates' clerk to rein in the hangers and floggers whom fate and a quiescent electorate allowed to become Their Worships.

Then again, it may simply have been merely her repetition of the word 'unlawful'. Whatever it was, it drove the Queen of Temple Regis into a tempestuous rage. The small oak-panelled room reverberated as its three occupants, each as strongly opinioned as the next, offered their version of what was right and what was wrong with the administration of justice in Temple Regis.

It slowly turned into something more gladiatorial, with Mr Thurlestone stepping back fearfully to watch the two women seek to impose their view on the other. Miss Dimont remained obstinately calm, but Mrs Marchbank's voice rose slowly up the scale as her arguments became less rational. It seemed that neither side would win the argument, but as it progressed, Mrs Marchbank's voice seemed to alter in some way, becoming harsher, shriller, less assured. Her mannerisms, too, shed much of their customary polish until the Queen of Temple Regis resembled nothing so much as old toothless Edith down the snug at the Fort.

The row was pointless, of course. The Chief Magistrate had passed sentence, and it would take the merest effort from those slothful men of the law who had parked their comfortable behinds in the defence benches to spring their charges from incarceration. Miss Dimont would write an excoriating 'Opinion' piece for the *Riviera Express* which Rudyard Rhys would water down before allowing it into print; but otherwise nothing much would come of this heated clash.

Yet for a moment the reporter glimpsed something new in the character of the woman who had reigned supreme in Temple Regis society since the War's end.

'It's as if her whole persona was just a stage act,' she told Auriol later. 'A complete transformation.'

'That's what they do, though, isn't it,' said Auriol, who despite a privileged upbringing always voted Labour. 'We have no idea how they behave at home but when they're out in public, it's always an act. You never see them other than perfectly dressed, or their manners other than completely polished. That way they maintain a respectful distance – you're respectful, they keep their distance.'

Miss Dimont thought this a bit harsh and tried to refocus on the matter in hand. 'You might almost think . . .' she started, but then plunged off into her own thoughts while Auriol kindly provided a cup of tea and a bun.

*

Hartley Radford was locked in conference with his leading light Marion Lake. She looked, as she sat on his sofa in the morning light, shorn of night-time allure, rather ordinary.

'So,' said Radford, in heartless fashion, 'you lost the father you never had.'

'Yes.'

'And now you will be taking time to get to know Prudence Aubrey in the hope you can be close friends.'

'Yes.'

'You'll be going home often to see your mother until the shock of Gerry's death subsides.'

'Mm.'

'No mention of the fortune you are likely to inherit.'

'Nn.'

'Or the fact that Gerry wouldn't let you appear in this last film of his.'

Miss Lake looked as though she had been prodded by something nasty. 'Of *course* I'm not going to mention that,' she said crossly, by now bored with this press briefing. 'Though why he refused to play opposite me . . . that part was made for me!'

'It may have been the director's decision, we have no way of knowing,' said Radford with a snakelike smile, even though he knew Gerry had threatened to walk out of the movie if his daughter were cast opposite him.

'He was so . . . *selfish*,' muttered Marion, and lit a cigarette.

'Careful. He may just have made you a very rich woman,' said Radford, as though the thought had only just occurred, adding as an afterthought, 'I'll have something to say to you about investments once the will is read.'

Marion ignored this olive branch. 'I'm on my way,' she snapped. 'I don't need his money. Though it would be nice,' she added hastily after a moment's thought.

'I remember Prudence making the same speech,' said Radford with only the merest hint of nastiness. 'Look what happened to her career. Just be careful what you say.'

'She'll be here in a minute,' said Marion, looking at her watch.

'I'm off,' said Radford. 'A few tears wouldn't go amiss.'

The nation's most admired film actress threw her agent a poisonous look. It bounced off him like a rubber balloon.

Moments later, Miss Dimont was knocking on the door of Marion's suite.

'It's only a tuppenny bus ride but sometimes it takes for ever,' she said. 'Sorry if I'm late.'

'Have a cup of coffee,' said Marion, who didn't care whether she did or didn't.

'No thank you,' said Miss Dimont, putting down her raffia bag but failing to extract the notebook which is the customary prelude to a newspaper interview. 'I want to ask you about Gerald's death.'

The actress took out a handkerchief. 'I lost the father I never had,' she said, and sniffed experimentally.

'I've been to see Prudence Aubrey,' continued an unmoved Miss Dimont, and Marion Lake faultlessly rose to her cue. 'It's time to get to know her,' she repeated faithfully, 'I hope we can become good friends.'

Miss Dimont doubted this, given the spectacular catfight at the inquest. 'Yes, yes,' she said and the lack of interest in her voice made Marion Lake realise this was not going the way she had anticipated.

'You travelled down in the *Riviera Express* with your father,' Miss Dim pressed on firmly. 'You were with him part of the time, but not all the time.'

'I was travelling with . . . someone else,' said Marion defensively. 'You know that.'

'That person never spoke to your father.'

'Given the circs—' a worldly sigh '—it would *not* have been a good idea.'

'Did you see your father eat a sandwich?'

'A sandwich?'

'Smoked salmon. Hovis.'

'I don't—'

'With perhaps a little extra garnish,' added the reporter, dangerously. 'Did you see him with a sandwich?'

'No, I don't think I did. He was learning his lines.'

'Did you, perhaps, make him a sandwich for the journey?'

Marion Lake looked puzzled. 'Me? No, why should I? If anyone was going to do that, it would have been Murgs. Er, Prudence.'

'Never put anything in his attaché case?'

'I thought this was supposed to be a newspaper interview!' exploded the actress. 'About the loss of the father I never had. That's what Mr Radford told me. About building bridges with my . . . um . . . stepmother.'

Miss Dimont smiled. What had she told the agent was the purpose of this interview? Sometimes reporters, when seeking urgently to speak to people, do not always give the right impression. It is not an admirable habit but, in the pursuit of truth, who's to say what is right and wrong?

'Your father was murdered,' said Miss Dimont, 'killed

by . . . something . . . in his sandwich. You never gave him a sandwich, you never saw his sandwiches?'

Marion reacted by lighting another cigarette from the one already in her mouth. Her hands were shaking as she did so.

'Murdered?' she whispered, in echo of her Miss Anderson in *The Cruel Are Lonely*. 'Murdered?'

Miss Dimont retraced her steps down a well-trodden path to give the actress some, but not all, of her findings. She watched closely as her narrative unfolded but could detect no agitation or alarm, merely incomprehension in the actress.

'I have the feeling you and your father did not get on particularly well,' she hazarded.

'It was fine to start with, I think he was pretty thrilled to have such a famous daughter out of nowhere. But, you know, he stopped paying the maintenance early on and my mother and stepfather used to say such horrid things about him, it was hard to forgive.

'And he didn't want it coming out that I was his child. He was reinventing himself for a new generation of fans and didn't want to be thought old enough to have a daughter of twenty-seven. And,' said Miss Lake, suddenly rallying, 'I thought we were going to do his new movie together. Suddenly he changed his mind when he inherited that money.'

'The money changed a lot of things in his life,' agreed the reporter. 'He decided to write his autobiography, to leave his wife, to alter his public image.'

'Wait a minute,' said Marion, baffled. 'When you asked if I made him a sandwich, you don't mean . . .'

'You had the motive,' said Miss Dimont very firmly. 'And the opportunity.'

'I don't know what you mean by opportunity,' snapped the actress, standing up. 'I hadn't seen him for two months before we met on the train. I arrived at Paddington just when the train was leaving – I'm always late – then I went with Mr Maltby and sat in our compartment. I popped in to see him just as the train reached Exeter to see if he was staying at the Grand, we had a few words, but he was keen to get on with his lines.'

'So you didn't see him after Exeter?'

'No.'

'Didn't give him any sandwiches?'

'I've already said I didn't,' snapped Miss Lake. 'You know – perhaps you don't know – girls with figures like mine don't keep their shape by eating bread and butter.'

Miss Dimont, who enjoyed the occasional fish-paste sandwich at tea, blinked crossly. 'So what were you doing, coming down to Temple Regis?'

'A happy weekend, darling,' sneered Marion Lake. 'Not that I'd expect you to know about such things.'

Miss Dimont gathered up her raffia bag and said goodbye. In the lift she mentally crossed Marion Lake off her list of suspects.

But only with difficulty. She was so obnoxious.

TWENTY-FOUR

Ray Cattermole stepped from the second-class carriage of the Riviera Express and looked about him. If he appeared a little jaded it was probably just his age – these little adventures never came to anything much, but they certainly took it out of you.

The once-famous actor-manager wandered languidly over to the bus stop unaware that, in his short absence from the side of Mrs Phipps, he had created a sensation for press and police. He was, according to which viewpoint you supported, either a murderer or had been murdered. Either way he was about to trigger the sort of personal publicity he had not enjoyed in half a lifetime.

Ray Cattermole was no longer, alas, young Lochinvar. As he awaited his conveyance he carried no shining broadsword, nor did his countenance offer youthful hope. Were it not for his palpable age and sagging waistline he might resemble nothing so much as a tired, naughty schoolboy needing to be sent to bed with a cup of Horlicks. Certainly Mrs Phipps was no Ellen and would not be racing away into the night with him – more likely she would be issuing a stiff talking-to across the brim of her gin glass.

All this was ahead. Now as the green and cream vehicle noisily approached, Cattermole dug in a pocket and fished out a threepenny bit for his fare.

The bus lumbered into view – like old Ray, it had seen better days, and the omnibus company should have retired it long ago. Still, it wheezed faithfully to a halt outside the station building and a single passenger alighted.

'Youm up town?' asked the conductor, displaying not the slightest shred of interest in his reply. Ray nodded queasily. He was not looking forward to explaining himself to Mrs Phipps. She was as easy-going as they come, but like all actresses she demanded attention and lots of it. Just occasionally Ray had to get away, for heaven's sake!

It wasn't just Mrs Phipps. Other factors had joined to precipitate his sudden departure from Temple Regis. That last night in the theatre had rattled him. He was doing his one-man show *My West End Life* and had just cheerily parked a trilby on his head to do his Tommy Trinder when one of the audience – there were only a handful in – got up and started heckling. Said they'd heard it all before, that half the anecdotes Cattermole claimed as his own came out of the Sunday newspapers.

It put him off. At half-time he had a drink and then decided he wouldn't go back on. He got his box-office lady Yolande to issue the refunds and sat in his office, brooding.

Old Ray had been heckled before – *Life* was never very

popular with the locals, but it was cheap to stage at the end of the season and he was generally thick-skinned enough to bear the occasional brickbat. No, what had rattled him was this Gerry Hennessy business. And then Arthur Shrimsley! Miss Dimont's double front-page stories of their deaths in the *Express* had left him with a sense of foreboding – a fear that the police might come asking questions, and worse, that his life might too be in danger . . .

*

Were she as gifted as most Temple Regents believed, Athene Madrigale might have sensed the tectonic shift which occurred in her hometown with the arrival of the 4.30 p.m. Riviera Express and the return of the bewigged native to his homeland. But at that moment she was in Lipton's buying her special tea and too busy struggling to get rid of the heavy brass coins which were weighing down her purse.

'So if I give you eight farthings and seven ha'pennies, that'll make up the difference?' she vaguely asked the shop assistant sweetly. The reply was no more than a grunt.

Athene stepped out into the sunlight, her wardrobe's luscious palette of colours creating a sudden splash in a street where most people wore variations on the colour grey. Though this was first and foremost a seaside resort, few of its townsfolk had altogether shrugged off the austerities of war and preferred to clothe themselves soberly and anonymously. Athene was given special dispensation because of who she was and what she could tell you: 'Pisces – a thrilling event is just around the corner. Prepare yourself for something special!'

She caught sight of Judy Dimont walking speedily back from the Grand Hotel, and waved across the street.

'Just got my special, dear,' she said as the two set forward towards the office. 'Got time for a cup?'

'Seem to be seeing a lot more of you in daylight these days,' said Judy conversationally. 'Normally I only see you at night.'

'Been a change, dear. I don't want to talk about it.'

Miss Dimont turned to look at her friend. 'What is it, Athene?'

Devon's most gifted astrologer suddenly stopped, and bowed her head. 'I'm losing touch,' she finally said. 'It's getting harder to read the stars. There are days, Judy, when I'm completely lost. Lost! I try to give my best, honestly, but . . .' It looked as though she was ready to burst into tears.

Her friend motioned to a bench in the market square and they sat down. This is a tragedy, thought Miss Dimont, that the town's shining light, its beacon of optimism and hope, its joyous ray of anticipation, should suddenly run out of inspiration. Her practical mind instantly hit on the solution – make it up, Athene, as the scribbled joke over the news desk tells you to do! Who, after all, was to tell what was right and wrong in her predictions? If they didn't work for one reader, they were sure to work for the next. And anyway, who could remember, next day, what their stars had foretold the previous lunchtime?

But the reporter instantly dismissed the thought. Ethereal, strange, out of place and out of time, Athene had brought a something special to Temple Regis which deserved preservation and protection.

'Would you like to come and stay the night?' she asked. 'We could have a nice long chat.'

Athene looked imploringly at her friend and nodded. 'That would be very kind.' More words might have been spoken but, just then, the green and cream single-decker of the South Devon Omnibus Company grumbled by and Miss Dimont, in the act of pushing her spectacles up her concave nose, glimpsed a familiar figure aboard.

'Athene,' she said excitedly, 'you're a genius! Look who you've brought me!'

Miss Madrigale had spotted him too. 'Raymond Cattermole,' she cried. 'I knew . . . I knew he would come back!'

Given her most recent confession, some might question the substance of that statement. However, in her presence something good had occurred, and when something good happens we all look to find the person to thank.

But Miss Dim was no longer there to issue words of gratitude. With remarkable speed she launched herself across the square, corkscrew hair bobbing in the wind, and jumped on to the bus's running-board just as it ground its gears and headed off down the hill to the seafront.

'Now, Mr Cattermole,' she called commandingly, half out of breath as she forged her way up the bus aisle, 'where have you *been*?'

The old thespian barely bothered to look up. 'Been up to London to visit the Queen,' he snapped. He knew coming back home was going to be disagreeable, but did he have to have the press harassing him even before he'd got his feet under the table?

'I wonder if you know what a fuss your absence has caused. Some people in the police force were beginning to suspect you'd been murdered. Along with Mr Hennessy and Mr Shrimsley.'

Cattermole turned white. The bus ground to a halt at some traffic lights and it looked like he might make a bolt for it.

'Erm,' he gibbered, 'erm? Murdered? What d'you mean? What's happened?'

'For a moment it looked as though you were the third victim.' Miss Dimont's wartime training was coming in very handy, for Cattermole was suddenly very rattled.

'You'd better let me know what's going on,' he spluttered. 'I've been away for three days and the world's gone mad in my absence! What I need is a . . .'

The bus stopped conveniently outside the Fortescue and the pair alighted, entered the saloon bar, and ordered drinks. Miss Dimont paid, and having scored this advantage wasted no further time.

'You were going to meet Gerald Hennessy when he came down to Temple Regis. You knew Arthur Shrimsley, and had met him recently. Both men are dead. That's no coincidence.'

Cattermole looked shiftily into his whisky. Miss Dimont intuited he was already in hot water with Mrs Phipps and did not have the reserves to put up much of a fight when it came to sharing information.

'Of course not!' he said finally. 'They knew each other of old – Shrimsley used to work in Fleet Street and used to write about Gerry when he was a stage actor in the West End.

'And *me*,' he snarled, 'there was a time when I was a bigger star than Gerry-ruddy-Hennessy and he used to write about *me*.'

'They're both dead,' Miss Dimont said stonily. 'What's the link? I think you know.'

Cattermole looked slowly round the empty bar. 'Gerald Hennessy was not all he was cracked up to be, you know,' he said. 'By the end of the war he was lording it around the place in his uniform as if he'd beaten the Nazis single-handed. It wasn't like that at all. He got called up like the rest of us but he managed to get away. He told the interview board he was an actor and had, ah, certain tendencies. To be put into a barrack-room full of rough soldiery would almost certainly bring about a return of the nervous breakdown he'd had.'

'I never heard about that,' said the reporter.

'Don't be soft,' growled Cattermole. 'There was no nervous breakdown. There were no certain tendencies.'

Miss Dimont was secretly relieved.

'But it meant his call-up was deferred and he escaped to Scotland. Pitlochry. Only after late 1942 when it looked like we had a chance of winning the war did he volunteer, and he went straight into ENSA. The rest of us had put our lives on the line for the duration but not Gerry, oh no.'

'Army Pay Corps for you, wasn't it?' asked Miss Dimont sweetly.

Cattermole ignored her. 'He came out of the war covered in glory and became every cinemagoer's dream of a war hero. Hah! Nothing could have been further from the truth.'

'What has this got to do with Shrimsley?'

'Well, they're both dead so it doesn't matter now. Arthur Shrimsley was going to ghost Gerry's memoirs. Gerry was coming down to Temple Regis to talk it all over with him and, I imagine, pop into the golf club he'd inherited from old Bill Pithers.

'Honestly,' he said angrily, 'you'd think that Gerry Hennessy was the Duke of Plaza Toro the way he waltzed around, when in fact his grandfather ran the most disgusting business in the world. Do you know, exactly, what fat-renderers do?'

It was Miss Dimont's turn to go pale and she swiftly pushed the conversation onwards with the order of more whisky from the bar.

'He inherited a huge pile of money from Pithers and didn't need to work any more,' said Cattermole bitterly. 'While some of us . . .' He paused. 'He broke my arm, you know.'

'I know.'

'It finished my career.'

'I know.'

'I used to get better notices than him, more press coverage, bigger parts. Then he broke my arm.'

'Is that why you decided to blackmail him?' asked Miss Dimont softly.

Cattermole looked stricken, like a curate caught with the Communion bottle. 'I . . . don't . . . know . . . what . . . you . . . mean,' he said, very slowly.

'No point in beating about the bush,' said Miss Dimont briskly. 'We went to Shrimsley's house and found a letter. You were going to tell Hennessy to cough up or you'd tell Shrimsley all about his draft-dodging. What would that do to his brand-new image as an actor of the people – that he spent half the War behind the reception desk at a hotel in Scotland using a walking stick as his alibi?'

Cattermole shook his head. 'Shrimsley was employed by Hennessy to write his memoirs, he wasn't going to put in a story like that. Why would he? There's no possible gloss you could put on that story and make it sound like the act of a war hero.'

'Shrimsley was a rat,' said Miss Dimont. 'He wouldn't hesitate to take Gerald Hennessy's money to write the memoirs, then sell the hotel story to his chums in Fleet Street. Just think of the headlines!'

'So yes, Mr Cattermole,' she went on, 'you were about to blackmail Gerald Hennessy.'

'Never happened. You can't prove a thing.'

'One thing I can prove is that he was murdered. And almost certainly Shrimsley too. Since there were three of you in this, isn't it just possible you may be next?'

The thought which had been lurking somewhere at the back of Cattermole's mind rose suddenly like a harvest moon and confronted him, with alarming results. He swallowed the remains of his whisky, took off his toupee and put it in his pocket.

'*Don't you say a word to anyone*,' he hissed, his eye scanning the bar for possible assassins.

'Mr Cattermole, this is a murder investigation. Nobody keeps anything from anybody – and if they do,' said Miss Dimont, pausing dramatically, 'well, you can see the likely consequences.'

The actor stumbled to the bar and brought back two drinks, both for himself. 'All right,' he said, 'OK.'

Sunshine fell through the Fortescue's stained-glass windows and splashed the table between them with a rainbow of light. 'Who killed Gerry?' he said, his eyes stretching wide. 'Who killed Shrimsley? Who's trying to kill me? What's this all about?'

'I think *you* must know the answer to that, Mr Cattermole. Why don't you start by telling me what you planned to do when you met up with Gerald Hennessy?'

'I was sick of it all. Do you know what it takes just to keep the Palace Theatre running? It's getting harder and harder to get people to come down here. They ask more and more money just to put in an appearance. They're all doing television these days, they can't be bothered with a six-week run at the end of the pier. The music halls are dead and the only people I can attract are all those out-of-work acts who were household names ten years ago but mean nothing now.'

Cattermole paused for breath. 'I gave up the West End and came here, to Temple Regis, with fire in my belly. I was angry at having my career cut short. I was going to show them all what a great actor-manager could do. And in the beginning it worked.'

Miss Dimont had her reservations about this claim, but let him speak.

'Now, it's almost impossible. I was angry with Gerry Hennessy – God,' he groaned, 'I've been angry with him ever since . . . my arm . . .'

'Go on.'

'When I heard he'd inherited Bill Pithers' fortune I just thought, Why him? Why should it always go right for him when I have to struggle from year to year, trying to keep my head above water?' He was becoming more and more tense as he spoke, his fists scraping the table, pushing the whisky glasses to one side.

'Did you mean to kill him?'

'What?'

'Did you mean to kill Gerald Hennessy?'

Cattermole barely paused before he gave his answer. 'Yes.'

Miss Dimont froze. Here came the moment of confession.

'Yes, I think I did mean to kill him. He was going to come here, to the theatre, ostensibly to take a look at the work I've been doing – maybe get a publicity photograph of the two of us together. Then I was going to go over to the golf club with him – I'm a member, you know – and show him around.

'I just had, in the back of my mind, an idea that we would take a healthy stroll down the pier at sunset and . . . over he would go . . . but I don't know,' snuffled Ray, 'I don't think

I've got it in me. Doing a scene where you're supposed to kill someone is all very well, and you can even fool yourself sometimes that you really mean to do it. But in real life . . .' He shook his head, and his shoulders slumped dejectedly.

'So it was blackmail instead.'

'He could afford it,' said Cattermole, rallying.

'You told Shrimsley about Pitlochry, why?'

'I knew he had contacts in Fleet Street. I wanted to find out how much he could make from selling the story, then I was going to tell Gerry, and ask him for double.'

'Shrimsley could have sold the story without coming back to you at all.'

'I hadn't thought of that.'

There was a pause.

'So,' said Miss Dimont, coolly appraising the man opposite, 'instead of your killing Gerry, someone else did it. Then Shrimsley. Who could it be, and why?'

Before he could answer Miss Dimont went on, 'You know Prudence Aubrey. You and she were . . . close . . . once upon a time. You know her well. Was it her?'

'How did he die?' asked Cattermole.

Miss Dimont told him. The bald-headed man laughed bitterly, twice, and fished in his pocket for the toupee. On it went again.

'Typical of Gerry,' he said bitterly. 'To be murdered by caviar! And him the grandson of a fat-renderer! I suppose it would have been too much to hope that he might have choked on a pork chop!'

'Who had the motive, who had the means? Apart from Prudence Aubrey?'

'I'll let you into a little secret,' said Cattermole, leaning forward.

'Yes, Mr Cattermole?'

'When I . . . knew . . . her, there was nothing she liked better than to go to Bertram Mills' circus and watch the wild beasts being tamed with a whip. You know those long fingernails of hers? She once just raked them down my cheek, no particular reason. Drew blood, left scars. She has a cold, cruel streak – mark my words.'

'You think she could have killed her husband, and then Shrimsley? Why Shrimsley?'

'Stands to reason,' said Cattermole. 'Even with Gerry dead, Shrimsley could still produce the biography she was dreading which would reveal the ghosts from her past. All those dressing-room secrets! But with both of them gone, the story would be buried with them. What's more, as the grieving widow of Britain's most popular film actor, what do you think the chances were of her stalled career taking off again?

'Of course,' said Cattermole with force, his eyes hard now, 'it was Prudence Aubrey. Who else?'

TWENTY-FIVE

It was rare for Betty to do The Calls. For one thing she was so easily distracted – someone might stop her in the street for a chat and she would forget the council offices, or the Magistrates' Court, or the police station – and she almost always forgot the great wooden board outside the Corn Exchange where Miss Dimont never failed to find a story.

This morning there was much on Betty's mind. Claud Hannaford had asked her to go away for the weekend, but on the other hand there was the Ladies' Inner Wheel reception on Friday night where she had met some very nice company in the past. And then there was the hockey on Saturday.

She had come up with a perfectly good front-page story – the ladies of Bedlington Bowls Club! – which was now being threatened by more of this Hennessy nonsense. What was it Claud had been telling her about it? Just as she was wandering into the cobweb-filled room which was her memory, Betty saw ahead of her Perce, the telegraph-boy, and quickly swerved across the road to the other pavement. Just in case.

She had to re-cross the road to make her way on to the

police station, and wondered if people had seen her execute this unusual manoeuvre, and if so, had been able to guess why. The trouble with Betty was she spent too long looking in the mirror and pondering; it had made her place in the universe more central than perhaps it actually was.

The station was looking gloomier than usual, which was saying something. One could never imagine the excitements of, say, *Dixon of Dock Green* occurring behind this uninspiring façade. There never seemed to be anybody about when Betty made her occasional calls and her imagination did not allow her to hope that stories were there, just for the asking.

After a longish wait, Sergeant Gull made his appearance accompanied by the usual lengthy discourse on the perils of allotment ownership. Clearly there was nothing to be had here, and Betty was making her farewells when he stopped her.

'You want a Page One story?' said Gull, mischievously.

Betty wanted nothing more.

'This Hennessy business,' said Gull, in no rush to part with the goods.

'Yes, Sergeant?'

'Fellow by the name of Radford was arrested last night. The charge is murder.'

Betty sat down hard. Her notebook, which had lain dormant in her handbag for most of the morning, was hauled out and a new page rapidly found. 'Who is he? What is this in connection with?'

Gull looked down pityingly on Miss Featherstone. The

times her name had appeared in prominent type on the front page of the town's only newspaper marked her, in most people's minds, as a leading practitioner in the dark arts of journalism, but Gull knew different. By now it was common knowledge that the champagne-quaffing lounge lizard holed up in the Grand Hotel was the agent not only of the murdered Gerald Hennessy but also of the town's most glamorous visitor, Marion Lake.

Furthermore, how many murders had there been in the parish of late? A quick sum of one + one might lead a competent reporter to the conclusion that the police thought Hennessy had been murdered by his agent, but for Betty it took a moment for the penny to drop.

'Hennessy . . . was murdered . . . by his agent?' She struggled with the words.

'Arrested last night by Inspector Topham. He'll be making a statement at lunchtime.'

It was as if all Betty's birthdays had come at once. This was the Page One of all Page Ones! She had dreamed often of leaving this life behind and arriving at last in Fleet Street – now here was her moment! And, as she raced back to the office to tell the editor, some small voice within sang with joy that she had beaten Miss Dimont at her own game. She had nabbed the story Miss Dim had been struggling so hard to get, she, Betty Featherstone!

Betty Featherstone of the *News Chronicle* here, Your Grace . . .

Miss Featherstone of the *Daily Herald,* if you don't mind . . .

Make way there! Featherstone here – Featherstone of the *Daily Sketch* . . .!

Rudyard Rhys had no idea how soon he was to lose the most talented and energetic member of his editorial staff. Otherwise her appearance at his door might have been greeted with a greater enthusiasm, tinged – possibly – with an expression of regret.

'Finally, Mr Rhys,' Betty almost sighed, as she lolled against the doorpost. '*Finally* . . .'

'Rr.'

'The Hennessy story, Mr Rhys.'

'Rr . . . rr.' The editor was doing battle with his pipe. It was not a good time.

'Could you just listen for a moment, Mr Rhys?'

Rudyard looked up and stared at his reporter. 'It's the splash,' he said, his tone making clear the editor's decision was final. 'Your bowls club story has been put back to page three.'

It took a moment for ecstatic Betty to gather her wits sufficiently to impart the latest developments, and indicate that Mr Rhys could take Judy Dimont's name off the story. She was going out now to cover Inspector Topham's statement – this story was hers from now on!

Rhys, who did not always feel he was in charge of the newspaper he ran, allowed her to scamper away. As he absorbed what Betty had told him he slowly prepared himself for the onslaught to come – the angry city fathers, the attack-dogs of Fleet Street who'd come and snootily requisition his offices, the loss of calm routine – and he called for his chief reporter.

'Coming,' trilled Judy, who'd only just returned to her desk.

The angry scenes which followed behind closed doors are part and parcel of everyday newspaper life. Accusations are hurled, recriminations vented, past failures revisited, human frailties dwelt upon and always, in the air, the noxious whiff of resignation. Miss Dimont emerged from their editorial conference in a state of turmoil.

She went in search of Athene.

*

Back at the station Betty was stirring her cup of Camp coffee and looking up into the eyes of Inspector Topham, seated opposite her in the police canteen. Other police forces laid on more lavish hospitality – biscuits too – if they had something to impart to the press which made them look good, but Temple Regis was limited in its resources, and Topham's press conference to announce an important arrest amounted to this – a cup of undrinkable coffee in the canteen with Betty. No other representatives of Her Majesty's fourth estate were present, for the simple reason the town had only one newspaper.

'Man aged forty-eight was arrested last night at the Grand Hotel in connection with the death of Gerald Hennessy,' he announced, with just the hint of smugness.

'Name and address?' Betty had never before taken down such thrilling information, but she knew the ropes.

'Hartley Radford, 13 Laurel Mansions, Primrose Hill, London. His actual name is Ronald Smith.'

'And he was Gerry Hennessy's agent?'

'That's correct.'

'And the charge against him?'

'We'll see when he gets into court, but we're not accusing him of cycling without lights.'

'Murder,' whispered Betty.

'You may very well assume that,' said Topham with a syrupy smile.

'Gosh, Inspector,' said Betty, laying down her pencil and looking through her eyelashes at her passport to fame, 'how brave you are! Were there lots of you went to arrest him?'

'Just me,' said Topham. He was enjoying this.

'But he might have . . . I don't know . . . he could have . . . Oh, you are brave, Inspector!'

As a matter of fact Frank Topham *was* brave, and had the medals to prove it. But there is nothing nicer than to be reminded of it, especially by a pleasant young woman who was so very much the opposite of the bespectacled reporter who usually dogged his footsteps.

'Anything else you'd like to know?' he asked invitingly.

'Well, of course, you've given me all that we can print – name, age, address, circs of the arrest and the possible charge. But,' said Betty, thinking now of the *News Chronicle* job coming her way, 'can you give me a little background? For use after the trial?'

'Early days yet,' said the inspector, but he didn't see why not. Now that Radford was behind bars there was little more he needed to do until court late this afternoon.

'The coroner ruled that he died of a heart attack,' said Betty, who it turns out had been listening to Miss Dimont after all. 'So how come Mr Radford, er, Smith, is to be charged with murder?'

'I didn't use the word "murder", Miss Featherstone, but yes. Radford administered poison in the form of fish eggs – or, as some people call it, caviar. Mr Hennessy did die of a heart attack but it was brought on by the fish eggs.'

'Go on,' said Betty, batting her eyelids furiously and hoping the inspector hadn't noticed she had taken up her pencil again.

'We retrieved the lost attaché case of Mr Hennessy,' said Topham, putting something of a gloss on the facts. 'When I opened it, I discovered various remnants of a sandwich which, when sent to the analyst, turned out to be salmon eggs – red caviar. From the breadcrumbs also retrieved it was possible to ascertain that the sandwiches had contained smoked salmon. He wouldn't have eaten a sandwich which contained only red caviar.'

'Why, Inspector?'

'Well,' said Topham, 'his widow – Prudence Aubrey, you know – confided in me that Mr Hennessy had an aversion, an allergy, to fish eggs which rendered him vulnerable to anaphylactic shock if he ate them. Heart attack, d'you see?'

'So someone hid the fish eggs in his smoked salmon sandwiches?'

'Precisely.'

'And that someone was Hartley Radford?'

'In cases like this,' said Topham, who'd never handled a case like this, 'you look for motive, means and opportunity. Those were not difficult to find.'

Indeed not – sharing a glass or two of Prudence Aubrey's champagne last evening, the inspector had been helpfully provided with all three. Curling her legs up on her sofa and allowing him to act as her butler, the actress scattered clues aplenty before her admiring interlocutor.

Radford, who had some time ago discontinued his professional relationship with Miss Aubrey – he could see she was on her way out – was clearly no favourite of hers. The motive, she happily explained, was that Radford had been milking Gerry's bank accounts for years and, though Gerry knew it, Radford was afraid his actions might be exposed in the forthcoming memoirs. Their relationship had deteriorated and with Gerry's new-found wealth, he could afford himself a new agent who was less sticky-fingered.

The means – Radford, as Gerry's agent, knew all about the allergy to fish eggs and had covered for him when he'd collapsed on the previous occasion.

The opportunity – shouldn't the inspector check whether Radford had accompanied Gerry to Paddington Station on his last fateful journey? Given him the sandwiches for his lunch?

Topham had fortified himself with a second glass of Prudence's Veuve Cliquot ('Not *again*, Stanley!') and walked across the hall to Radford's suite. The ensuing conversation lasted no more than twenty minutes and convinced the inspector he had got his man. Radford, taken aback at Topham's attack on his integrity, agreed to continue the conversation down at the station and there he was later arrested.

Betty's pencil came to a standstill. 'Murder By Caviar' was the screamer – front-page headline – she dreamed up for herself, a headline which would grace her exclusive story when she was newly installed in Fleet Street. She felt like kissing the inspector.

For now, the rules of court reporting allowed her only a limited number of facts regarding Radford's sensational arrest, but these could be dolled up with innocuous background information – the clothes he wore, the suite he had taken at the Grand, the list of illustrious clients which read like a *Who's Who* of the British cinema. She couldn't wait to get back to the office.

When she did so she found that Miss Dimont, anticipating her arrival, had helped clear up the mess on her desk and had even provided Betty with a cup of tea. 'Athene's miracle cure,' she said nicely enough.

Betty was not quite sure how to take these generous acts. She had stolen Judy's story and made it her own – and now, possession being nine points not only of the law but of journalism, the story would be hers until Radford went to trial, was found guilty, and sentenced to be hanged. The Hennessy case was, at last, her big break!

Miss Dimont, she could tell instinctively, was covering some hurt. Given her fiery relationship with Mr Rhys, it was likely that there had been an exchange of views, and by the look of it the chief reporter had not come out of it very well. She seemed to have lost her perpetual bounce.

'If you need any help, dear,' said Miss Dimont, as Betty threaded her copy-paper sandwich into her typewriter – and by the sound of it, she meant it.

'I can't believe it,' said Betty. 'A real scoop, murder on our doorstep – the most famous actor in the land murdered, by his agent. Unbelievable!'

'That's right,' said Judy Dimont, almost to herself. 'Unbelievable. He didn't do it.'

Betty wasn't listening.

TWENTY-SIX

For others it might be a bitter pill to swallow, to have your story stolen by a trusted colleague, and then be made to add extra paragraphs to it. But then for that someone else to take all the glory is like landing on that square in Monopoly where you go to jail *and* are fined £40.

But as ever, Miss Dimont rose above. The editor had sent her to court to cover the remand hearing, not as a punishment for wasting company time on her ill-founded theories, but because she had a better shorthand note than Betty and could be trusted not to miss a single drop of information that was allowable in law to be published.

As every cub reporter knows, at a remand hearing only skeleton details are permitted to be reported as a precaution against prejudicing a forthcoming trial. But there are ways and ways of building up a picture for the readers – and for sure, *Riviera Express* subscribers would want to have every last morsel from this quite extraordinary turn of events. Miss Dimont was adept at describing the clothes and behaviour of the accused, the atmosphere in court, even the demeanour of the prosecuting counsel, solicitor or policeman – details which could never prejudice a trial jury against the accused (should they even read them), but which were meat and drink to *Express* readers. The more detail she could legitimately squeeze from the proceedings, the happier her editor would be.

But Rudyard Rhys was happy already. Today was Thursday, press day, and the story would lead his newspaper's front page the following morning. No national press were aware of Radford's arrest, and they would only learn it through the pages of the *Riviera Express*. Naturally, as its editor, Rudyard Rhys would be taking the full credit as his nationwide scoop was gradually followed up by *The Times* and its lesser brethren.

The court was empty when Miss Dimont arrived at 4.30 p.m., though fairly soon Mr Thurlestone came in and slid his eyes towards the press bench. He and Miss Dimont looked at each other, and tacitly agreed to put yesterday's business between them to one side. Life was long in Temple Regis, and for the forseeable future these two players in a bigger drama would be meeting twice a week in this very room. It was best to make up.

Soon the motley handful of people who inhabit Magistrates' Courts with no definable role found themselves seats, Inspector Topham took his place in the front bench, and two prison warders brought Hartley Radford up into the dock.

The accused looked remarkably fresh. His night in the cells, away from his daily intake of champagne and cigars, had if anything put a spring in his step. He looked not the least apologetic at having brought together, at a time when they should have been sitting down to their tea, this disparate group of players and onlookers.

'All rise,' barked Mr Thurlestone. The door behind the bench opened and in walked two old warhorses, their faces pink from the late summer sunshine they had so recently been enjoying in their gardens. Behind them came their chairman.

But no, it was not Mrs Marchbank! Miss Dimont could not believe her eyes. How could the town's self-appointed scourge of wrongdoing miss an opportunity like this, to send onward to his ultimate destruction a man who so wilfully had robbed one of Britain's best-loved characters of his life? Where on earth could she be?

Instead in her place was Colonel de Saumarez, a man of immense rectitude and beautifully pressed tweed suits. The accused might well be assured of a fair hearing from him.

'You are Ronald Hartley Smith, also known as Hartley Radford?'

'I am,' said Radford, who didn't seem to mind anybody knowing.

'You live at 13 Laurel Mansions, Primrose Hill, London?'

'I do.'

'State your age.'

'Forty-eight.'

'Ronald Hartley Smith, you are charged that on the twelfth of September of this year you did wilfully murder Gerald Victor Midleton Hennessy. How do you plead?'

A smooth-looking fellow in dark jacket and striped

trousers eased himself languidly to his feet and said, 'Your Worship, I represent Mr Radford whom you charge as Smith. He will plead not guilty.'

Colonel de Saumarez peered down his nose at this stranger in his town. He did not like what he saw. Like the accused, the barrister was clearly from London and that did not count in his favour.

'You are?' he said, uninterestedly.

'Henry Montagu, senior counsel.'

'Mm,' said the colonel, this monosyllable loaded with ambiguity. The ensuing battle over Hartley Radford's liberty was not helped by the mutual contempt shooting like electric currents across the bench, and despite Mr Montagu's perfectly reasonable arguments as to the probity of his client and of his personal guarantee that he would turn up for the trial, Radford was remanded in custody for a week.

'I'd like the usual reports,' said the colonel importantly to Mr Thurlestone, as if he knew more about the law than Mr Montagu. Thurlestone nodded and straightened his wig.

And that was that. All Miss Dimont had to do now was convert this dull exchange of meagre information into magical prose which would transform an automatic, almost robotic, event into high drama. But she was good at that.

Back in the office she sought out Betty to let her know what she'd be writing to accompany the star reporter's own version of events. 'You know,' she said, as they settled down with a cup of tea, 'the oddest thing was that Mrs March wasn't in court. I can't understand it – she wouldn't miss the opportunity to give Radford a bit of a lecture about behaving himself when in Temple Regis – you know the usual thing.'

Betty nodded, but in truth she did not know. She avoided court reporting because it made her go to sleep. And then she would be in trouble with the editor.

But not for much longer! Soon, oh let it be soon, she would be in Fleet Street!

Just then Terry appeared behind the desk and whispered in Judy Dimont's ear. The pair of them left Betty to finish her report and stepped together out of the newsroom.

'You heard what Topham's gone and done?' said the reporter as they stood at the top of the stairs.

'Got the wrong man,' said the photographer.

That was Terry for you – no information, yet he came up with the right answer. It infuriated her.

'I think the old inspector was nobbled by Prudence Aubrey,' she said crossly. 'He's sweet on her.'

'We're all sweet on her. That twirl!'

'Oh pipe down, Terry!'

'Don't see too many like her around this parish,' he said, waggling his eyebrows.

'Concentrate!' ordered Miss Dim crossly. 'She was dropped by Radford because her career was stalling. This is her revenge, her chance to plant it on someone else.'

'Not necessarily,' he said, but he seemed more interested in polishing his camera lens than in the conversation.

'Well, all I can say is we're going to look pretty stupid tomorrow when our paper points the finger of suspicion at the wrong man. We'll have Fleet Street down here again, pulling the story apart, coming up with the real murderer.'

'We're going to the town hall now,' said Terry, changing the subject. 'You taking Herbert, or coming in the Minor?'

Miss Dimont sighed in a frazzled sort of way.

'Come with me,' said Terry kindly, sensing her frustration, 'we can pop into the Grand afterwards. A nice gin and tonic.'

The couple sailed down the stairs, steeling themselves for the task ahead – of finding a new way to tell the town, for the umpteenth time, how magnificent it was.

The town hall was a bit like a wedding cake – built a hundred years ago by city fathers who dreamed one day all Temple Regis would look like this. Its crenellations, stained glass, over-elaborate door handles and wealth of plasterwork were a grim reminder of Victorian grandiloquence at its maddest, but Terry and Judy, immune to its excesses, strolled through its elaborate doorway and headed for the council chamber where a party was being held to celebrate the end of the holiday season. The high point of the evening would be when the mayor revealed how successfully Temple Regis had seen off all competition to be the county's favourite seaside resort. It was the same story every year.

Terry and Judy were there out of duty, not interest, and readily accepted a glass of sherry each while they awaited the speeches.

'Hear you and the memsahib had a bit of a dust-up,' said a voice in her ear. She turned to find Patrick Marchbank, the chairman of the Rural District Council, looking down with an amused smile on his face.

'Well, you know . . .' said Miss Dimont, somewhat at a loss. Lord Mount Regis's younger brother was an old charmer, and she had written many paragraphs extolling his even-handed management of the Watch Committee. She liked Mr March just as much as she cordially disliked his wife, but she was far too polite to make any criticism.

Marchbank elegantly smoothed back his silver hair and gave her a grin. 'She's been having a rough time of it lately,' he said. 'Not quite herself.'

'I'm sorry to hear it,' said Miss Dim, not really very sorry.

'You're a writer,' said Marchbank, 'what do you know of biographies?'

'I've always liked Boswell's *Life of Samuel Johnson.*'

'History as biography, hmm. But what I meant was – when people decide to tell their life-story. Memoirs, d'you know what I mean?'

'People who tell their own story usually leave the best bits out,' said Miss Dimont. 'People who write someone else's life never really get the whole story. Neither is very satisfactory. You're better off with a novel.'

'Ah, yes. Well, I see your point.'

Terry had wandered off. This was not his kind of conversation at all.

'It's just – I think Mrs Marchbank has been overly worried about the death of a cousin and oh, I don't know, the possibility of some things being said. She's a very sensitive woman, you know.'

'Yes,' said Miss Dimont, uncaring of Mrs March's frailty.

'Her cousin – he was impetuous, you know. Looked solid as a rock but very impetuous. You couldn't be certain what he would do next.'

'Mm.'

'And then when he said he was going to write his memoirs, there was no knowing what he might say. I mean,' added Patrick Marchbank, 'he was always very nice to me. But he and Adelaide . . .' His voice trailed off as the mayor's sergeant rapped his gavel and prayed silence for His Worship.

The proceedings took their usual course – long, self-congratulatory, repetitive. Temple Regis was indeed the jewel of the English Riviera, etc., etc., and Miss Dimont's shorthand flew across the page. But while she scribbled her mind was elsewhere – looking, searching, teasing out hidden facts and long-lost scraps of information. When the speeches were over, she went in search of Mr March, now deep in conversation with a large lady in a black hat (so inappropriate on a sunny day, thought Miss Dimont) and begged a further word.

'Mrs Marchbank's cousin. May I ask who that is?'

'Was. He's dead now. It was all over your front page.'

'Not . . .?'

'Gerald Hennessy.'

Miss Dimont went white. Terry arrived just in time to grip her elbow and guide her towards fresh air.

'I've been stupid, so stupid,' she gasped, as he found her a glass of water.

'Not for the first time,' said Terry blandly. 'Remember the time you—'

'Pipe down, Terry. I've been heading in the wrong direction all this time. Come on.'

'The Grand? Or would you prefer the Fortescue?'

'No, no, no,' said Miss Dimont impatiently. 'You come with me!'

Terry unlocked the Minor and they drove off. Miss Dimont did not stop talking.

*

Lummacombe Manor stood at the far end of the Mount Regis estate, occupying a breathtaking position on top of a small knoll looking far out to sea. Its drive led up from the hamlet of Lummacombe past fields newly harvested and ploughed, the red Devon earth like blood spilled profligately across the landscape.

At the cattle grid, where Terry slowed the Minor, Judy Dimont captured a glimpse of the seascape below. Clouds, which had momentarily shrouded the sun, allowed enough of its rays through to cast a brilliant shaft of light on the water below, turning the surface into an iridescent mirror which sent the sun's rays back upwards as if returning a lover's glance. The broad estuary was filled with small boats at anchor, still but animated, like dogs patiently awaiting a walk with their master.

Across the valley the church bell struck seven and seagulls chattered in the air, diving and swooping for no good reason. There could be no more heavenly place.

The manor house stood low and sturdy ahead, and as the Minor crunched its way into the large gravel circle laid out before it, a grey cat ran across its path. Otherwise there was silence.

'Go round the side,' said Terry, who had an instinct on such occasions.

'I think we have to be firm,' said Judy, and Terry nodded. He knew what she meant.

As they turned the corner of the old stone house there stretched before them a perfectly shorn greensward which seemed to end in infinity, its furthermost edge disappearing into the greying horizon. At a wooden table on a small terrace sat Adelaide Marchbank, perfectly still, her features partly obscured by large dark glasses.

'Don't you know this is private property,' she said, a statement rather than a question. She had not even turned her head. 'Go away.'

It was difficult to judge whether Mrs March was looking at them or at the sheaf of papers in front of her. Terry and Judy continued their advance towards the table.

'Go AWAY,' snarled Mrs March, 'or I shall call the police.'

'They're on their way,' said Miss Dimont quite curtly. 'I think you may have some clue as to why.'

'Those . . . hobbledehoys who came to Temple Regis looking for a fight. Maybe they will get out on bail, but a short
sharp shock is what they needed. I have no regrets.'

'No,' said Miss Dimont. 'This is about something else.'

'Their solicitors could have appealed at the time. I think
they were happy to see their clients go to jail. Now that
National Service is coming to an end, they have to learn
discipline somehow.'

Miss Dimont ignored this. 'Can you tell me why you
weren't in court this afternoon for the remand hearing?'

Mrs March did not look at her. 'There is no obligation for
the Chairman of Magistrates to be present at every sitting.
Colonel de Saumarez is a very competent man.'

'The remand was on account of the murder of Gerald
Hennessy.'

'I am perfectly aware of that.'

'Your cousin.'

There was a long silence. 'Yes,' said Mrs March finally,
cautiously, as if opening a door on a dark night to see who
was there.

'You might have said that you could not sit on the Bench
because of a family involvement.'

'I might, but I didn't. It's really none of your business.
You know, people always complain about press intrusion
. . . I have never taken their side. But now I begin to see what
they mean. Has your editor, that Mr . . .'

'Rhys.'

'Has Mr Rhys sent you here to harass me?'

'No. He doesn't know I'm here.'

Mrs Marchbank took off her dark glasses. Her eyes were hard. 'Then I shall telephone him and tell him to instruct you to leave my property. I will not be harassed by . . . a court reporter who quite clearly has a personal animus against me. You've got a bee in your bonnet. She's got a bee in her bonnet!' she railed, turning to Terry for support.

'That's not true.'

'Yes it is. Look at your behaviour yesterday in Mr Thurlestone's room. All those critical pieces in you opinion pages. Quite inaccurate. Quite contemptible!'

'There is such a thing as fair comment,' said Miss Dimont, unmoved by the magistrate's chilly hauteur. 'But I am here to ask you questions about the death of Gerald Hennessy.'

'That's quite improper. I am a magistrate. I know the law. And I know that you are trespassing. If you don't leave now, I shall—'

The clear air was punctured by the sound of car tyres on the gravel.

'Topham,' said Miss Dimont. Terry nodded and wandered off.

For a moment the two women eyed each other combatively, but before anything untoward could occur Terry returned accompanied not only by Inspector Topham and his two anonymous henchmen but by Mrs March's husband, wiping his brow with a silk handkerchief.

'What is this?' panted Patrick Marchbank as he approached, more in alarm than anger. 'I tell you my wife isn't well and you come all the way out here and start badgering her. It really won't do!'

Miss Dimont turned her back to the horizon and addressed the small group gathered round the old oak table. 'I regret to say, Mr Marchbank, that I asked Inspector Topham to come here to arrest Mrs Marchbank for the murder of Gerald Hennessy. And of Arthur Shrimsley.'

Topham blinked. He already had his man. As far as he was concerned Radford was on his way to the gallows. 'I don't really think, you know . . .' he started, but then stopped. This was not the first time he and Miss Dimont had found themselves in such a situation.

'Mrs Marchbank murdered her cousin because of the book he was about to write. She then murdered Shrimsley, the book's ghostwriter, because he knew what was in the book and could very well cash in on Mr Hennessy's death.'

Miss Dimont turned to Mrs Marchbank. 'You have spent half a lifetime in Temple Regis living on a knife-edge, knowing that your grandfather, William Pithers, could at any time claim you as his own. You had built up a reputation as the town's leading light and you did not want it known that your grandfather was a fat-renderer and, let's be honest, one of the least attractive characters Devon has ever known.'

Mrs Marchbank reached for her husband's hand.

'You have lived in perpetual fear of exposure, yet people would have judged you by your works, not because of who your grandfather was. You have given a huge amount to

Temple Regis and people have reason to be grateful for all you've done.'

'Huh!' said Mrs Marchbank, and lit a cigarette.

'For the past year you have known that with the death of your grandfather things were likely to change. You and Gerald were his only remaining relatives – your mother, and Gerald's mother, are both dead. You were to share Mr Pithers' substantial fortune.'

'How do you know all this?' said Mr Marchbank, who seemed less surprised than perhaps he should.

'I'll come to that,' said Miss Dim. 'But I think you'll confirm that when you both had dinner with Mr Hennessy in London to discuss the will, he told you of the intended change in direction insofar as his career was concerned. And that to help people to look at him a new way, he was going to write his memoirs.

'The new audience he was seeking – the kitchen-sink lot, I think he called them, the people who like the plays of John Osborne and Arnold Wesker – would be thrilled to learn that he wasn't so upper-crust after all. That despite playing all those public-school types in the cinema, his grandfather was in fact a fat-renderer.'

'I can't see why . . .' said Mr Marchbank, with genuine puzzlement.

'The memoirs would inevitably involve the tale of his mother and her sister, who fled the family home after a childhood of abuse and horror. That sister,' said Miss Dimont, 'was your mother, Mrs Marchbank.'

Inspector Topham looked embarrassed. He couldn't yet see where this was going.

'As if the worry about your origins weren't enough, you were concerned about your husband's family too. Lord Mount Regis has no children, and Mr Marchbank will inherit the title. That would make you Lady Mount Regis, and the joint head of an ancient family. You did not want them all knowing about Mr Pithers and his fat-rendering business.'

'My husband knows everything about my family,' retorted Mrs March. 'I have never tried to conceal my origins from him.'

'Not from him, but you never wanted anyone else to know. Gerry Hennessy was about to blow that secret sky-high.'

'That doesn't mean I murdered him. What a ridiculous idea!'

'The night before he died, he had a row with Prudence – over the way he was conducting his personal life, but also about this wretched book. He walked out – and came to stay with you in your London flat.'

Mr Marchbank shot his wife a sharp look.

'He told you that night he was coming down to see Mr Shrimsley to get going on the first chapter and – let me guess – he said he was going to start off with his childhood memories of running around the fat-rendering factory amongst all the dead carcasses and entrails and boiling fat with his cousin – you.'

'You can't possibly know that.'

She didn't – she was taking a chance. 'In the morning

you said you'd make him a sandwich for the journey and nipped across the road to Fortnum's to buy not only the smoked salmon, but the salmon caviar. You went back to the flat, made him the sandwich, then left and caught an early train back to Temple Regis. I know that,' said Miss Dimont, cutting short an interjection from Mrs Marchbank, 'because Mr Mudge kindly told me.

'There was only half a chance your plan would work. He might not have wanted the sandwiches. You may not have concealed the caviar well enough. He may have eaten them and suffered no more than a blackout. But I suspect if he survived that first attempt on his life, you had other plans.

'As it is, you were successful. Gerald Hennessy ate the sandwiches and almost immediately suffered anaphylactic shock. The pathologist was too lazy – or too much in awe of this public figure he had under the knife – to analyse the contents of his stomach and draw a proper conclusion.'

She turned to Topham. 'Inspector, I think we have our murderer.'

The inspector nodded, for though Mrs Marchbank remained rigid and aloof, no words of protest or denial were issuing from her lips. 'But Shrimsley?' he said.

'Ah, yes, Shrimsley. I will say this for Mrs Marchbank, she is resolute. When she decides upon a course of action, she gets on and does it. She had telephoned Shrimsley from the London flat on the morning of his death and presumably told him some tale which might add spice to the fat-rendering anecdotage. She asked him to meet her off the train and she drove him in her car to Mudford Cliffs.

'They went for a walk along the cliff edge – we'd had a big story in the *Express* the week before about how dangerous they were – and my guess is Mrs Marchbank encouraged him behind the barrier so they were out of sight of any dog-walkers who might stroll by.

'With it being so unstable underfoot, it wouldn't have taken much of a push to send him over. Shrimsley tried to cling on, but it was lunchtime and he'd already had some drinks. He managed to grab hold of Mrs Marchbank's scarf and—' she turned to Terry '—that's what we saw in the photograph you took. It wasn't a letter, it was a piece of Mrs Marchbank's scarf. What was left was found by Captain Hulton.'

Mrs Marchbank put a hand to her throat. 'Yes,' said Miss Dimont, 'the scarf was round your neck. It must have been a difficult struggle before the cliff gave way under him.' Mrs Marchbank looked up, glanced around hysterically at her husband, reached out to him, then started to sob.

'Mrs, er, Marchbank,' started Inspector Topham, unsure of the correct etiquette when collaring the sister-in-law of a peer – does one use Honourable? Or is what she has done so dishonourable the title is superfluous? – but he forged manfully ahead. 'Mrs Marchbank, I am arresting you on suspicion of causing the unlawful deaths of Gerald Hennessy and Arthur Shrimsley. Anything you say may be taken down and used in evidence.'

The accused stared out to sea, her back straight, her eyes brimming. 'I did it for you, Patrick,' she said very slowly. 'You have always been so kind to me. All our lives together. I could not allow the Mount Regis title to be allied with . . . that man Pithers. He was a scoundrel, a liar, a fornicator and a cheat. And he was my grandfather.

'If it had come out, what would people say? Especially since your brother is dying and you will inherit the title soon. Oh, Patrick . . .'

Her husband took her hand. 'I have said to you,' he almost whispered, 'how many times have I said to you that it doesn't matter who your people were? You have done a wonderful job representing my family in the town over all these years. Why did you have to kill Gerry? Nobody would have taken the slightest bit of notice of what he said in his memoirs – he was an *actor*, you know. Not of the real world.'

'You will never understand,' said his wife. 'Your family history stretches back to the Domesday Book. You know who you are, nobody can dislodge you. People like me, however long we live alongside you, spend our lives constantly worrying we will do or say something which doesn't quite chime. Old families are so very tribalistic – they view with suspicion anybody who comes to join them. I've always felt that.'

There was a long silence.

Topham courteously said he would accompany Mrs Marchbank so she might get her coat and pack a small bag. Marchbank said he would come along too. The two plain-clothes men marched back to their car, and Terry turned to Miss Dimont.

'You know,' he said, 'you're a ruddy marvel, you are!'

'Oh Terry,' said Miss Dimont. 'It's horrible – so sad. She killed out of shame – shame of who she was. You can see the only thing she ever wanted to do was live up to her husband's family name, she's essentially a good person – a very good person. It's tragic.'

'There, there,' said Terry, and he put his arm round her shoulders. The pair looked out to sea as the purple clouds of night gathered on the horizon, readying themselves for their long journey inland.

TWENTY-SEVEN

Athene was making the tea – '*Not* the Lipton's, dear, I save that for drinking at home – this is my special.'

Miss Dimont expressed her delight and collected the cups in preparation. Around her desk in the otherwise deserted newsroom were her dear friend Auriol, Terry, and Peter Pomeroy, the chief sub-editor whose Herculean task of re-drawing the front page was at last complete.

'Nifty headline,' mused Peter, who'd encapsulated the complex saga in two decks of Bodoni 48pt. 'But I'd rather have written MURDERED BY CAVIAR.'

'You will, Peter, you will – but there has to be a trial first.'

'Now, dear,' said Athene, bringing over the tea and some welcome Bourbon biscuits, 'you have to tell me everything. I can only see *so* far, you know.'

Miss Dimont pushed her spectacles up and took a sip. 'I made so many mistakes,' she started.

'Livin' up to your name,' cut in her photographer. 'Miss Dim.'

'Pipe down, Terry. It was such a difficult case, made all the more complicated by the disappearance of old Cattermole. All the while he was missing I thought he was dead, but trying to fit his death in with the other two meant I was aiming in the wrong direction.'

'You thought it was Prudence Aubrey,' said Auriol.

'Yes, I did. She had reason to kill all three men – Hennessy because of his desertion, Shrimsley because of his part in writing the memoirs *and* the threat that he might leak some of the contents regarding her past life to the Sunday newspapers, and Cattermole because – well,' she said, scratching at her corkscrew hair with a pencil, 'because he had been a beast to her years ago and she thought he'd told Shrimsley all about it. She clings to her reputation.

'Remember,' she went on, 'this is a highly volatile woman, as some actresses can be, Athene.' But Athene was already lifted to another plane, looking at Miss Dimont's aura, and was very pleased with what she saw. 'Yes, dear,' she said contentedly.

'She is capable of violence, certainly of violent thoughts, she even told me she had contemplated killing her husband.'

'I should have discounted her the moment those words left her lips,' said Auriol, ever the sage.

'Oh, pipe down, Auriol.'

Terry helped himself to a biscuit. 'She might have murdered

Hennessy, but how could she have pushed old Shrimsley over the cliff? She was in London.'

'She said she was, but we had no way of knowing. She has a devious mind – look how she managed to frame that odious agent Radford. Quite took Inspector Topham in.'

'Certainly made my life difficult,' said Peter Pomeroy, gazing with pleasure on his page-proof of tomorrow's *Riviera Express*. Like all deskbound journalists he wanted to write himself into the narrative. 'Imagine if the paper had gone to bed saying Radford had done it and was going to swing while all the time it was Mrs March!'

'You did a wonderful job, dear,' sighed Athene. 'And you always make my page look so nice.'

'A pleasure,' said Peter. 'My wife loves what you write. She even reads all the other star signs too. Says they give her hope.' Athene blushed.

'What about the message Hennessy left on the railway carriage window?' said Terry, still proud of having captured it with his masterful f5.6 at 1/60th. 'You know, M . . . U . . . R . . .?'

'Well, that had me scuttling around,' admitted Miss Dimont. 'When you first showed it to me, it had to say "murder". It was our first clue, remember? Later, when I suspected Prudence Aubrey, it convinced me it must be her because he called her Murgs.

'But,' she said shamefacedly, 'I had the answer all along. When I went into the carriage there was a piece of newspaper on the floor. It seemed so wrong that the death-place of someone so famous should have litter so I put it in my handbag and shoved it in Herbert's pannier basket. Only when I remembered it did I discover it was a *Daily Telegraph* crossword which Hennessy had started but not finished. I looked in it for clues, and then I came across this one – *rum conversation behind closed doors: hush-hush.*'

'Murmur,' said Auriol, quick as a flash.

'Oh Auriol, you're so *blankety* clever,' said Miss Dim, exasperated. 'Took me some time to work that one out. Poor Gerald wasn't accusing anybody when he wrote on the window, just trying out a crossword clue.'

'Just as well Topham isn't here,' said Terry, 'he'd have you clapped in irons for tampering with the evidence.'

Miss Dimont smiled. 'Inspector Topham is in many ways a wonderful man,' she said. 'Unlike many of his calling, he has humility. He was quite sweet to me about having got it wrong.

'But,' she added, 'I think that particular clue would have passed the inspector by. He is not one to spend time with a crossword.'

Athene poured more tea. 'I did for a moment consider Marion Lake. She had the motive – tangled feelings about her father, topped off with a sense of rejection because he wouldn't allow her a part in his new film. She had the opportunity – she was in the train with Hennessy when he ate his sandwiches. But you have only to look at her to see that although she's pretty competent with a script in front of the camera, she's not much good at the rest of life. Look at that unfortunate fellow she dragged down here.

'And then, of course, it could have been Cattermole. He had a deep-seated hatred of Hennessy – reckons he put paid to his career. But I don't think he has it in him.'

She paused. 'And,' she said, 'then I went back to see Captain Hulton.'

'Captain Hulton?' said Terry. 'Who's that?'

'Lives up on Mudford Cliffs. An honorary member of what he calls the She-Club – ladies who walk their dogs. He has a very sweet dachshund called Bruce. You know I never really liked dachshunds, but—'

'Yes, yes,' said Terry, who could see Miss Dimont's story taking a lengthy side-turning. 'Captain Hulton, Judy!'

'Captain Hulton is rather shy. He doesn't talk to people very much. But the She-Club are kind, and they chat to him. I went back on the off-chance that he talked to some of their number after our conversation, and they'd come up with something more.

'They had,' added Miss Dimont. 'Or, actually they hadn't.'

'Come on now,' said Auriol. 'Which?'

'The women who were out walking at midday saw a well-dressed woman with no dog. That was strange – why would a woman be up on Mudford Cliffs, that well-known dog-walking place, with no dog?

'Anyway, they said she had a smart-looking car. That same

car was back the next day – still no dog. Captain Hulton persisted, and they said it was a Wolseley.'

'There was a Wolseley in the stables at Lummacombe,' said Terry.

'And Inspector Topham found the torn silk scarf still in the glove compartment,' said Miss Dimont. 'No doubt it will match the fragment of material in Shrimsley's hand which you and I, Terry, thought was a letter.'

'Never said it was a letter.'

'Oh, come on, Terry! You can't be right all the time!'

Terry responded with a smug smile.

'Poor old Betty,' said Peter Pomeroy. 'Her beloved Page One taken away from her again. Did you notice I gave you an extra-big byline, Judy?'

'Yes, Peter, and thank you.'

'She'll be hopping mad.'

'Betty,' said Miss Dimont slowly, 'knew all along that Mrs March was Pithers' granddaughter. Her new boyfriend Hannaford told her. She had seen my notes – she was keeping an eye on me for Rudyard, silly old fool – and she could quite possibly have made the deduction for herself.'

'Not her boyfriend any more,' said Athene. 'She had to choose between a weekend away with him or the hockey team. She chose hockey.'

'I thought she liked his big Rolls-Royce.'

'Obviously not that much.'

All this went over Auriol's head. 'So Rhys was spying on you? Trying to find out what you knew?'

'Auriol,' said Miss Dimont, 'that's not spying, not as *we* know it.'

Her friend laughed. 'He never was much good at the Admiralty – *Rusty* Rhys! It's a wonder you work for him.'

'It suits me.'

'Time to go home,' said Terry. 'It's gone midnight. Want a lift in the Minor?'

There was a pause.

'Yes, Terry,' said Miss Dimont, looking up at him. 'Why ever not?'

Everyone got up to leave. Then Auriol said, 'Better give you this. She says you never answer her letters, so she sent it to me to pass on.'

'Oh,' said Miss Dimont, 'oh dear . . .'

Auriol had passed her a stiff white envelope whose frontage was adorned with a beautifully formed copperplate hand. It read:

> Mlle Huguette Dimont,
> c/o Cmdt. Auriol Hedley, WRNS,
> Crabrock Cottage,
> Bedlington-on-Sea,
> Devon.

With heavy reluctance she drew from its interior a short note.

Dear Huguette,

I have been very worried about you. Since you do not answer my letters this is the only way to reach you.

I am coming down on the Riviera Express on Friday which arrives at 4.30. Please do me the courtesy of meeting the train.

Your loving,
Maman

'Oh Lord,' said Judy Dimont. 'Terry, I don't think I can take that lift after all.'

Missing Temple Regis already?
Read more of the Miss Dimont Mystery series in

RESORT TO MURDER

Coming November 2017

ONE

Pale aquamarine and milky like the waters of Venice, the sea moved slowly inland. The shoreline at Todhempstead welcomed the advance reluctantly, giving up its golden sands inch by inch, unwilling to concede a single yard of the most beautiful beach.

The body lay some way distant from the incoming tide, but sooner or later it would have to be moved.

For the moment, though, it lay there, surrounded by a frozen tableau – a small group of people immobilised by what lay at their feet. Death changes behaviour patterns, imposes a protocol of its own.

She was young, she was blonde, and she may have been pretty but for the hideous open wound that claimed half her face. Her dress was glamorous in an inexpensive sort of way, arranged around her decorously enough. It was still dry, a sure indicator it had not been here too long.

Frank Topham looked down with some discomfort. The long shallow beach had at its furthest end a high embankment, surely too far away for the victim to have fallen from and landed here. The injuries which claimed her life were too severe – that much was evident – for her to have walked or crawled to her final resting place, yet there were no footprints around the body apart from those made sparingly by the small group of eyewitnesses.

Nor was there any blood.

These contradictions jarred Inspector Topham's usually tranquil state of mind, but were swept aside for the moment as he looked down on the wretched girl.

'Twenty, I should say,' he murmured to the two faceless acolytes standing at his shoulder.

'No shoes,' said one.

'No handbag,' replied Topham.

The other lit a cigarette and looked up at the sky. He didn't seem terribly interested.

Whatever passed next between these custodians of the peace was drowned by the arrival of the up train from Exbridge, a billowing, grunting triumph of the steam engineer's art, slowing as it made its long approach into Tod-hempstead Spa station.

'Better get her away,' Topham said to the police doctor. The man on his knees looked over his shoulder at the advancing waves and nodded.

'No evidence,' said Topham wretchedly. 'No clues. We're moving the body and there's no clues.'

Taking his cue, the second man moved vaguely away and came back. 'Tizer bottle.'

'Is the label wet?' asked Topham without even looking at it.

'Yer.'

'Chuck it,' snapped the inspector. 'No use to us.'

He moved swiftly off to the slipway where the car was parked, not wanting the men to see his face. There had been too many deaths back in the war, but wasn't that why he had fought? So there wouldn't be any more? It was a man's job to die, not a woman's.

For a moment he turned to look back at the scene below. The dead body claimed his focus, but, beyond, it was as if nobody cared that the world had lost a soul this morning. In the distance two sand-yachts raced each other across the broad beach, and overhead an ancient biplane trailed a long banner flapping from its tail. Smith's Crisps, according to its message, gave you a wholesome happy holiday.

Far in the distance he could see a solitary female figure, dressed in rainbow colours, standing perfectly still and looking out to sea as if what it had to offer was somehow more interesting than a dead body. It was as if nobody cared.

Inspector Topham got in the car and pulled out on to the empty road. He reached Todhempstead Spa station in a matter of minutes, but already the Riviera Express was pulling out, heading on towards Exeter at a slow roll – huffing, grinding, thumping, clanging. He could get it stopped at Newton Abbot to check if there was evidence on the front buffers of contact with human flesh from the downward journey, to quiz the train guard and the driver. But they'd all be back again this afternoon on the return trip, and he doubted, given the distance of the body from the railway embankment, that this was a rail fatality. Though, with death, you could never be sure about anything.

As he drove back to the Sands, his eyes lifted for a moment from the road ahead. It was already mid-June and the lanes running parallel to the beach were bursting with joy at summer's arrival. Though the bluebells and primroses had retreated, the hedgerows were noisy with young blackbirds testing their beautiful voices, while, beneath, newly arrived wild roses and cow parsley reached out, begging to be noticed.

How, asked the policeman, could anyone wish a young girl dead at this season, when hope is in the air and the breeze is scented with promise? His years in the desert, those arid wastes of death, might be long behind but still they cast their shadow. He drove down the slipway on to the beach, got slowly out, and nodded to his men.

'Body away,' said one.

'Come on then.'

Topham removed his hat and got back in the car. His square head, doughty and in its own way distinguished, grazed the ceiling because of his ramrod-straight back. Despite the rising heat he still wore the raincoat he'd donned in the early morning when he got the call. He'd been too distracted by what he'd seen to take it off.

Too honest a man, too upright, perhaps too regimented in his thinking to see life the way criminals do, Frank Topham was both the very best of British policing and, some might argue, the worst. There was a dead woman on the beach, but if it was murder – if – the culprit might never be caught. No clues, no arrest.

No hope of an arrest.

The car approached Temple Regis, the prettiest town in the whole of Devon, and, as the inspector drove up Cable Street and over Tuppenny Row, his eyes took solace in the elegant terrace of Regency cottages whose pink brickwork blushed in the summer sunshine. Further down the hill he could hear the clanking arrival of the 10.30 from Paddington, its sooty steamy clouds shooting upwards from Regis Junction station. Life was carrying on as if nothing had happened.

Topham entered the police station at his regulation quick-march. The front office was empty apart from the desk sergeant.

'Frank.'

'Bert.'

'Anything for the book?' The sergeant had his pen poised.

Topham hesitated. 'Accidental. Woman on T'emstead Beach.'

The other man gazed shrewdly at him. 'You sure? Accidental?'

Topham returned his gaze evenly. 'Accidental.' He tried to make it sound as though he believed it.

'Only I got a reporter in the interview room. Saying murder.'

'Reporter?' barked Topham nastily. 'Saying murder? Not – not that Miss Dimont?'

'Nah,' said Sergeant Gull. 'This 'un's new. A kid.'

Topham's features turned to granite at the mention of the press. Though Temple Regis boasted only one newspaper, it somehow managed to cause a disproportionate amount of grief to those police officers seeking to uphold the law. Questions, questions – always questions, whether it was a cycling without lights case or that unpleasant business with the curate of St Cuthbert's. As for Miss Dimont . . .

To Frank Topham's mind – and in the opinion of many other Temple Regents too – the local rag was there to report the facts, not to ask questions. So often the stories they printed showed a side to the town that did little to enhance its reputation. What good did it do to make headlines out of the goings-on the magistrates' court? Or ask questions about poorly paid council officials who enjoyed elaborate and expensive holidays?

And how they got on to things so quickly, he never knew. What was this reporter doing asking questions about a murder? It was only a couple of hours ago he himself had clapped eyes on the corpse – how had word spread so fast?

'So,' said Sergeant Gull, picking up his pencil and scratching his ear with it, 'the book, Frank. Murder or accidental?'

'Like I said,' snarled his superior officer, and strode into the interview room.

*

You can be the greatest reporter in the world but you are no reporter at all if people don't tell you things. A dead body on the beach is all very well but if you're out shopping, how are you supposed to know?

In fact Miss Judy Dimont, ferocious defender of free speech, champion of the truth and the thorn in the side of poor Inspector Topham, hardly looked like Temple Regis' ace newspaperwoman this afternoon. As she ordered a pound of apples in the Home and Colonial Stores in Fore Street she might easily be mistaken for a librarian on her tea break: the sensible shoes, the well-worn raincoat and the raffia handbag made it clear that here was a no-nonsense, serious person who had just enough time to stock up on the essentials before heading home to a good book.

'One and sixpence, thank you, miss.'

The reporter reached for her purse, smiled up at the young shop assistant, and suddenly she looked anything but ordinary. Her wonderfully erratic corkscrew hair fell back from her face and her sage-grey eyes peeped over the top of her spectacles, which had slithered down her convex nose. The smile itself was joyous and radiant – the sort of smile that offers hope and comfort in a troubled world.

'Tea?'

'Not today thank you, Victor.' She didn't like to say she preferred to buy her tea at Lipton's round the corner. 'I think I'll just quickly go over and get some fish.'

'Ah yes.' The assistant nodded knowledgeably. 'Mulligatawny.'

This was how it was in Temple Regis. People knew the name of your cat and would ask after his health. They knew you bought your tea at Lipton's and only gently tried to persuade you to purchase their own brand. They delivered the groceries by bicycle to your door and left a little extra gift in the cardboard box knowing the pleasure it would bring.

'I tried that ginger marmalade,' said Miss Dimont, with perfect timing. 'Delicious! In fact it's all gone. May I buy some if you have any left?'

The assistant in his long white apron hastened away and, as she wandered over to the marble-topped fish counter, she marvelled again at the interlocking cogwheels that made up Temple Regis' small population. Over by the coffee counter the odd little lady from the hairdresser's was deep in conversation with the secretary of the Mothers' Union in that old toque hat she always wore, winter and summer. Both were looking out of the window at a pair of dray horses from Gardner's brewery, their brasses glinting in the late sunlight as they plodded massively by.

They'd all meet again at the church fete on Saturday, bringing fresh news of their doings to share and deliberate upon. While the rest of Britain struggled with its post-war identity crisis – move forward to the brave new world? Or go back to the comfortable past? – life in Devon's prettiest town found its stability in the little things of here and now.

'Do you have any cods' heads? If not, some coley? And a kipper for me, please,' just in case anybody should think she was reduced to making fish soup for herself, delicious though that would be!

It had been a perplexing day, and the circular rhythms of

the Home and Colonial had a way of putting everything back in perspective. The magistrates' court, the one fixed point in her week that always guaranteed to provide a selection of golden nuggets for the front page of the Riviera Express, had failed her – and badly. Quite a lot of time today had been taken up with the elaborate appointment of a new Chairman of the Bench, and that had been followed by a dreary case involving the manager of the Midland Bank and a missing cheque.

It shouldn't have come to court – everyone has the occasional lapse! – and under the previous chairman the case would have been thrown out. But the Hon. Mrs Marchbank was no longer with us, her recent misdeeds having taken her to a greater judge, and in her place was the pettifogging Colonel de Saumarez, distinguished enough in his tweed suit but lacking in grey matter.

'Anything else, miss?'

'That's all, thank you.'

'Put on your account?'

'Yes please.'

'Young Walter will have it round to your door first thing.'

'I'll take the fish with me, if I may.'

The world is a terrible place, thought Miss Dimont, as she emerged into the early evening sunlight, what with the atom bomb and the Suez Crisis, but not here. She waved to Lovely Mary, the proprietress of the Signal Box Café, who was coming out of Lipton's with a wide smile on her lips – how aptly she was named!

'All well, Judy?'

'Couldn't be better, Mary. Early start tomorrow though, off before dawn. A life on the ocean wave, tra-la!"

'See you soon, then, dear. Safe journey, wherever you'm goin'.'

Miss Dimont walked down to the seafront for one last look at the waves. After the kipper, she would sit with Mulligatawny on her lap and think about the bank manager and the missing cheque. It had been a long day in court and she needed a quiet moment to think how best the story could be written up.

*

Things were less tranquil back at her place of work, the Riviera Express.

'What about this murder?' roared John Ross, the red-faced chief subeditor. It was the end of the day, the traditional time for losing his temper. He stalked down the office to the reporters' desks. 'Who's on it? What's happening?'

Betty Featherstone clacked smartly over from the picture desk in her high heels. She was looking particularly radiant today though the hair bleach hadn't worked quite so well this time, and her choice of lipstick was, as usual, at odds with the shade of her home-made dress. The way she carried a notebook, though, had a certain attraction to the older man.

Betty was the Express's number two reporter though you wouldn't know that if you read the paper – her name appeared over more stories, and in larger print, than Judy

Dimont's ever did, but that was less to do with her journalistic skills than with the fact that the editor liked the way she did what she was told.

You could never say that about Miss Dimont.

'Who's covering the murder?' demanded Ross heatedly.

'The new boy,' sighed Betty.

The way she said it carried a wealth of meaning in an office that was accustomed to the constant stream of new talent washing through its revolving doors – in, and then out again. Either they were so good they were snapped up by livelier papers, or else they were useless and posted to a district office, never to be seen again.

'Another rookie?' snapped Ross, the venom in his voice sufficient to quell a native uprising. 'When did he arrive?'

HQ
One Place. Many Stories

The home of bold, innovative
and empowering publishing.

Follow us online

 @HQStories

 @HQStories

 HQStories

 HQ Stories

 HQMusic

HQ_SM